FRANCES ELLEN

A World To Lose

For Carlota,

My Spanish partner in crime. Without you as my sounding board, some beautiful scenes and unexpected plot twists would have never happened.
I am eternally grateful.

Contents

Preface

The events in this book take place a week after *A Queen To Come*, the first novella in the Asters Prequel Trilogy. I advise that books in the Prequel series are read in order.

If you'd like to be the first to hear about the progress of other books in the Asters series, free bonus content, and more, I encourage you to sign up to my newsletter; details are on my web site:
https://francesellenbooks.com/newsletters/.

Trigger words
There are scenes of bloody violence and death that may be distressing for some readers.

Grand Canyon
Saluverus
Glacialis
Amazon Basin
Gayle's village
Auro
Viria

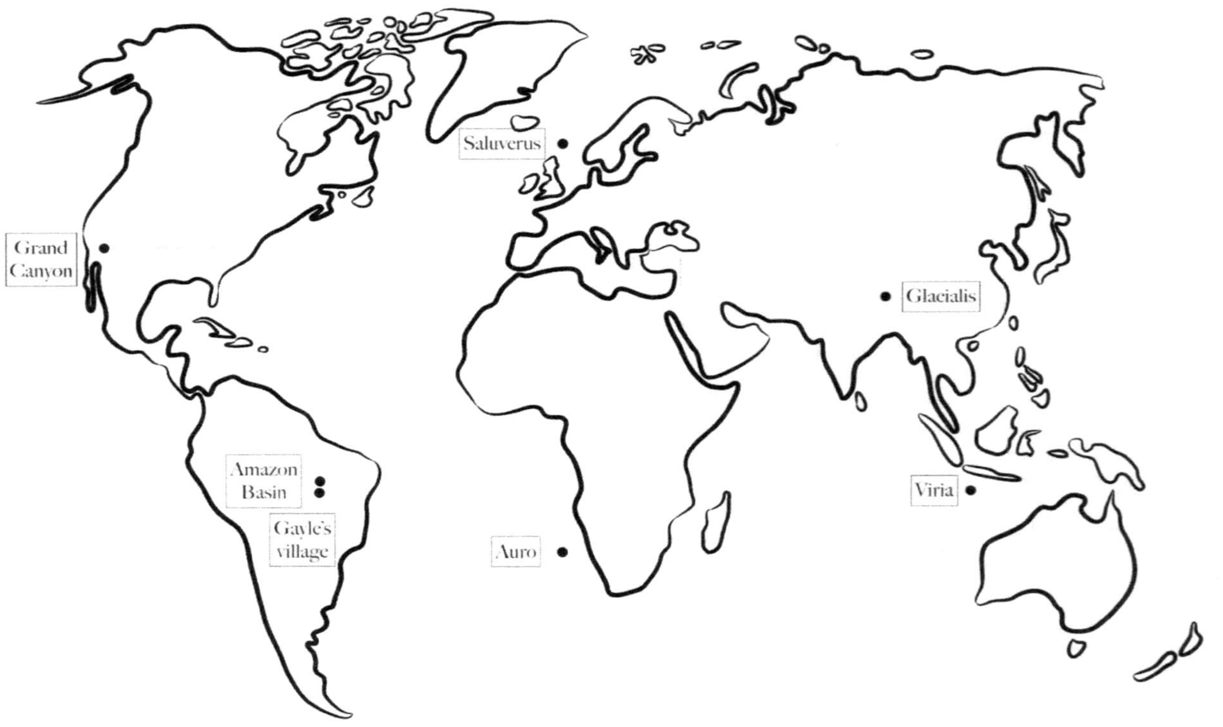

iv

Chapter 1

The coppery tang of magic stung Sky's nose as he stepped into the crypt. The moon shone bright enough in the cloudless sky that he didn't need a torch to find his way. Two thick, large candles burnt on either side of the entryway into the crypt.

Sky knew Sophie would be here. The smell of magic proved it.

It had been three days since Gayle Mendosa died, and it hit Sophie hardest. It was no surprise that she was here using her magic trying to prove that Gayle was still alive.

Sky blinked in the dim light and searched for his sister. He started to get slightly nervous. How many times had she cast the same tracking spell? The remnant particles of the magic stung his eyes and prickled on his skin. He stepped further into the Mendosa crypt.

Because of ancient tradition, Affinites and Asters weren't buried. Queen Aiyana had been a descendant of the earliest Vikings in Denmark, and had brought her beliefs to Saluverus. The dead were burnt on high funeral pyres, with the belief that the smoke of the flames would bring them to the stars. The same stars that had given Aiyana the power to defeat the Higher Kings to begin with. The remaining ashes were then buried within the cliffs, making the dead a part of Saluverus, and Affinite and Aster history forever.

Only later were the family crypts created. And the ashes were now encased in glass boxes; to be placed within the walls. A golden plaque with a name and two dates was placed over the opening, sealing them inside the rock.

Three new plaques had been placed in the Mendosa crypt this morning, but there were no ashes encased in glass within the wall behind them. Sophie was kneeling before the wall underneath them, and she was chanting softly.

For two days straight the current generation of Asters had been working together with the four remaining Ceders and the three Elders. All these living Asters had spent day and night casting any spell they could find to see if Gayle might still be alive. Countless possibilities were considered, and they had clung on longest to the hope that something was blocking their magic to find her. Yet even with three generations of Aster magic they couldn't detect any life or magic.

Gayle Mendosa and her magic were gone, and they were not coming back.

"Soph," Sky said, moving towards his sister.

Sophie stirred, registering Sky's arrival. She paused her chanting only for a second before continuing. Her long, wavy blonde hair floated around her head as the magic of the spell took hold. As Sky stepped closer another smell aside from the copper of magic hit him.

Blood.

Stronger than it should be. A lot stronger.

Sky broke into action. He didn't care that he was interrupting Sophie in the middle of her spell. Even though he knew that doing so could be extremely dangerous; an unfinished spell could have catastrophic consequences if left unstable and up in the air. Sky fell to his knees beside Sophie and saw what he dreaded when he first smelled the blood.

Sophie's left palm was cut open and bloody. She'd been using her own blood to strengthen her magic for the spell. But what he saw... *cut open* was too nice a description for how her palm looked. *Shredded* was a better way to describe it. She should've been using blood from the vials in the laboratory. That was the whole reason she and the other Asters gave blood every few weeks; so that they didn't have to cut into their hands every time they needed blood as a stronger agent for a more effective spell.

"Soph, stop it!" Sky commanded.

Sophie only shot him a *look*, but didn't break her chanting. She started to lean forward, ready to draw her blood on the ground below the map of Brazil that lay unrolled in front of her.

"No!" Sky reached out and took her wrists in both his hands. He raised them up, so that Sophie couldn't reach the ground with her bloodied, shredded hand. There was a crackle in the air as the spell was interrupted, but Sky didn't pay any attention to it. Sophie's face was ghostly pale and her lips were blue. Her grey eyes were bloodshot and wild. The state of her absolutely appalled him. He couldn't imagine what effect the tracking spells had on her every time they drew a blank.

Spells took a toll on an Aster's energy as it was. Combine that with Sophie's desperation for the spell to work when clearly there was nothing to find... She would cast the spell again and again, hoping the next would lead to something different. It was draining her utterly in the process.

How many times had she cast the spell already? How close was she to casting that one spell that took whatever energy she had left, and kill her? By the looks of her grey skin, Sky guessed she wasn't far off that point at all. He didn't want to think about what would have happened if he'd been any later.

"Let me go!" Sophie struggled, but Sky was stronger. There was barely any energy left in his sister, and her efforts were an incredibly weak attempt at loosening his grip on her.

"You need to stop! Are you out of your mind?" He held up her torn left hand and showed it to her. "What were you thinking? You know this will kill you if you keep this up!"

"I have to keep this up—even if it kills me... it has to work!"

"It won't work! If it didn't work the first time, then the second, third, *tenth* time isn't going to be any different! Dammit Soph, you're supposed to be the smart one around here!"

Tears were rolling down her ashen face now. "It has to work! She has to be alive—I have to find her!" she sobbed.

"If she was alive, we would have found her already. You know that," Sky said. He tried to keep his voice calm, but the urge to throw her over his shoulder and shimmer the both of them out of there was hard to ignore. She needed to get to the Medical Bay as soon as possible to get her hand checked out and her strength and energy restored before it was too late.

"Come on," he said, his voice softer this time. "I'm getting you out of here."

Sky started to guide her to her feet, but she once again resisted him. Sophie shook her body and pulled on her arms. This tug was even weaker than her first attempt to shake him off. It sent a shock of worry through him.

"No. One more time! Once more, you'll see! She's not dead. I'll cast the spell. You can help me; with our magic together the spell will be stronger. We'll break through whatever has been blocking me so far. You'll see. She's still alive. She has to be..."

"No! Listen to me." Sky crouched back down again and took her ghostly face in his hands. He stared into those thunderstorm grey eyes that he'd known all his life. There was always such strength in them; so much more than he had ever expected to come from that scrawny little girl he saw for the first time when he was just four years old. That strength was gone now. She was terrified. She didn't want to face the consequences of what it meant that Gayle Mendosa, their Queen, was dead.

"Take a breath," he said. She stopped struggling. Her shoulders slumped but she kept her eyes on him. Her eyelids drooped slightly, but Sky could tell that she was holding on to every word he was saying. Utter exhaustion was closing in on her, and it wasn't the natural kind. It was the kind that would take her away into a deep sleep; one that she might never wake from if he didn't get her to the Medical Bay *fast*.

"Take a breath and think. I know you want it not to be true, but it is. No number of spells is going to change that. You know that what you're doing here is useless. You are only hurting yourself by doing this. And I won't let you. She's dead, Soph. Gayle Mendosa is dead. I'm sorry."

Sophie's bottom lip quivered. "Then we're doomed."

"We're not doomed."

"She was born for a reason," Sophie whispered. Her voice was so raspy it was like she'd inhaled a large amount of dust. "Our magic won't be enough. She wouldn't have been born the Queen if we didn't need that magic. Something's coming, and the Asters won't be strong enough to stop it. She was born to save us."

"Save us from what?" Sky asked. He knew there was a sliver of truth to Sophie's words, but he couldn't let her think he believed it, too. And since there was no immediate danger detected on the radars, there was no reason to worry yet either.

"I don't know," Sophie breathed. "But it's coming, and *she* won't be here to help us stop it."

There was another crackle in the air that broke Sky's stare with Sophie. He looked around and saw that the magical particles floating around them had started glowing and swirling with life. The ground under their feet rumbled. Sky's gaze shot to the map on the ground next to them. It was covered in Sophie's blood, which now seemed to hiss and brighten with energy.

"Right now we have other problems," he said flatly. He jumped to his feet, pulling Sophie up with him. The unfinished spell stirred in the air.

"Dammit," Sky muttered as he pulled Sophie behind him towards the entrance of the crypt. He would've preferred to shimmer the both of them out of there on the spot, but if this spell was going to explode the way he expected it to, he first needed to make sure there was no one else in the vicinity who could get hurt.

Blood from Sophie's shredded hand coated Sky's skin and the cuff of his coat. Sky hardly registered the warmth of it.

"You're the one... who stopped me," Sophie huffed, dizzily.

"For all I knew that was the one that would kill you," Sky said, almost one hundred per cent certain that he was right, considering it was an all-time miracle that Sophie was even on her feet right now.

Sky pulled her out of the crypt and onto the stone walkway. He whirled around, checking that there was no one else near the Mendosa crypt. When he was certain no one was, Sky turned around. Sophie's eyes had closed entirely now, and her knees buckled. Sky shot forward and managed to catch his sister before she hit the ground, unconscious.

The second he held her comfortably in his arms he glanced back into the crypt. A bright light shone from its depths and was getting brighter.

"Crap," Sky muttered. "Someone's going to have to clean that up."

He gripped Sophie tighter in his arms and shimmered before the unfinished spell exploded.

Once the blue light of his shimmer had vanished, Sky was standing in one of the patient wings of the Medical Bay.

A woman behind the desk near him shrieked as he appeared out of thin air.

"Show me to an empty room and get me Bianka Mazur!" Sky ordered.

The woman didn't hesitate for a second. She gestured to a young nurse, no older than Sky, who had just come around the corner. Sky recognised her. "Marlena, find your mother immediately," the woman commanded with an accent Sky couldn't quite place.

Marlena Mazur was a Polish nurse and the daughter of the Chief Medical Officer of the Medical Bay on Saluverus. Sky didn't want anybody less than Bianka treating Sophie.

Marlena and Sophie had been friends for years now, and she shot a worried glance at her unconscious friend in Sky's arms before dashing off to find her mother.

The woman behind the counter, in her thirties Sky guessed, hurried around her desk and led Sky all the way down to the end of the corridor and gestured for him to go into a room on her right.

"I need a phone, *now*," Sky snapped. He didn't bother being polite. He would thank the woman *after* he was sure that Sophie was all right. Right now, by the way he was holding his sister he couldn't tell how well she was breathing.

The woman nodded and ran back down the corridor.

Sky hurried to the hospital bed and laid Sophie down on top of it. On the dazzling white sheets, it was even clearer how grey Sophie's skin had become. Sky reached over and placed two fingers under her jawline.

She still had a pulse, thankfully. It wasn't strong, and it was getting weaker, but it was there.

"Mum!" Sky shouted urgently up at the ceiling. "I need Katherine or Diana now! No questions, please!"

He knew his mother would hear him. It was both a blessing and a curse that came with their shared magic of Speed and Flight. If anyone who possessed magic would call out their name loudly, they would be able to hear it, along with any short message that followed. Sky just hoped that his mother wouldn't come shimmering to him first, without Sophie's mother or grandmother, just to see what it was all about.

Sky kept his fingers on Sophie's throat and an eye on his watch to monitor her pulse. It was getting weaker by the second and he didn't know how much time she had left.

The woman from the patient's desk returned to the room with a phone in her hand. Sky beckoned her to come to him, since he wasn't about to step away from his sister, or lift his fingers from her skin. The woman hurried closer, holding out an unlocked phone to him. Sky gave the woman a short nod before closing his free hand around the phone.

The woman understood that he had no need for her anymore, and retreated. She did, however, remain by the door.

Smart nurse, Sky thought.

It wasn't every day that Asters came to the Medical Bay, and no nurse here wanted to be the one on duty if something were to go wrong with them.

There were running footsteps in the hallway and Bianka Mazur appeared in the doorway. She dashed into the room, Marlena on her heels. Bianka stood on the other side of the bed to Sky and placed the palm of her hand on Sophie's forehead. She then took the stethoscope she had resting around her neck, put the earpieces in her ears and placed the chest piece over Sophie's heart. She looked up briefly and barked something in her native language at the woman by the door.

Sky watched as the woman disappeared out of sight.

At that moment there was a blue light, and a second later Madeleine Mayne appeared with Katherine Griffiths at her side.

"Sophie!" Katherine shrieked and she rushed to her daughter's bedside. Sky moved away from the bed so that Katherine could get closer. Sophie remained unconscious when her mother touched her daughter's forehead.

The woman from the patient's desk appeared again with a bag of fluid hanging from what looked like a weird coat rack. She was holding the long end of a plastic tube that was connected to the bag of fluid.

Bianka Mazur looked up and, again in Polish, told the woman to come closer.

Sky stepped further back to let the doctor and nurses do their thing. The magical Band, with black inked lines and the symbol of the staff of Caduceus, on Katherine's wrist had started to glow golden, which meant her healing magic was working.

A hand gripped Sky's arm and drew him roughly aside. Sky pulled his arm away angrily and turned to find his mother glaring at him. "What the hell happened?"

Sky shook off his mother and turned his attention to the phone in his hand. "Not now," he said as he started typing in a number.

"Yes, *now*," Madeleine pushed. "It looks like she's dying. *What happened?*"

Sky stared into his mother's deep blue eyes, identical to his own. He brought the phone to his ear as it started calling. "She over-used her magic on tracking spells," Sky said.

"*What?*" Madeleine spat. "How could you let that happen?"

Sky frowned indignantly. "Excuse me? She is nineteen *and* the Aster of Knowledge and Health! She should know not to herself," he whispered angrily.

"These are extreme circumstances," Madeleine hissed. "You should keep a better eye on each other."

"Then where were my brothers, huh? At least *I* found her," Sky barked back.

"Yes..." Madeleine said, her voice softening slightly. Her eyes drifted over to the hospital bed. "At least you did."

Sky was about to say something else. He didn't want his mother to go over to his brothers in a fury, demanding to know why they weren't keeping a better eye on their sister. But when he opened his mouth to speak, the person on the other end of the line finally picked up his phone.

"Hello?" Axel Reed said.

"It's Sky," he replied. And Sky began telling the Ambassador what had happened in the past twenty minutes. He didn't leave anything out.

"Oh, and the unfinished spell exploded in the Mendosa crypt. That'll probably be quite a mess," Sky said finally. On hearing this last bit, his mother turned her attention away from the hospital bed long enough to glare at him again.

Sky shrugged innocently. He ended the phone conversation before Axel could respond. He wasn't in the mood for the shouting of another angry adult. He would get enough of that from his own mother. But none of that bothered him right now.

The only thing he cared about was that Sophie, still unconscious on the hospital bed, would be all right. Sky watched as Katherine held her glowing hand above her daughter's face and Bianka cleaned and bandaged Sophie's bloodied hands. Both of them looked extremely tense, which sent a spike of anxiety through Sky's body.

He had to have made it in time. She had to be all right.

But Sky knew that even if Bianka and Katherine healed her physically, Sophie needed a different kind of healing that neither the Chief Medical Officer nor the Ceder of Health and Knowledge could provide. She needed rest, and lots of it.

Sky moved through the room and sat down in a chair closest to the bed, but still out of the way from the doctor and nurses. He didn't know how long it would take for Sophie to recover, but he did know that he wasn't going to leave her side until she did.

Chapter 2

Five days after Gayle Mendosa had been killed, Lian ventured into the dining hall for breakfast around the same time as most of the castle did. He always liked the bustle at breakfast and being around all the people going about their normal lives. But in the days after the Queen's death, Lian had avoided most people. Ever since the terrible news had spread, angry and disappointed stares followed him wherever he went. He'd only really shown himself at the funerals of Logan Brown, Dara Jasman, Fiorella Soto, and Lorenzo Benanti. The four Affinites had lost their lives in the days leading up to the Queen's death. Only Darra and Fiorella had been burnt atop individual funeral pyres - since the other two bodies were lost in the explosion at the Perth townhouse - but the funerals were for all four of them.

Axel had sent out a broadcast announcing the news not just to every Affinite on Saluverus, but also to the other two islands, Viria and Auro, to those working in Glacialis and to every Affinite still on the Surface. The broadcast had been brief, and not many details were given about how Gayle and her parents died.

The stares that followed Lian and the other Asters around were a mixture of anger and despair. Some Affinites had come up to him to ask him what happened. Other Affinites had gone so far as to accuse him of not doing his job properly.

Lian hadn't been able to take it the first few days. He was in despair himself. It hadn't been their direct job to protect Gayle Mendosa. That job had been given to the four Ceders, Gayle's parents and ex-soldier Percy Kelly. Still, it felt like it had been Lian's job, too. And he had failed. They'd all failed.

On the fifth morning Lian was done with his own sulking. He couldn't change what had happened, and he wanted to find a way to shake off the intense sadness inside of him. Before this morning, he'd gone down to the dining hall in the hours he knew no one would be around. But in those isolating moments, he felt the sadness only press in on him harder. So today, especially after what had happened to Sophie two days ago, Lian forced himself out of hiding. His sister had almost completely over-used her magic on tracking spells because of her desperation and probably oncoming depression. Lian didn't want to end up like that.

He stepped into the dining hall and found it quite busy. Lian forced himself to walk tall and confident. He would not shy away from the glaring eyes and the sad stares around him.

People were quieter than usual, but at least they were talking to each other. As Lian walked past the long tables a few Affinites stopped their conversations to watch him pass. They didn't say anything to him, and returned to their conversations after Lian was once again out of earshot. He forced himself not to care that they were probably talking about him and his siblings. It wasn't hard to imagine what the Affinites must think of them.

In the broadcast, Axel had said that the attack on the Mendosas had been planned many years ago, and that there was nothing the Asters of any generation could have done to foresee what unfolded in the small town on the edge of the Amazon Rainforest.

There must have been something more they could've done, was what most Affinites were saying to each other. Lian didn't disagree with them. For the past five days he'd played and replayed the events of the past few weeks in his head. From the moment they received the emergency call from Eidi Okoth in Nairobi, to the moment they saved the kidnapped Affinites. Lian still so clearly remembered the moment when Josephine Stewart, Matu's girlfriend and one of the hostages, revealed that the South American King had known of Gayle Mendosa's location all along, and had planned it all so that the Asters were in the South American Underworld and couldn't help their parents when the attack on Gayle, Tomas and Cara happened.

It didn't matter how many times Lian replayed the events, it all led to the exact same conclusion: the King had planned everything, and had accounted for everything. He knew Gayle's location, probably for years already. The Small Council and the Asters hadn't known that; there had been no indication from the King or his Disciples, and no intelligence from Felix's Watchers or Mergers, to raise suspicions. And so they were one step behind from the start, all the way through to the end.

In the last part of Axel's message, he sought to reassure everyone that Saluverus' Spymaster, Felix Hauser, had his Watchers and Mergers on high alert in case any of the Higher Kings began activities that indicated they were making moves on the Surface, such as stationing a large number of Disciples near entrances to the Underworlds, or even make direct attacks on Affinites or humans. Lian wasn't sure how comforted the Affinites on the island were with this message. It seemed to him that there was a collective, and understandable, sense of unease as everyone on the island went about their business.

After filling a bowl with cereal and piling toast on a plate Lian turned away from the breakfast buffet. Out of the corner of his eye he saw someone waving at him. Lian looked over and saw that Anna was sitting alone at the end of one of the long tables. Lian headed over to his friend and sat down opposite her.

"I haven't seen you here in a while," Anna said. Her long, light brown hair was tied in a messy knot atop her head. She was wearing her signature eyeliner and had three small rings in her right ear. With her bright red jumper she stood out amongst the other, less colourfully clothed, Affinites in the dining hall.

"I wanted to avoid the staring and whispering," Lian said.

Anna looked around; Lian kept his eyes on his breakfast.

"Some are still staring and whispering," Anna observed. "But you still decided to come out of hiding?"

Lian glanced up from his breakfast and nodded at his friend. She smiled back at him, the expression warming her face. There was still a hint of sadness in her eyes.

"Are you all right?" she asked.

Lian shrugged. "I don't know. It shouldn't have happened this way."

"It shouldn't have happened at all," Anna said.

Lian looked up, frowning. He wondered if even his best friend was going to accuse him and his siblings and their parents of not having done everything they could.

"I know there was nothing more you could have done," Anna reassured him.

"How do you know?" Lian whispered.

"Because I believe Axel Reed," Anna said. "The man might be mean and *very* scary—" Lian chuckled at this, "—but he is good at his job. And so are you."

Lian hadn't realised how much he needed someone to say those exact words until he heard them coming from Anna. She offered him a kind smile again before taking a bite out of her vegetable omelette. Lian turned back to his breakfast as well, and the two of them continued to eat in companionable silence.

After a while Anna asked, "How is Sophie?"

"Still asleep. She was awake for a while last night. She's still recovering from all the energy she lost. Bianka Mazur said she should be fully conscious tomorrow," Lian said. In the last two days he and the other Asters had taken turns sitting at Sophie's bedside as she slept. Sky had done well, shimmering her away when he did. Katherine Griffiths and Bianka Mazur had worked together impeccably to bring Sophie back from the brink of death. It had taken most of Katherine's healing magic to pull together what energy Sophie had left inside of her and rally it to keep her alive.

"That's good," Anna said.

Lian smiled ruefully as he remembered something Sky told him the evening before. His brother had been at Sophie's bedside when she woke up. She was quite clear-headed for the short while she was awake.

"What?" Anna asked, frowning at Lian's expression.

"Sky said Sophie doesn't want her hand to heal magically. One of the first things she said when she woke up, apparently." Lian shook his head at his sister's stubbornness. "She even fought her mother on it when she tried to magically heal it."

"Why on earth would she want that? I thought it was shredded."

Lian nodded, his expression sombre. "It was—it is. She just... wants it as a reminder or something."

"Well," Anna said, placing her knife and fork on her empty plate. "Whatever works for her, I guess."

"Such sympathy from a future doctor," Lian teased lightly.

"Hey, that's unfair! I will always offer sympathy to my future patients," Anna retorted.

"Sure you will. Though you will also joke about them when you're out of the room." Lian grinned at his friend, whose eyes were now narrowed and blazing. Then Anna closed her eyes and smiled.

"You're right, all doctors do it. Bianka more than any of them," she said.

"Bianka Mazur? *Chief Medical Officer*, Bianka?"

"I'm telling ya," Anna said, shaking her head.

Lian was laughing when the chip in the top of his right arm started vibrating. He stopped laughing abruptly. Anna noticed the change in him immediately. "What's wrong?"

Lian was already getting up from the bench when he said, "They're calling me."

"What do they want?" Anna asked.

He looked down at his best friend. "How many times have I told you? I don't know 'till I get there. Can you put this away for me? I have to go," Lian said, gesturing to the plate and bowl on the table.

Anna narrowed her eyes at him. "At your service, *Aster*," she said sarcastically.

"Thanks," Lian said, leaning down to kiss his friend on the cheek. "I owe you. I'll see you later, all right?"

"Yeah, yeah. Get out of here." Anna brushed him off, amusement, but also a hint of concern, written across her features. Asters being summoned did not necessarily mean trouble, but these days, it was more likely than usual.

Lian thanked her one last time before leaving the dining hall and heading down the corridor to the other side of the castle towards the Board Room. When he entered, all the other Asters were already there. Only Sophie wasn't – she was still in the Medical Bay. Lian hoped Bianka Mazur was right and Sophie would be fully awake again tomorrow evening.

Without saying anything, Lian made his way over to the large, round, oak table in the middle of the Board Room and sat down between Matu and Nathan. All five members from the Small Council were there. Sylvia, the Consul, was standing in between Nicholas, the Emissary, and Felix, in front of the large window overlooking the island. Though not a member, Jackson's twin brother, Percy Kelly, was also there. He had moved back to Saluverus permanently now that his job of training Gayle Mendosa no longer existed. This wasn't the first time since

Gayle's death that Percy was in the Board Room when the Asters were summoned. He seemed to have unofficially become the sixth member of the Small Council.

"Thank you for coming," Axel said once Lian sat down. The Ambassador was standing at the head of the table, looking down at the four Asters in front of him. "I have just spoken to Bianka Mazur. Sophie was awake again this morning for longer than she was last night. Bianka is positive that she will make a full recovery by tomorrow evening, and be up and about again the following morning."

Next to Lian, Nathan let out a sigh of relief. Lian looked past his American brother towards Sky. He didn't show such obvious relief as Nathan did, but Lian knew that Sky still wasn't back to being his nonchalant, arrogant self. Not outside of the public eye, anyway. He'd barely left Sophie's side in the past three days. Lian knew that the first night had been touch and go. Both Katherine and Bianka never left Sophie's room in those first twenty-four hours so they could step in if Sophie's condition worsened. Thankfully, it now seemed that she was not only out of the woods, but on her way to recover completely.

"When she is able, she will be seeing therapist Olga Masalis so that she can work through whatever brought her to the brink of over-using her magic. Doctor Masalis will be responsible for her recovery and is the only one who can clear Sophie for Aster missions," Axel continued.

It was to be expected. Though already in her sixties, Doctor Olga Masalis was Saluverus' leading therapist. Originally from one of the smaller Greek islands, she specialised in trauma psychology and was especially known for having treated countless soldiers after the war against Astaroth.

"Now, on to other matters," the Ambassador continued. "In five days there will be a memorial for Gayle, Cara and Tomas Mendosa. The service will be led by the Elders, and the Throne Room will be open to anyone who would like to attend. You are all expected to be there."

Axel looked at every one of the Asters sitting around the oak table.

"We wouldn't miss it," Matu said. The other three Asters murmured their agreement.

Axel nodded slowly. "Good. Right then. Something else relating to the Mendosas. Percy?" The Ambassador looked over his shoulder. Both Jackson and Percy were leaning against the corner desk behind Axel. They were near-identical twins. Lian was only able to recognise Jackson because he'd been trained by the man for the past fourteen years and noted the distinct small scars on the Commanding Chief's face.

Percy Kelly pushed himself off the corner desk and stepped forward.

"We will be sending some of our best soldiers to Brazil," Percy began. Another difference Lian noted; his voice was smoky where Jackson's was rough.

Lian straightened at hearing this news. Why were soldiers being sent to where Gayle Mendosa and her parents were ambushed and killed? And why was it Percy who seemed to be in charge of this mission? And most importantly, why were they sending soldiers instead of the Asters?

Lian decided to keep his mouth shut, giving Percy the chance to explain himself.

Sky was not so patient.

"Why send Affinites when you can send us?" Sky asked bluntly, clearly offended.

"They will be accompanying Affinite researchers to investigate the manner of Gayle Mendosa's death," Percy responded calmly.

"We can do that," Sky snapped. "From what my mother told me that area is a magical minefield. You're going to need magic, and we should be the ones to provide it."

It was true. In that dreadful night, a dark veil had been erected around the town. If there was any sort of veil left behind, the Affinites sent in wouldn't stand a chance of getting through it. They would need magical assistance that only the Asters could offer.

"If you would look at the screen," Percy Kelly said, his voice still a deadly calm. "You will see that the Disciple activity has gone down considerably in South America."

"So, why aren't we—" Sky started.

"If you would let me finish, you will learn what we will have the Asters do," Percy interrupted. The way his voice was strong enough to cut Sky off mid-sentence, while remaining so icy calm, was almost freaky.

"So you are having us do something?" Sky said acerbically.

Something unreadable flickered across Percy's face as he looked down at Sky. "As you said so eloquently, *Aster of Speed*, the town might be a magical minefield. Local Affinites have been working hard to preserve the Mendosa's house and are using memory potions to keep the news from reaching the media. But there are still remnants of the veil and other traces of Dark magic. The Small Council has agreed that the four of you will go there tomorrow, to work with the local Affinites over the next three days to clear the area. Only after the Memorial will my soldiers be sent in."

Lian blinked at these last words. Now they were *his* soldiers? He wondered if his brothers noticed the change in emphasis. It looked like Percy had taken over some of his twin brother's responsibilities for the Affinite fighting forces. The two men did share many responsibilities back in the war, Lian was just surprised how quickly Percy had stepped in, now that he was back on the island permanently.

"To accompany the researchers to find out what happened?" Matu asked.

Beside Percy, Axel nodded.

"Precisely," Percy replied. "That mission will henceforth be code named the Queen's Case."

"Why not just keep us on?" Sky asked.

"Because," Percy said, nodding towards the screen, "there are no Disciples anywhere near the town where the Mendosas lived. Once you've cleared the veil, Affinites will be able to handle the mission without your magical assistance."

Lian looked at the screen. Percy Kelly was right; there weren't as many Disciples on the Surface of South America as there had been in previous weeks. In the days that led up to Gayle's murder, South America had been swarming with black dots, each indicating the life of a Disciple.

But then Lian noticed something different. Something not related to South America at all.

"What about North America?" Nathan asked, spotting the same thing Lian had.

"I will get to that," Percy replied. "To finish with South America, we have entrusted the mission to some of our best soldiers. They will go into Brazil straight after the Memorial. Their task is to methodically scour the area and determine the exact order of events from the moment Gayle fled her house to the moment she was killed. We want to know everything we can about how the new South American King works. How Gayle was killed will give us some information on that."

"Still don't understand why we're not helping with that," Sky muttered.

Percy cast him a glance. Anger flared briefly in the soldier's eyes. "You will be back here for not only the Memorial, but also because you will be on stand-by for what might be happening in North America. Word has spread that the Queen of the Asters and Affinites is dead. Knowing that she was alive caused a great deal of fear in the Underworld. The news that she is no longer a threat, however, could possibly lead to an uprising on any continent. We have assessed Disciple activity on the Surface and in the Underworlds where Felix has Mergers. The North American King seems to be the only one who might be attempting this. At seventy-two years old this King is young and inexperienced. He is not a threat you can't handle, but you cannot be off in Brazil when you might be needed elsewhere."

Percy paused for a moment. He turned his attention fully on to Sky and narrowed his eyes. "Satisfied, *Aster of Speed*?"

Sky held the soldier's gaze. Lian and the other Asters held their breath. They knew Sky could be impulsive and reckless. Now was not the time to answer with another snippy remark. Especially since they didn't know Percy Kelly well enough to know how he would react.

All Sky did, however, was give the soldier a short nod, while still not breaking the man's stare. Percy seemed to accept this and turned his attention to the rest of the group. Lian tried not to let out a sigh of relief. He didn't feel like witnessing an unnecessary argument.

Axel cleared his throat, breaking the tension. "There is more you need to know. Sophie will be updated on this tomorrow evening when she's back to her full strength." He paused, as if anticipating the reaction his next words would cause. "We will be considering the deaths of Cara and Tomas Mendosa as deaths of Asters who have not yet passed on their magic to the next generation."

Lian stared at the Ambassador. He wasn't quite sure where Axel Reed was going with this, but he had a feeling...

"Yesterday the Ceders cast a spell to try and detect the bodies of Cara and Tomas Mendosa. While not able to pin point where the bodies are, the spell did detect a signal. This means that their bodies can still be found," Axel continued. "Aside from the Queen's Case, we are also planning to send a recovery team to Brazil to find the bodies of Cara and Tomas. Once the bodies have been found and brought back here, we will be taking their magic, and passing it on to two worthy Affinites around your age. The Aster magic must live on, and it will," Axel said.

There was absolute stillness in the room as the Small Council waited to see the Asters' reactions.

Lian suddenly felt very uncomfortable. He saw next to him that Nathan was shifting in his chair. Matu was staring at Axel with an unreadable look on his face, and Sky looked like he was about to jump up and throw his chair across the room.

When an Aster died before having a child, a spell was used to extract the magic from the dead body, and place it into a worthy Affinite. That Affinite would then possess the dead Aster's magic, and become an Aster. He or she would then also pass on the magic to the single child they would have. As a result, the Aster magic would remain strong, and would never become extinct.

"You're going to bring in two new Asters? Are you out of your mind?" Sky exclaimed.

"Yes, we are. And no, we are not," Axel replied simply. His voice was calm, but Lian could detect the Ambassador's impatience simmering underneath the surface. Sky either didn't detect the same thing, or merely didn't care. Lian assumed the latter.

"This generation was never going to have more than five Asters!" Sky declared.

"This generation was supposed to have five Asters and *the Queen*," Axel's voice thundered through the room. He had obviously had enough of Sky questioning them at every turn. In a more controlled voice he continued. "If Gayle hadn't been born the way she had, then Cara and Tomas would've had twins, one of them having Tomas' magic of Endurance, and the other having Cara's magic of Mind. You all know this to be true."

They did. Something that had never quite been explained other than *magic has a way of keeping itself strong*, was that every Aster only ever had one child. The magic would never be diluted amongst siblings. Two children were only ever born to an Aster couple; one inheriting the father's magic and the other the mother's. This was what everyone had expected when Cara became pregnant.

However, eighteen years ago, Cara Mendosa shocked the world by giving birth to a single girl, who wasn't born with a symbol within the Band of black lines identical to either her father or her mother's magic. The dark lines on Gayle's wrist enclosed the symbol of a wolf that signified the Queen's magic, visually announcing her fate that one day she would wear a crown and rule them all. And face a threat greater than anything any generation of Asters had faced since the Original War.

Axel referenced that threat in his next words as he said, "You also know that she was born to help you fight a threat you won't be able to defeat on your own. We don't know what threat that might be, but we do know that we will not be sending you to fight it without giving you the best chance possible. Two extra Asters, with the magic that Tomas and Cara used to have, will increase your chances of survival considerably." Axel paused and then emphasised, "The chances of *all our survival.*"

Sky grumbled something under his breath, but said nothing outright.

Lian had to admit that he understood the reasoning. Ever since Gayle's death this unknown threat had loomed over all of them.

"What about Gayle?" Nathan asked quietly.

Lian turned to the Ambassador. He'd only mentioned the bodies of Cara and Tomas Mendosa. What if they could find Gayle's? There was no Transfer protocol when it came to the Queen's magic, because Queen Aiyana was the only one to ever possess it, and her magic had died with her.

Axel Reed raised his chin. "Of all the spells we've cast in the days after her death, we have no reason to assume Gayle's body can even be found. The spells that would find her body, even in death, have come back blank. We will cast them again before the soldiers and researchers in charge of finding out what happened to her leave Saluverus. We do not know yet what we will do with her magic if we are lucky enough to find her body—if there is anything we *can* do. It is different to Aster magic, and much stronger. We don't even know if we can extract it from her body, let alone give it to someone else.”

“But you would if you could?” Sky snapped.

“Nothing has been decided, and it is not up to you to do so,” Axel said, annoyance edged his voice.

“Oh, but it’s up to you?” Sky said sharply.

“Sky...” Matu warned.

“No!” Sky snapped, whipping his head round to his eldest brother and standing up from his chair. “They don’t get to decide if that magic gets to be used; no one does! How can they possibly make such a decision? Who is worthy of becoming the most powerful creature in the world? It’s not the same as Aster magic. We are privileged enough to have it and were trained to become what we needed to be, to be worthy of it. We understand that. Even Transfers understand that! Gayle didn’t receive her magic through blood and she wasn’t picked out from the Transfer list. She was specifically chosen to bear the Queen’s magic by the stars! Now you’re just going to pass it along to some random Affinite we might not even know? No! I won’t stand for it. That magic was Gayle’s and no one else’s. The stars *chose* Gayle like they *chose* Aiyana. I’ll accept the two new Asters, because it would be insane not to. But *no one* is worthy of making the decision of who gets the Queen’s magic, let alone being worthy of possessing it!”

Without another word Sky stormed from the Board Room. Sylvia Allen called Sky’s name once in an attempt to get him back, but he was not going to turn around. The door slammed shut behind him.

The three Asters remaining stayed silent as Axel stared at the door for a moment. Then he turned his attention back to the three boys and said, “All we wanted was to bring you up to speed. No decision has been made yet regarding the Queen’s magic. The chances her body can even be found are next to none. We will speak to Sky about his behaviour later.”

“I don’t think you want to do that,” Matu said. During the moment of silence when Axel had been staring at the door, Matu looked at both Lian and Nathan to see where they stood on what Sky had proclaimed. None of them needed to speak to know what the others were thinking. That connection was the result of years of training and working together. They all believed the same. Sky may have acted rashly, but he was not wrong. Far from it, in their eyes, anyway.

"Excuse me?" Axel asked, his voice turning dark.

Matu raised his head, placed his hands on the armrests of his chair and pushed himself up so that he stood. "You are the Ambassador," he said. Lian and Nathan followed suit. "But for what it's worth, we do not think Sky is wrong."

Axel narrowed his eyes, but Matu continued.

"The stars entrusted Gayle with her magic just like they entrusted Aiyana. We don't believe anyone has the right or the worth to possess a magic so specifically and strategically granted."

"We are trying to help you as best we can. That magic will give you a better chance against whatever threat you will face," Axel said through gritted teeth. Lian doubted Axel had expected resistance from all four of them. Especially Matu, who was known to never oppose Axel or any other member of the Small Council.

"We will face the threat with Aster magic, if that's all that is available when the threat comes. We will not fight alongside a leader whose magic was not bestowed on them by the stars," Matu said. And without saying another word, the three remaining Asters left the Board Room.

Chapter 3

The following afternoon the four boys stood in the Board Room once more. None of the Asters, nor any member of the Small Council, mentioned the disagreement they'd had over Gayle's magic the day before. Today wasn't about that. Today was about helping the local Affinites in Gayle Mendosa's hometown.

They weren't expecting any Disciples to be there. None had been detected in the town, and the surrounding countryside and villages were also free from any Dark activity. Still, there was a bag at their feet containing a few weapons, and the Asters were strapping on their signature weapons just in case. It felt strange for Lian, as he slung his bow and quiver across his shoulder, that Sophie wasn't there with them. Even though they were heading somewhere where they shouldn't meet any resistance, Lian still felt slightly less safe. He never imagined going out into the field where she wasn't there. Perhaps he should've put more effort into the magic-free trainings where he *should* avoid getting hurt if he could. But as strange as it seemed, getting hurt was his best tactic. No one saw it coming, and Sophie was always there to save him. They did have plenty of her blood with them if one of the Asters really did need healing, but that always took more time; time they may not have in the field.

"Upon arrival you will meet Karla Morais. She is in charge. It is better that she tell you herself what has been happening in the last few days,"

Axel said. "Just to give you an idea, most of the veil is still up around the town, and it will be your job to bring it down. There was also a lot of destruction in the main street. That will be mostly for you—" Axel looked at Nathan, "—to clean up and close up with your magic."

Nathan nodded.

Lian wondered what Axel meant by *destruction*, but it didn't seem like the right time to ask. He would see for himself soon enough.

"Being who you are and what you will be doing there, we do not want the local inhabitants of the town to know. And seeing as you will look like *that*, we would rather that you will not be seen at all," Jackson said.

Lian sniggered. They never really put much effort into blending in. All four Asters were wearing black gear, and their weapons were hard to miss. Seeing that humans didn't know about magic, the Asters couldn't afford for them to start asking questions about their presence in town.

"Come on," Matu said. He cast Lian a glance that shut him up. Yes, the mission was serious. Matu always seemed to be the one to remind them of that.

The four Asters moved to form a circle. There were two bags on the floor; Sky and Matu both grabbed one each and slung it across their shoulders. Jackson and Sylvia had packed them especially for anything they might encounter. Lian could tell that one of them was quite heavy, by the way Sky grunted as he picked it up.

"What the hell is in this thing?" Sky grumbled.

"Spell books," Sylvia replied simply.

"Are you serious?" Sky answered.

Sylvia looked at him inquisitively. "How were you planning on taking down the rest of the veil?"

"Matu's strength."

"And if that doesn't work?"

Sky narrowed his eyes. Lian could detect the slight twitch at the corner of Sylvia's mouth as Sky tried to come up with an answer.

"I do know some spells, you know," Sky countered.

"Do you now?" Lian teased, taking Sylvia's side. He caught even Matu smiling to himself.

"*Yes*," Sky snapped. "I know how to cloak us from human eyes."

Sylvia smiled at the Aster of Speed. "Go ahead then."

Sky snatched up Lian and Matu's hands from either side of him and closed his eyes. He started whispering the words to a spell Lian didn't know. Wanting to remain known as the greatest Aster of his generation, Sky could never back down from a challenge. Lian would've just outright admitted he didn't know the spell. No shame in that. Though, without Sophie it did make him wonder if it hadn't also been a good idea to pay more attention in the spell classes Sylvia had made them take.

When Sky finished whispering, Lian felt a little shock in his body. Sky opened his eyes and looked around the room. He found Sylvia and looked at her.

"Well, you used the right words," Sylvia said, with a touch of surprise. "But we're all Affinites. You'll only know it has worked when you get there."

Lian had to laugh.

"*It worked*," Sky snapped irritably.

"All right, you're ready," Axel said testily. "Remember your mission. Get rid of any traces of Dark magic you can find and help clear up the main street. Then return home. The Queen's Case will take it from there."

The four Asters didn't respond to Axel's instructions. They didn't need to. Sky craned his neck to the television hanging above the corner desk. The world map started zooming in and soon enough it was focused on a small town somewhere in Brazil. Lian saw a great expanse of green along one side and guessed it must be the Amazon Rainforest. Never in his wildest dreams did he think he would ever visit the hometown of their once future Queen. It pained him that it was under these circumstances.

Blue light appeared all around him and the four boys were swept away from the Board Room. Lian could distinctly hear an echo of Sylvia's voice wishing them good luck as they vanished from Saluverus.

When the blue light darkened and disappeared from his vision, they were standing in a small side street. The first thing Lian registered was the warmth. It reminded him of the jungles of Indonesia. It was such a huge contrast to the November cold they'd just shimmered from.

Matu looked around him and headed down the side street. "Are you sure the cloaking worked?" he called over his shoulder.

"Why does everyone automatically assume I don't know my spells?" Sky retorted.

Lian slung an arm across Sky's shoulder. "Because you've never cast a proper spell without Sophie's help in your life."

"Well, I'm sure this one worked," Sky huffed.

Lian cast his brother a sideways glance. "You visited Sophie before coming to the Board Room this morning, didn't you?"

Sky kept his eyes firmly forward as they followed Matu to a bigger street. "I may have."

"She told you what spell to use?"

Sky didn't respond, but a smile played on his lips.

Lian laughed, clapping his brother on the back. "I knew it! And the world makes sense again."

Sky pushed Lian to the side, making him bump against the wall of the side street. Matu and Nathan had stopped in front of them at the end of the passageway. Sky and Lian were still laughing when they came to Matu's side.

Their laughing died away immediately as they saw what was in front of them. There was no doubt that this was the main street of the town. It was like a gigantic knife had been pulled across it. Two rows of rubble, a mixture of earth and stone, lay along each side for the whole length of the street. The rubble was at least three feet high, and the surrounding road was filled with cracks and tears and open holes.

"What the..." Matu breathed. The Asters stepped forward towards one side of the rubble. Lian looked over the edge and down. He had expected a chasm deep into the depths of the Underworld below. But instead, he saw it was only a few feet deep. As if the gorge underneath had been covered up once again, but not very well.

"Do you think this is how they got to Cara and Tomas?" Sky asked.

"Must be," Matu said. "They met your mother and Percy with a car. From what I've heard they haven't found the car either."

"You mean the King got the earth to swallow them up?" Lian said, shocked. "Does he even have the power to do that?"

"Astaroth didn't," Matu said.

"Does anyone? Other than you?" Sky asked. He looked at Nathan as he posed the question. Nathan had the power to do this. But they had never heard of a King with powers that could control the earth. Astaroth's power was that of lightning. The new King would have that same power as well. In hindsight, it was no surprise that there had been a thunderstorm the night Gayle was killed. The new King would be able to cast spells, too, but none so powerful as to be able to do this, surely.

"No one does," Nathan answered. "Only my bloodline."

"Then how did he do this?" Lian wondered.

"No idea," Sky said.

"We can be sure about one thing. The King was definitely here in person. Look." Matu pointed a little further along the shallow gorge. Lian saw what he meant. All along the gorge, tiny blue and black particles floated in the wind; remnants of Dark magic. They glowed a little, as well. As Lian looked along the complete mess the King had made, he realised the remnant magic particles were not only near the shallow gorge, but everywhere; around the houses and floating through the side streets. If Lian would guess, the entire town was awash with what remained of the Dark magic used the night Gayle and her parents were killed.

Then Lian realised that they weren't the only ones near the destruction site. There were at least ten people walking up and down the street as if nothing had changed. None of them looked at the rubble, or seemed to notice anything was different. One man in particular was walking right towards the Asters. Lian had to step aside so that the man didn't bump into him. The man walked past and climbed over the first line of rubble, jumped down the few feet into the chasm, climbed over the other line of rubble and continued as if it was the most normal business in the world.

"I think it's safe to say your cloaking spell worked," Lian said, staring after the man.

"Thank you, Sophie," Matu said.

Sky just grinned.

"Asters," came a quiet voice from behind them.

The boys turned around and found a slender woman in a black pantsuit standing behind them. She had short black hair, which accentuated her small round face and pinched nose.

"Karla Morais?" Matu said.

The woman nodded and stepped towards them. She extended her hand and shook all of their hands firmly.

"Thank you so much for coming," Karla said. Her voice was high as she spoke. Lian didn't fail to notice how good her English was. "There is lots you need to do."

"We can see," Sky said, eyeing destruction behind them.

Karla shook her head. "Not just the gorge, I'm afraid."

"What happened? Do you know?" Lian asked.

Karla shook her head again. "We have never seen anything like this before. We hoped you would know more. Please, come with me."

She headed off down the main street. She waved her hand in front of her every few steps to keep the floating Dark particles away from her face. Matu walked alongside her. Sky and Lian walked behind them, and Nathan took up the rear. Lian looked over his shoulder. Nathan didn't seem at all interested in the information Karla was telling them. All he was doing was staring at the gorge. Lian noticed that his Band was glowing green, and he wondered if Nathan was trying to communicate with the earth to discover what had happened here.

"How come the humans act like they can't see the gorge?" Matu was asking.

"We spelled them with the use of the Council's potions. It's the first thing we did the first morning. They are spelled to act like everything is like they've always known it. It won't last, but that's why you're here."

"But what about new people coming into town?" Sky asked.

"The Dark veil is keeping people out. The King created it not just to keep Asters and Affinites out, but it also influences people to stay within it, or to stay away from it. No one from the town has left since that night, and no one from outside has even come near the town. We've been supplying the stores ourselves because not even food delivery trucks have been coming. Your parents only broke the veil momentarily, but did not destroy it completely. It's been weakened. That's why we could come in and you could shimmer in without a problem. But we need it gone so these people can return to their normal lives."

Karla took them down a side street and towards a tall rectangular building. It was old looking, with brown bricks, rectangular windows only near the roof and a large wooden door. Karla led them inside.

Aside from a few tables and chairs and a pile of boxes, there were only a few fitness machines stored up against the back wall, to suggest this was once a gym. A group of about fifteen people were standing around them. They looked up as Karla and the four Asters approached. One man near the front looked Lian directly in the eye. Being able to see him, Lian knew immediately these must be the other Affinites from around the area helping out.

"This is Igor, my husband," Karla said, gesturing to the man who had looked at Lian when they arrived. Igor shook hands with the Asters. "He has been in charge of preserving the scene at the Mendosa's house."

"The neighbours on either side are not in. We've asked around, and they both seemed to have gone on vacation a few days before that night. We assume that was the King's doing as well. Better to influence them and have it look as though they left of their own accord, so as to not raise suspicions. No one knows when they will be back, so we're trying to finish up before they do," Igor explained.

"This King was really thorough," Lian spoke aloud.

"That's why he succeeded," Sky muttered under his breath.

"We've packed up all the Mendosas' belongings in these boxes here. We will be keeping those here, along with our initial investigation report for Saluverus' researchers when they arrive. It will still be good to have you come to the house first, though."

Matu nodded. "We will."

"And afterwards? Where would you like to begin?" Karla asked.

Matu thought for a moment. "Sky and Nathan will take the house while Lian and I will take a look at the veil. I think it's important we work on the remnants of Dark magic throughout the town first. That might take a few days. After we've got rid of all Dark traces, we'll work on the veil and the gorge."

Lian thought about all the glowing particles he'd seen around the gorge, but also on their way to the old gym. Even though the town was small, he estimated that it would take them at least till late afternoon of the next day to get rid of it all. A spell as great as the one cast in the main street was bound to leave behind a lot of traces, and they couldn't just leave the particles floating around the town. Dark magic, even remnants of it, had a bad influence on humans.

Karla looked over to her husband before nodding. "Then follow us."

Nathan didn't know what to expect, but for some reason he thought the Mendosa's house would be bigger than this. But it was a small, two-story house, with a small kitchen, dining and living area on the bottom floor, and two bedrooms on the top. It felt strange walking through the living room, knowing that Gayle had lived here. It almost felt like an invasion of her privacy. The Asters were never meant to know where she lived, even after she'd come to Saluverus. For the protection of the people in the town, no one was to know where the most powerful creature on earth had lived. The first thing a King would do was take someone she grew up with and cared about, to use against her.

Though none of that mattered now.

Most of the personal belongings had been taken away, already in the boxes stacked in the gym. It was hard to imagine that two Ceders had lived here. Two powerful beings hidden away in a small house in a little town on the edge of a great jungle.

Even in his cold, focused state, it was hard for Nathan to keep his concentration, knowing that the immense beauty of the rainforest was so close to him right now. He could feel the pull of the nature around him. That great, massive strength of green, most of it never explored. It felt like it was something alive that he needed to see, needed to be a part of. He'd never felt anything close to this before. Not even in the jungle in Indonesia. Then again, no jungle compared to this one. No expanse of nature even came close.

Sky and Igor were in conversation in the living room when Nathan walked up the stairs and stepped into what used to be Gayle's bedroom. There were no personal belongings anywhere. Her cupboards had been cleared out. There were no notepads or books on the little desk, nor any picture frames on the walls or shelves. Nothing in this room said someone had lived here all their life up until only a few days ago. Igor and his people had done a good job of clearing it all out.

Just like outside, glowing black and blue particles floated through the room. Nathan held up his right hand and cast a spell to expel Dark magic. He didn't need a spell book to know what spell to use or what the words were, but it took him more effort to remember spells than it did Sophie. Her magic probably played a great part in her memory and knowledge. But he'd put in the effort. Nathan didn't want to be dependent on the other Asters if he didn't need to be. And also, Sophie always seemed both impressed and grateful that she wasn't the only one in their group to know enough spells. Matu had quite a range, too, but Nathan knew more. Sky and Lian barely knew anything. They were always joking around together instead of paying attention in class.

The Band on Nathan's wrist prickled as he finished the spell and his magic started working. His right hand glowed a bright white. He started moving his hand around the room, and every particle near him got sucked towards the white glow and vanished. The spell didn't last long enough to get rid of all the Dark magic in the room. Nathan would have to cast it at least twice more to expel all the particles on the top floor.

After Nathan finished clearing the Dark magic from her parents' bedroom, he headed into Gayle's room once more and looked out of the broken window. Madeleine was sure Gayle had escaped this way. Nathan hadn't been able to get a good idea of what had happened in the main street. Something terribly evil had been involved there, and it was blocking his communication with the earth. Like the ground had been tainted by something much more powerful than he was. Although, Nathan wasn't even sure if it was tainted by something evil. Just something... impenetrable... something ancient. Not that that made any more sense to Nathan.

He didn't know if Gayle had been swallowed up by the earth in that main street. He did know that she hadn't been killed in this house. Madeleine was sure Gayle had managed to run. But where to? The Amazon was his best bet, but Nathan couldn't imagine she'd have made it. Not with the King actually being present in the town that night. And not with whatever Dark magic the King had used to create the gorge in the street. Knowing nothing about her own magic, Gayle wouldn't have stood a chance.

Nathan couldn't imagine what she had experienced; how she must have felt when all she knew, her comfortable and loving world, was obliterated before her eyes. He shut those thoughts away and headed back down to the ground floor, where he found Sky, Igor and the two other Affinites who had accompanied them.

"Clean?" Sky asked. Nathan nodded. When they arrived, Sky and Nathan had already expelled the Dark magic floating around on the ground floor.

"Then we're done here," Sky said. He turned to Igor and shook the man's hand. "We'll cast a protective spell on the house that will deter humans so Axel's researchers can work in peace and you won't have to manipulate the minds of the humans anymore. Then we'll go and join our brothers and start working on the rest of the leftover Dark magic in town."

"Thank you," Igor said.

The five of them stepped out of the house. Nathan remembered being told that the front door had been completely thrown off its hinges. It seemed to have been replaced. The current door creaked as it closed behind them. Nathan turned back to the door and placed his hand on it. He closed his eyes and whispered the words of the spell to cloak the house. Once he was finished, all human onlookers would just see the house. They would not see if Affinite researchers were walking in and out. They would see nothing and they would remember nothing. Nothing of the three people who had lived there for almost eighteen years. The Mendosas would be completely erased from all of their minds. As if they had never existed at all.

Chapter 4

A light breeze kissed Sophie's face as she walked across the stone walkways that were built into the cliffs that made up the western edge of Saluverus. If Sophie leaned over the wall that reached up to her hip, she could see the deep plunge down to the Norwegian Sea below. A few passages led through the cliffs to the rest of the island. Queen Aiyana had created the stone walkways on this side after she and the first generation of Asters won what was now called the Original War.

All along the western side of the cliffs were stories upon stories of walkways, which led to the thousands of family crypts right inside the cliffs.

Sophie didn't know why she was on the stone walkway now. She just felt the need for the open yet private space after her first session with Doctor Masalis that morning. Sophie had no aversion to the idea of therapy. She knew of countless soldiers who had gone to Olga Masalis after suffering traumas from the war. She knew even her own mother had seen Olga on occasion to work through the things she experienced during the final battle against Astaroth. Sophie would've preferred not to need a therapist's approval to go back on missions, but she knew better than to fight Sylvia, Axel, or Doctor Masalis on it. Better to go along with it. Maybe she would actually get something out of it.

Sophie thought of her brothers in Brazil. She should be there with them. Even if she was still not up to her full strength, they needed her. Casting spells might not be good for her recovering body right now, but the fact that Sky needed her for a cloaking spell and Matu had called her for another matter as well...

Sophie chuckled to herself. They would be fine without her, but it was nice to know that her brothers still felt like they needed her there. There were no Disciples anywhere near the town. She could have been there. From what Matu told her about the destruction in the main street... Not even Nathan knew how it had happened. Maybe she could've figured it out, if only she had the chance to see it. But Sophie knew there was no chance of that happening.

Sophie let out a long breath. She looked over her shoulder to the entrance of the Mendosa crypt. She knew she wasn't ready to enter it at this point in time, even though she was only a few feet away from it. Since her accident, the rocky walls had been reconstructed, the inside of the crypt repaired, and the gold plaques and glass casings replaced. Sophie felt a sense of guilt at the trouble she'd caused and the ashes that'd been lost because of the explosion.

Sophie leaned on the stone wall and stared out over the Norwegian Sea. With her right thumb she rubbed over the bandages around her left hand. She didn't want her mother to heal her flesh wounds. Sophie knew her shredded palm would heal horribly, but she wanted to keep it as a reminder. She'd lost it, just for a moment. If Sky hadn't found her in time the spells would have killed her. Sophie had felt hopeless and desperate. She never wanted to feel that way again. And she would keep the scars to remind herself of that. Even if it would take time—and therapy. Even if she wouldn't completely recover from what losing Gayle Mendosa had done to her. It was enough for now.

Sophie stared at the point in the distance where the sea met the sky. The sun was already starting to set, casting the darkening sky with beautiful shades of purple and pink. She liked it up here. There was something peaceful about the dead lying at rest all around her. Here, Sophie didn't feel so important. She didn't feel like she was the Aster of Health and Knowledge, one of the most powerful creatures in the world. Someone everyone turned to for guidance and wisdom. One of the only people in the world who could stand up to and question the Ambassador.

And who could possibly kill a King.

Sophie sighed and closed her eyes. Nathan and Sky had told her about Axel's plans to have two Affinites take the vows and receive the magic to become Asters. That news had been fine. Even though she'd trained with her brothers ever since they were four years old, and she couldn't quite imagine what it would be like to bring in two outsiders to their close-knit, diverse family, she knew it was necessary to have Aster magic live on.

It had been done ever since the first generation of Asters had lost two of their own in the Original War. Throughout the centuries Asters had been killed and new Asters had come in their place. There was no arguing that the "birth" of two new Asters was necessary. They would not be the first generation to lose an Aster and bring in a Transfer, and they most certainly wouldn't be the last.

But a new Queen...

Or King, even...

Sophie chewed her bottom lip. No. They couldn't. She'd told Axel Reed as much when he came in to see her. There was a reason for everything, Sophie had said. She believed as much. Only twice in history had the magic of the Wolf – the magic of Fauna – been gifted. There was a reason for that. There was a reason that Aiyana's children hadn't inherited her magic. It wasn't supposed to live on the way Aster magic did. Not through generations. It was far too powerful and ancient for that. No one knew precisely why Cara and Tomas' child was born with the ancient power, but it wasn't a coincidence. The child had been gifted with the magic just like Aiyana's almost five hundred years ago. Sophie would never believe that the people who had been given that magic were just a random choice. It was specific and strategic and beyond what any Aster or Affinite knew in the world.

Sophie doubted the magic could even be extracted from Gayle's body, let alone placed into someone else. Not that she herself even believed in that miniscule chance that they could find what was left of Gayle's body, for any of this to matter at all. Sophie would find out more tomorrow, when she, the Ceders and the Small Council planned to have a meeting on how to strategically handle the two separate missions in South America; Cara and Tomas' Bone Recovery, and the manner of Gayle's death. They would also cast one final tracking spell to see if Gayle's body could even still be found. If the King was smart enough, he'd have burnt her body and obliterated her bones. Sophie suspected he was.

Sophie was glad to have been invited to the meeting. Just because she wasn't cleared yet for missions, it didn't mean the Small Council didn't appreciate her input. Now that her brothers were in Brazil, the meeting made her feel like she wasn't completely useless.

Footsteps sounded on the stone walkway, and she opened her eyes. About thirty feet to Sophie's left was a staircase that led to the walkways below. The sandy, blonde hair was the first thing Sophie saw of Jacob Henderson as he walked up the stairs. On reaching the top, the boy hesitated as he saw Sophie leaning against the wall.

"Sophie," he said, surprise in his voice.

Sophie watched Jacob as he walked slowly towards her. She had never liked him much. He was never unkind to her, but he always made a point of getting under her brothers' skin. Especially Sky's, for some reason. Aside from that, he always walked around like he owned the place, very cocky as he smiled his crooked smile, which made his pale brown eyes light up. He had girls following him wherever he went; though, to give him his due, he didn't take advantage of them in the way Sky did.

"What are you doing here?" Sophie asked, not unkindly.

"I er, come here sometimes," Jacob said. There was nothing of the arrogant air around him now. Rather, there was something calm and peaceful about him, as if he'd let down that cocky shield; it revealed a somewhat sad serenity underneath.

"Your parents?" Sophie asked. Jacob was an orphan. He had lived in the castle for as long as Sophie could remember. All Affinite orphans came to live either on Saluverus, Viria or Auro, the three undetectable islands created by Queen Aiyana.

Jacob came up beside Sophie and placed his hands on the stone wall. He looked out over the Norwegian Sea as he nodded. "Yeah."

"I'm sorry," Sophie admitted. She had never seen Jacob like this.

Jacob shook his head as if dismissing her condolences. Sophie doubted he even remembered his parents much, considering how young he must have been when he lost them. Saluverus was the only life he'd really ever known.

He turned his head towards her and searched her face. "Are you all right?"

Sophie smiled slightly. "You don't have to pretend to care, you know," she said, remembering the crappy interactions he'd had with her brothers. Sophie reminded herself of how much Jacob wanted to be an Aster, and how she or one of her brothers would have to die for him to have a chance at becoming one.

"I do care," Jacob said, turning his gaze back to the Sea. There was no offence in his words. "Though that might be hard to believe."

"You're horrible to my brothers," Sophie pointed out.

Jacob turned his head to look at her again. "I'm never horrible to you."

"We're family. If you come after them, you come after me, too," Sophie said sharply.

There was a hint of a smile on his face. "That's nice."

Sophie felt a pang of empathy then. Even though her "real" family didn't live on Saluverus, but in England and Canada, Sophie had never once felt alone. The other Asters were her family.

The orphans on Saluverus were well taken care of, Sophie knew that much. But did they ever have the feeling of having a real family? Did the orphans come together and become a make-shift family like the Asters had done?

Sophie looked at Jacob and saw the longing in his eyes as she had spoken of the Asters being like her family. She realised then that probably no one on the island had ever seen him like this; so open. Sophie wondered why he was showing this side of himself to her. The two of them had never really had a long conversation, since she was mostly in the company of her brothers, and they and Jacob never hesitated to say something to get on each other's nerves. Sophie felt bad for the boy now, but she still didn't fail to remember.

"It's also no secret you want to be an Aster," Sophie said.

"Not *just* an Aster," Jacob said.

For a moment a wave of panic soared through Sophie's body. Did Jacob know that there was that tiny chance the Small Council could be looking for an Affinite to get the Queen's magic? Then Sophie shook herself. No, no one outside of the Asters knew. And *no one*, not even Jacob, could possibly dream of the Queen's death, just in case the unlikely scenario would arise that he might become King himself.

"Do you know why I train the way I do?" Jacob asked.

Sophie gave him a pointed look. Her silence was enough of an answer.

"If the opportunity would arise to become an Aster, I would take it yes. *But—*" Jacob said as Sophie couldn't hold back rolling her eyes, "—not for the reasons you might think."

Sophie let him go on. This was the most honest she had ever seen him. She still wondered what was in it for him to tell her these things.

Sure, he had flirted with her from time to time, but Sophie had never taken it seriously. She always thought he'd just done it to annoy her brothers some more.

"I wanted to fight alongside her," Jacob said. "If I couldn't be an Aster and fight with her the way you all would've done, then I wanted to be like Jackson and Percy. I wanted to be that one Affinite soldier the Queen trusted beyond anything."

"You could still be that for the Asters," Sophie said quietly.

Jacob shook his head. "No, I can't. It's not what I trained for. It's not *who* I trained for. It was never about the Asters. If I had the opportunity to become one, I'd jump at it because it would bring me closer to who I wanted to serve and fight for. Anyway... it doesn't matter now." He paused, and then said quietly, "I haven't been here in a while, you know?" After another pause he shook his head, as if to clear away that line of thought, and continued in his original tone. "I was *so sure* of myself." He paused a third time and corrected himself, "I still am, don't get me wrong. I'll make the best soldier."

A small grin appeared on his face, and Sophie couldn't help but do the same, all the while shaking her head. He was right, though. He would make one of the best soldiers. Aside from all his arrogance, he trained harder than any Affinite the Asters trained with. And they had all just thought he was preparing himself for the day he might be asked to become an Aster. He was of the proper age, and there was a secret list for who could be chosen for the Transfer of Magic. Sophie didn't doubt that Jacob was somewhere near the top.

"You would make quite a decent soldier, yes," Sophie admitted.

"*Quite a decent soldier?* Come on, you know I'm better than that," Jacob said, exaggerating his offence, his brown eyes sparkling.

"I don't want to feed your ego," Sophie remarked, trying to hide her own smile and how much she was enjoying having a conversation where they weren't talking about how *she* was doing. Jacob treated her like a normal person, instead of some fragile piece of glass that could shatter at any moment.

"Oh, you don't have to worry about feeding my ego. My ego is pretty *decent* sized already."

Sophie laughed. "I have no trouble believing how true that is."

The two of them laughed for a moment before falling silent. The sun had nearly set and the lanterns hanging on the walls and inside the crypts had magically turned on, the fires within them crackling softly.

"So why did you come today?" Sophie asked.

Jacob frowned at her.

"You said you hadn't come for a while," Sophie clarified.

Jacob shook his head. "I don't know. Everything I trained for... Now that she's gone, I'm not quite sure of anything at the moment. It's like the lights have been turned off and I've been left in the dark. And I'm just waiting not to feel lost anymore."

Sophie caught her breath. He understood. Sophie hadn't expected it to come from Jacob, but he understood. Better than anyone how it felt that the Queen had died. Sophie felt lost, too. She'd given herself into her magic because she couldn't stand the feeling of being so lost. She'd almost given her life, hoping to prove that what had made her feel this way wasn't true. That the Queen – that Gayle Mendosa – might still be alive. And everything Jacob had done; everything he had lived for, was for Gayle, too. What would happen to him now that he had lost that one focal point? That one thing that motivated him beyond anything else?

"You just need a distraction; something else to fight for. You will find your way out of the darkness eventually. Just keep fighting," Sophie said.

Jacob glanced at her bandaged hand. Without even realising it she had started rubbing the bandages again. It suddenly made her feel very self-conscious. "I will if you will," he said quietly.

Sophie stared at him. Jacob offered her a smile before sighing and leaning down on the stone wall on his forearms. He was now at the same height as Sophie, their faces at the same level. He turned his head to face her.

"How do you think she died?" he asked her.

Sophie closed her eyes for a moment. She'd thought about that night a hundred times, imagining every possible way Gayle had lost her life. For only a moment she would have witnessed the magical world she had always been a part of but had never known, before it was all ripped away from her. "Alone," she breathed. "Alone and afraid."

Jacob let out a long breath beside her. "I can't think of a worse way to go."

Sophie shook her head. Neither could she. For what worse way was there to die than not knowing who you are and why it was the end?

"Our darkness is nothing compared to hers," Sophie said softly. "She'll never come out of hers."

Jacob looked at her again. "What about you? Have you found your way out?"

"Not yet," Sophie admitted. "But I'm less lost than I was before."

For a moment Sophie worried that she'd steered the conversation right to what she didn't want to be talking about. Almost every conversation she'd had recently was about how she was feeling, that she needed to be careful, that she needed to take things slowly for a while. Every single person she talked to would have this worried look in their eyes, ready to catch her in case she broke again. But they didn't get it. The worst was behind her now. She wasn't going to break again. She would be sad for a while, yes. She would feel lost for a while still, yes, that too. But she wouldn't break.

"You don't seem so lost to me," Jacob observed. At his words, a weight lifted off her chest. One person. At least there was one person who didn't treat her like she was damaged and a danger to herself. She suddenly realised she wanted to be around that more; around someone who treated her like a normal person.

Sophie smiled at the boy who understood her. He probably opened up to her because she understood him, too. There was something strange about that, and yet it was extremely comforting.

Before Sophie knew what she was doing, she was already leaning towards him. She pressed her lips against his. For a split second he didn't react, but then he leaned into the kiss, too. He stepped closer to her and his hands were in her hair before she even realised what was happening.

Then, before it became anything too intense, Jacob pulled back. Even in the illuminated darkness Sophie could see his cheeks were flushed and there was a glaze over his light brown eyes.

"What's wrong?" she asked softly.

Jacob breathed once. His hands were still in her hair and his face was still so close to hers. "I don't want to be just a distraction," he breathed. "I don't want... I *want*..."

Sophie placed a hand on his chest, and felt his heart hammering underneath. She could feel him tense the second she touched him. "You're not a distraction, Jacob," she told him.

Jacob smiled slightly and whispered, "Call me Jake."

"Okay," Sophie whispered.

Jacob's eyes sparkled in that way that made her heart beat faster. "Okay."

And he kissed her again.

The next morning the Board Room was filled with people. Not only was every member of the Small Council there, including Percy Kelly, but every Ceder and Elder was there as well. Ceders became Elders the moment a third generation was born. Aside from Diana Griffiths, only Sky and Nathan's grandfathers were the other Elders left alive.

Sophie stood in between her mother and grandmother near the window, looking out over the island as they waited for Madeleine to ready herself for the final tracking spell she was to cast to find Gayle's bones. At this point the hope that she was still alive, but behind some magical barrier blocking their spells was gone. Now all they hoped for was if they could possibly still find her bones, which would then lead to the highly charged question of what to do if the Transfer of Magic spell could work on them.

The table and chairs had been moved to the side, and a large circle of salt had taken its place. Madeleine knelt inside it, a map of the area of the Amazon Rainforest near Gayle's hometown spread out in front of her. At the top of the map stood a small dish filled to the rim with the blood of the four male Asters of Sophie's generation. Because they were still in Brazil and couldn't help with the spell, their blood would have to do. A candle stood in the dish.

Madeleine straightened the map in front of her, before looking up and holding out her hand. Sylvia leaned in closer and handed her a lighter and the last remaining vial of Gayle's blood, provided by Cara and Tomas on the night that it all went wrong. At the same time, Sophie stepped forward, together with the other three Ceders and the three Elders. They created a circle around Madeleine and linked their hands together.

Madeleine looked up at Katherine. "Ready," she said.

Katherine nodded and closed her eyes. As she started whispering the spell to lend Madeleine the strength of everyone around her, Sophie saw her mother's Band glow golden. Sophie's right hand, which was holding her mother's, started to warm, and soon enough her own Band started to glow golden as well. On Katherine's other side stood Diana, Sophie's grandmother. Her Band glowed golden, too. As Sophie looked around the circle, everyone's Bands started glowing their distinct colours, one by one.

After finishing the spell, Katherine opened her eyes and looked straight at Madeleine. Without even using her own magic yet, Madeleine's Band turned from black to a glowing blue the colour of the sky. The moment this happened, Madeleine first took the lighter and lit the candle in front of her. Then she opened the vial of Gayle's blood. She held her eyes open as she murmured the words to the spell that specifically tracked a dead body. Madeleine tipped the vial over the candle, causing a single drop to fall out and into the flame.

There was a bright flash. Sophie closed her eyes instinctively against the light. When she opened her eyes again, she looked down at the map in front of Madeleine. There were a few glowing sparkles near where Sophie knew Gayle's hometown was, but they died down almost immediately. If there was a dead body to be found, or even a few bones, the sparkle would have remained at the place Gayle was killed for a moment, before moving to the place the body was now. But the sparkles didn't move; they slowly died away. There was nothing to be found.

Sophie heard someone outside of the circle of three generations of Asters sigh disappointedly. Madeleine dropped her hands by her side and blew out the candle. Everyone in the circle let go of each other's hands.

Behind Sophie, Sylvia cleared her throat. "It was a fool's hope," she said.

"It was still hope," Katherine said.

Sophie looked up at her mother and remembered something she always told Sophie when she was a little girl.

When all seems lost, don't give up on hope. Sometimes hope is all you have left.

Her mother had still had hope. Maybe not that Gayle was alive, but that her magic didn't have to die with her. Now that hope was gone, too.

Axel turned to Percy. "Ready the troops. The Queen's Case will start their investigation the day after the Memorial."

Percy nodded and left the Board Room.

"Is it necessary to research the exact manner of how she died?" Sky's grandfather, Harrison, said. "What will it bring us but more sadness that we couldn't save the poor girl?"

Axel kept his voice quiet and respectful as he answered the oldest Elder. "Whatever we come to learn will help us when we need to face the new King again. It is no longer about Gayle, but about preparing our Asters for the future. We know too little about him."

Harrison Mayne inclined his head but said nothing more. Sophie wondered if this was a good enough explanation for him, or if he knew that questioning the Ambassador further didn't have any effect on the plans that were already set in motion.

"We need to move on," Sylvia said. She walked over to a bag lying on the corner desk and pulled out another vial of blood. She handed it to Madeleine, who was still kneeling within the circle of salt. Sophie knew that this vial contained the blood of both Cara and Tomas Mendosa. A spell cast a few days earlier had indicated that their bodies could still be found. Gayle's body must have been incinerated for not even her bones to be able to be found. Why the King hadn't done the same to Cara and Tomas, Sophie didn't quite understand. Perhaps he didn't think an extra two Asters would be a threat. Killing Gayle seemed to be his main priority.

The three present generations of Asters locked hands again. Katherine once again recited her spell to connect the powers of everyone in the circle, and one by one the Bands on everyone's wrists started to glow. Madeleine's glowed last. She lit the candle once more, all the while murmuring the words to the tracking spell, and let a few drops of blood fall into the flame.

There was a bright flash again, but this time when Sophie opened her eyes, the sparkles on the map in Brazil remained. First the sparkles came together to form one little bubble of light, and then it began to move east and north. Sophie expected as much. At a certain point, the bubble would pause and remain at a certain spot. Because the map was pretty detailed, it wouldn't take the Bone Recovery team long to find the bones.

The light bubble started to slow down, but, to Sophie's surprise, it never stopped. Instead, the bubble split into two, both of which split again. And again and again until there were tens of tiny glowing sparkles covering a significant area of the Amazon Rainforest.

"What on earth..." Madeleine whispered. Everyone looking at the map was momentarily dumbstruck; no one had been expecting this. And no one quite knew yet what it meant.

"Quick, make a note of the coordinates of that whole area," Axel instructed sharply.

Nicholas Nelson, the Emissary, leaned over to get a good view of the map in front of Madeleine. All along the edges were numbers and angles. He scribbled them down on a piece of paper and said, "Got it."

No sooner had he said so, than Madeleine dropped her hands and blew out the candle. The sparkles vanished the second the flame was gone.

"What does that mean?" Diallo asked.

"It can only mean one thing," Katherine said, answering Matu's father and looking down at her daughter to see if she knew it as well.

Sophie did and swallowed. "The bones are not in a single place. They are scattered throughout that area, most likely after the bodies had been cut into pieces."

Katherine nodded beside her.

"Oh no," Harrison said, horrified. Sky's grandfather stepped back and took a seat in the desk chair of the corner desk. Sophie caught Madeleine close her eyes in disgust. She was clenching and unclenching her fists by her side.

"They didn't deserve that," Nathan's mother whispered.

Sophie felt the deep sadness and growing anger of the Ceders in the room. Like the Asters, they too were like a family to each other, bound by their magic and their duty to Affinites and humans the world over. And they had just lost a brother and sister in the most tragic of circumstances.

Katherine squeezed Rose's shoulder. "We will find what is left of them, and give them a proper burning. Even after the Memorial."

Rose nodded.

"This is offensive," Axel ground out. No one could miss the anger in the Ambassador's voice. That the two Ceders had been treated with such disrespect was mind blowing. This new King was breaking all known bounds of Dark magic and behaviour. A heavy silence reigned as the enormity of his latest atrocity began to sink in.

"We need a bigger research team than the one we assembled," Nicholas pointed out practically, bringing everyone's thoughts back to the present.

Axel nodded. "You're right." He looked up at Rose and Katherine. "You will get at least triple the people. You will go the day after the Memorial. You need to cover the entire area. It could take weeks, if not months."

Katherine nodded. "We will search for as long as it takes."

"Agreed," Rose said.

Axel turned to Nicholas and Jackson. "I am trusting you to gather a research team of one hundred strong. Make sure you cover all bases and specialities, including soldiers. We don't want to take any chances. Rose and Katherine, why don't you join them? Since you will be leading the Bone Recovery mission."

Both Rose and Katherine nodded. Sophie remained quiet. She hadn't known her mother would be in charge of the search. It seemed to have been known and decided before today, though now wasn't the time to ask about it.

Axel turned to address the others in the room. "Thank you all for coming. I know it was difficult, but we needed this information. You are all dismissed. Except for Madeleine and Diallo, I would like to have a word with the two of you. Thank you all again."

Everybody except for Madeleine and Diallo exited the Board Room. Felix vanished around a corner almost immediately, while Sylvia led the three Elders down the corridor. Sophie remained outside the Board Room. Katherine turned back to her daughter and whispered, "I will see you later, all right?"

Sophie nodded and smiled at her mother, who then joined Rose, Jackson and Nicholas. The four of them headed down the hallway to the left. She herself stayed by the door a little while longer. She stared sightlessly down the corridor, everything that had occurred in the last few minutes hitting her at once. How had any of this happened? A few weeks ago, she was happily jumping around in anticipation of the Queen arriving on the island. Now they had with all certainty determined that she and her magic were lost. And the focus was merely on gathering information on how the King had done it. Not to mention a whole other research team, one hundred strong, being sent to Brazil since they discovered that Gayle's parents had been killed and hacked to pieces. How was that possible?

A chill went up Sophie's spine and she shivered, suddenly feeling quite alone. She shook her head and headed for the arena, where she had arranged to meet up with Jacob, all the while hoping her brothers would be back soon.

Chapter 5

For the past two days the four Aster boys had spent most of their time walking through every single street of the town casting the exact same spell to expel the remnant particles of Dark magic. Matu had been right when he said it'd take them a full two days to get rid of all of it.

On the evening of the third day, the four of them stood at the edge of the town in front of what remained of the veil. The sun had already set and darkness had fallen over the town. The only light came from the street lamps a few feet away from them, and the small blue shining orbs that Sky had called up with his magic.

The veil wasn't like a physical wall; it was more like a slightly darkened sheet. As if Sky was looking through sunglasses to the cultivated fields surrounding the town. And it was moving in the wind, like a curtain would if a breeze blew in softly through an open window.

"Karla couldn't see it," Matu said. "She said she could only sense its presence on the brightest days."

"Sense it? You mean like Eileen can?" Sky asked, referencing Josephine's mother, whose affinity was for sensing Light and Darkness.

"Hmm-mm," Matu replied. "Though Eileen's affinity is much stronger. She would have known the veil was still here the second she encountered it."

Sky stepped forward and raised his hand. If the local Affinites couldn't see the veil, he doubted the humans in the town could either. Perhaps it was the magic in it that made it only visible to those who possessed magic themselves. When Sky's hand touched the veil, he half expected it to send a shock through his body, but it didn't. Instead, the veil moved slightly at his touch and felt extremely cold. The feeling of cold in the warmth of the Brazilian afternoon sun was utterly contradictory, and Sky pulled his hand back in surprise.

"Strange, right?" Lian said, who'd done the exact same thing seconds earlier.

Sky nodded. "Yeah."

"It's not like any veil we've seen before," Matu stated.

"Seen... heard of, read about," Sky added.

Lian snorted. "When would you have ever read about veils?"

Before Sky could come back with a comment, Matu said, "I called Sophie. She said veils usually disappear the second they've been broken." They all stared at the undeniably still present veil. "It shouldn't be too hard to get down. It's been weakened by my father."

"Looks like I'm not the only one who used Sophie," Sky smirked.

Matu cast him a glance. "Just because she's not here, doesn't mean we can't use her for what she's best at."

"I'm sure Axel would disagree. Why else would he give us all those books?" Lian said.

"Axel isn't here. And calling Sophie just saved us a lot of time," Matu said.

"Well, well, would you look at that. Disobeying Axel's orders to get a job done quicker." Sky grinned and slapped Matu on his shoulder.

"Axel didn't specifically say *don't call her*," Matu said in his defence.

"Whatever technicality works for you, brother."

"You said calling Sophie saved us a lot of time. Did she tell you what spell to use?" Lian asked.

Matu nodded. "There are multiple ones we can try. Most of them come with a pretty big explosion at the end, which we need to try and avoid."

"Mum said there was a big red flash when your father broke through it. How are we going to hide that from the locals?" Sky asked.

"We're not. The spell we're using won't lead to a big bang, just a bright flash. That's why we're starting now that it's dark. It will take us a few hours to break the whole thing down. We have to cast it at multiple places in the veil to weaken it further, until it is so weak that it will disappear on its own. By that time all the locals will be asleep in their homes and won't notice the flash," Matu explained.

"A few hours? Seriously?" Sky moaned.

Matu glared at him.

"We've been casting a single spell for the past two days," Lian pointed out. "I'm sure you can handle another spell for just a few hours."

Something mischievous sparkled in Sky's eyes. "How are you so sure? Those other spells really took their toll, you know... Maybe I'll just sit this one out."

Lian raised his eyebrows. "Nice try, brother."

"Here," Matu interrupted, handing each of them a piece of paper with two sentences scribbled on them. "It's the spell we'll be using. Place your hand against the veil and cast it. Do the same thing again every thirty feet."

"You're right, that will take us hours," Sky grumbled.

Lian held up the piece of paper. "You know what, I think this is one of the spells I already knew."

Sky snorted. "Yeah right."

Lian snickered.

"While we're working on the veil, Nate will be working on the gorge in the main street. Right, Nate?"

After a few seconds, Sky and Lian also turned to their youngest brother to see why he hadn't responded to Matu. There was something about him today that Sky couldn't quite put his finger on. He'd noticed it first in the Mendosa's house. There seemed to be a crack in that frozen façade he always had during missions. His mind was somewhere else. Now again, he was staring in the direction of the Amazon Rainforest, at the back of the town. He had a hand on his stomach and a thoughtful look on his face, as if his gut was trying to tell him something. His Band wasn't glowing, so he wasn't in contact with the nature around him. So, what was it?

"Nate?" Matu repeated.

Nathan seemed to shake out of the state he was in and turned to his eldest brother.

"What's going on?" Matu asked.

Nathan shook his head. "Nothing. It's the feel of this place, that's all. The nature's calling me."

Sky slapped his brother on the back. "Well, tell the nature to call back later. We have work to do."

Nathan shook his head again. "You're right."

"You work on the main street, while we work on the veil, all right?" Matu said.

Nathan nodded.

Sky glanced at his brother one last time. He still hadn't put whatever it was out of his head, Sky could tell. But at least his attention was on the task at hand again. Nathan turned on his heel and headed back into town towards the main street. Sky dug into his magic and flew into the air to start casting the spells higher up. Matu and Lian separated as well. From his height, Sky looked out over the town. None of these inhabitants had any idea what Darkness had happened in their town. There was something peaceful about that. Somehow, luckily, no humans had been hurt the night Gayle was killed.

Sky found himself smiling slightly with relief as he raised the piece of paper in his hand and got to work.

While his brothers were casting their spells at various places along the veil to weaken it, Nathan's focus was the destruction running all the way up and down the main street. Every now and again, he caught a flash of blue light as Sky flew overhead.

Nathan crouched next to the shallow chasm in the main street. He was the only one there; even the local Affinites had gone to bed already. Not a single light shone from a window. The entire town was asleep.

Nathan placed his hand on the ground and closed his eyes. He shut out the calling of the Amazon Rainforest behind him. The Band on his wrist started prickling as his magic started to work. He sent his magic into the earth. He forced it to race through the ground, along the insides of the chasm and report back to him. He wanted to know what had happened here. He wouldn't be able to get a clear picture, but he should be able to feel what the ground had experienced and what sort of people had been near it when it happened.

As his magic swept through the chasm, Nathan opened his eyes. Tiny streaks of glowing green were shooting from his hand and snaking away across the earth. More and more shot out of his hand, lighting up the chasm from end to end.

The glowing streaks of light shot through the chasm, moving faster and faster, until suddenly they all turned and raced back to Nathan's hand. The magic he'd sent out crashed back into him so hard that he almost toppled over backwards. The second his magic returned his head was overrun by a hundred different impressions at the same time. Nathan held both hands to the side of his head, keeping his eyes firmly closed as he tried to handle the chaos unfolding in his head. There was screaming and the sound of rain crashing down. The bright white light of lightning flashed behind his eyes. There was the clashing of metal on metal. Another deathly scream. And then the sensation of Darkness swept through his body with such force that Nathan heaved and threw his dinner up onto the street.

But the magic wasn't done. The sound of thunder crashed through his head. Nathan dug his nails into the skin of his head. Another flash of bright light blinded him from behind his eyes. Then came another clash of metal, but this time on rock. And a tearing noise unlike anything he had ever heard before. He couldn't see it, but he could hear and *feel* the earth being torn apart. Like an earthquake shattering the very foundation of the ground and ripping it open. He could feel it like it was his own skin, his own life. And another scream. Another wave of Darkness. A ferocious roar that had Nathan clap his hands across his ears.

And then nothing.

From one split second to the next it was all gone. No pain, no Darkness, no sound. Nathan could no longer hear the rain clattering down, or the thunder, or the screaming. The bright light of the lightning had gone, too. As if none of it had been in his head to begin with.

It was unlike anything he'd ever experienced before. Any time he'd asked the earth for its memories, Nathan was like a passive spectator. He couldn't physically feel anything, yet a second ago he definitely felt the rain coming down on top of him and his clothes sticking to his skin.

He tried to piece together the things he'd experienced, but as quickly as they had come, they were also vanishing from his memory. Only vague and indescribable feelings and sensations remained. He still remembered the storm and there was still a remnant of the sensation of the earth being torn open. But for the life of him he couldn't remember what had preceded it; what had been done to be able to destroy the fabric of the earth like that and break it open. He also couldn't sense who had been in the main street when all of it had happened. He couldn't tell if it was Tomas and Cara, or if it had been Gayle. The magic memory was fading ever faster.

Nathan only then realised how heavy his breathing had become. He closed his eyes for a moment and raked a hand through his wavy brown hair. He took a moment to bring his breathing back to normal.

He opened his eyes again and stared down at the shallow chasm in front of him. From what he could vaguely remember, he knew that the chasm had been much deeper. When the earth had been torn open before, it must have led straight down into the Underworld. The King had put in some effort to close it back up, but it was up to Nathan to finish the job.

The earth felt cold as he placed both his hands on the inside of the chasm again. He looked down the main street on both sides and put his magic to work. The Band on his wrist glowed a bright green once again and Nathan threw his magic into the earth around him.

Nathan was surprised at how quickly the earth responded to him. The ground morphed and moved under his knees, and the two tall lines of rubble started breaking apart and floating up into the air. Soon he was completely surrounded by earth and rock and stone as all the loose pieces hovered in mid-air before coming down and fitting into the chasm perfectly. The cracks in the pavement on either side started to vanish and, quicker than Nathan had thought possible, the chasm began filling up.

Nathan looked up and down the main street. His magic was coming to him quicker and faster than he had expected. He looked up to his right. He couldn't see the Amazon Rainforest in the darkness, but he knew it loomed over the town like a mighty guardian. He could feel the power in that jungle, and he could feel it feeding him. There was something otherworldly about it that he couldn't explain. But at this moment he didn't care. He loved the extra strength surging through his body as his magic worked all around him. His cold state softened slightly as he took in the wonder of the completely destroyed street rebuilding itself, until there was absolutely nothing left of the earlier destruction but a single piece of rock that couldn't find its place.

Nathan's magic wasn't hard to miss from above the town. Sky even hovered for a while, as he watched his brother control all the earth and rock around him and fill the chasm up completely. Sky had seen Nathan morph the earth before. He'd made a whole earthen staircase right down into the South American Underworld not so long ago. But Sky had never seen his brother work as fast as this. The main street of the town wasn't a short road, and the chasm had stretched all along it. This was one of the more powerful pieces of magic that Nathan had performed. Or maybe he could always morph the earth like this; Sky had just never seen him do it this fast before.

Sky smiled as he watched his brother get up from a crouched position and look up and down the main street. There was nothing left of the chasm. There was not a single crack in the street to be seen.

Looking around the town from above, Sky found it strange to think that Gayle had lived here all her life. It was a simple town, not too big. Nothing like where a Queen should live, that was for sure. Sky looked over to his left. Lian and Matu had finished on the western side of the village and they had each gone north and south respectively to tackle the rest of the veil. He himself had already done what he could with the veil. He didn't know how many times and at how many places they would have to place their hand on the veil and recite the spell to get it to finally disappear, but from what Sophie had told them he knew they should be close.

Sky looked further around the town. It was deadly silent. There were no lights on anywhere, except for... Sky narrowed his eyes as he looked over to his right. One house had a light on. No, two lights even. Sky remembered that house better than any other in the whole town. That was Gayle Mendosa's house. And there was a shadow moving around inside.

Without even thinking to tell his brothers, Sky stopped hovering and flew across town to see what was going on.

It was the middle of the night and Matu was getting tired. He didn't know how many times he'd recited the spell now, but he'd lost track at around thirty. He forced himself not to think about what the strength of the Dark veil said about the power of the South American King; that it needed so much Aster magic to counteract it. Now once again, he placed his hand against the veil. It felt just as cold as all the times before, and it swayed slightly under his touch. Matu closed his eyes and started whispering the spell. The Band on his wrist started prickling as his magic started to work.

He was about halfway through the spell when his phone started ringing. As fast as he could, Matu finished the spell. He knew what stopping in the middle of a spell could do; the explosion in the Mendosa crypt was a prime example. Once he'd finished, he grabbed his phone quickly and picked up just in time before the caller was sent to voicemail.

"Hello?"

"It's Felix."

Matu could sense tension in the Spymaster's voice. He didn't know why Felix was calling instead of Axel, but he didn't question it. "We're almost done with the veil. When Nathan's done with the street we'll be coming back."

"Stop with the veil," Felix said.

"What?"

"Get to the Mendosa's house, now! Sky is already on his way. It's Disciples."

Matu swore and ended the call. Of course Sky was already on his way. Why Matu expected time and time again that his reckless brother would act responsibly for a change, and get the other Asters first before heading straight into danger, he would never know. Maybe Matu just hoped that one day Sky would be smarter than this.

As Matu ran back into town he dialled a number on his phone.

"Matu? What's going on?" Lian asked.

"Saluverus' sensors detected Disciples at the Mendosa's house. Sky's going in alone!"

Lian didn't even answer him. The phone line had gone dead. Matu swore in Swahili, the most obvious sign that his emotions were running high.

As he dialled once again to reach Nathan, Matu turned another corner and ran towards the house. He couldn't imagine what Disciples were doing here now, but he just hoped they weren't in the King's higher ranks. If so, Sky would have quite the battle on his hands until the other boys got there.

As Sky flew closer, he could tell that there was more than one Disciple present. For starters, there were two guarding the replaced front door, which was now standing open. Apparently, the protective spell was strong enough to deter humans, but not Disciples. Sky used his super-human speed to fly closer still. He gripped his short spear tighter. He was ready for a fight. He'd wanted one ever since Gayle's death. And now he'd get one, in the town where she died. His magic hummed through his veins and he shot forward.

The guards saw him coming from the sky. Both of them turned their heads and barked something to inside the house. One of them fell silent a second later; Sky was already there, and his spear had gone right through the Disciple's abdomen. The other Disciple was on top of him a second later. Only thanks to his magic of Speed did Sky evade him in time. With his spear still stuck in the first guard, Sky dodged the second guard. He reached for his waist, only to realise that he wasn't wearing a weapons belt.

Sky swore inwardly as he avoided the slashing sword of the second guard. The Asters and the Small Council hadn't expected any Disciples to be in the town. The Asters had carried their signature weapons just in case, but the bag with more weapons was far away in the town gym right now.

Sky darted backwards. The second guard was in between him and his spear. He had no other weapons on him. He balled his fists. The guard wasn't carrying a double-bladed axe, which gave Sky some relief.

The guard came at him again. Sky used his shimmer to vanish momentarily, and appear right behind the Disciple. From there he used his fist to punch him across the side of his face. He lifted his leg and kicked the Disciple in the back, making him stumble forward. It was enough of a break to give Sky the time to turn around and yank his spear out of the first guard's body.

As he retrieved his spear, Sky was shocked to hear multiple footsteps clattering down the staircase. When Sky turned around, he saw two more Disciples appear in the hallway from the living room, and another three coming down the stairs. They looked just as shocked to see him as he was to see them. Sky didn't have time to take them all in, for the guard came at him once again. The guard wasn't a bad fighter. He wasn't good enough to stand a chance against Sky, but rarely any Disciple was. The guard was, however, good enough to buy his friends some time. Because the other Disciples were not armed, and were not planning to fight at all. Instead, they headed for two windows to the left of the front door. During his one-on-one battle against the guard, Sky caught glimpses of the other Disciples opening the windows and jumping outside.

Sky couldn't believe his eyes. Why weren't they fighting back? Sky was almost completely unarmed and he was alone. Why weren't the Disciples taking their chance?

Anger flared up inside of him. He dug into his magic and moved faster than the guard could possibly handle. Within seconds the guard was impaled and lying on the ground. Sky stomped on the man's hand so that he lost the grip on his sword. Then he leapt on top of the Disciple and clasped his hand around the man's throat.

"What are you doing here?" Sky spat.

The Disciple glared at Sky but said nothing. Sky tightened his grip around the Disciple's throat.

"Answer me!"

With a strength Sky hadn't expected the Disciple to have, he was thrown backwards. The Disciple sat up and pulled a dagger from a sheath at his hip. Sky braced himself, with spear in hand, for a final attack from the already heavily bleeding Disciple. But instead, the guard brought the knife up to his face, and cut his own throat.

"No!" Sky shouted. He darted forward, but it was too late. The Disciple had already toppled backwards, blood spraying out in an arc, soaking his clothes and the floor, and splashing over Sky. He was dead seconds later. Sky swore and kicked the knife the man had dropped. He wiped the blood from his face with his sleeve, and turned around to see if he could catch up with one of the other Disciples that had run for the hills. As he did so, he was taken completely unaware by a fist that was heading right for his chest. Sky couldn't put his magic to work fast enough, and the punch threw him backwards, into the house.

"What the hell was that for?" Sky exclaimed, recognising immediately the only person who could rally strength in a single punch like that.

Matu appeared in the doorway, glaring. "What the hell is wrong with you?"

Sky scrambled to his feet. "We don't have time for this! We need to catch up with one of them and question them on why they're here!"

"Can't," Lian said, appearing next to Matu. "Those we did catch cut their own throats before we could. Even if we could catch up with the others, they'd do the same before we even come close."

Sky looked past Lian and Matu. Nathan was standing a few feet further away, in between two dead Disciples. Both of them had blood pooling around their neck and throat.

"What the hell, Sky!" Matu thundered again. "You were unarmed and alone!"

"I had my spear," Sky said indignantly.

"Don't make me throw you on your arse again," Matu warned. "If they were all soldiers you would've been screwed, and you know it."

"If they were all soldiers, I would've shimmered out before things got too bad."

"Would you though?" Matu questioned.

Sky growled at Matu, but said nothing. No, probably he wouldn't have. He would've fought to the end no matter what.

"You don't go charging in when you don't know what you're facing.

There were seven in there, Sky! We're a team for a reason. You don't have to prove you can do everything alone. That could've gone very wrong!"

"He's right," Lian agreed.

Sky looked past Lian and found Nathan's eyes. They showed him no emotion. All Nathan did was shake his head. He agreed with his brothers, too.

"For *once*, can you be responsible?" Matu said with exasperation.

Sky looked at his older brother. He suddenly wished Sophie was there. She would probably have had the same opinion, but at least she'd temper Matu's anger slightly. There was no need to react this strongly to him going in on his own. Especially since he was unhurt.

"Let's just drop it, all right?" Sky said. "It's over now."

Matu gave Sky one last long look, but said nothing. He muttered something unintelligible under his breath, still furious with Sky, and turned to Nathan. "How's the main street?"

"Like nothing happened."

Matu nodded. "Good. Can you clear this up, too?" He gestured to the two Disciple bodies lying not too far away from them.

Nathan pointed at the two guards Sky had killed. "Bring those out here, too."

Sky and Lian each took a guard by the ankles and dragged them towards the other two Disciples. When the four dead Disciples were lying closely next to each other, Sky and Lian stepped back. Nathan raised his right hand. The Band on his wrist started glowing and the ground started to tremble. The earth underneath the bodies started to give way, lowering them slowly down into the ground. When they had vanished just under the surface, new earth appeared above them. When Nathan lowered his hand, nothing indicated the ground had ever been touched. It was like the Disciples had never been there at all.

Sky leaned on his spear. He couldn't believe how quickly the second guard had chosen to take his own life. He had known something... Something he didn't want the Asters to know about. Aside from the two guards, none of the Disciples in the house were soldiers. So, what type of Disciples were they? And what had they been doing here?

"They were looking for something," Sky said, speaking his thoughts aloud. "You guys have any idea for what?"

Matu and Lian shook their heads. Nathan had a distant look in his eyes that Sky couldn't read.

"It's not up to us to figure that out," Matu said.

"Of course it's not," Sky muttered.

Lian shot him a glance. Sky rolled his eyes, but knew that he really needed to watch what he said. Matu was done with his reckless behaviour, and it showed. One more snarky comment from Sky and the Aster of Strength would probably explode.

"Let's just finish what we came here to do so we can go home," was all that Matu said. He sounded extremely tired.

Without saying anything else, Matu headed down the street towards the eastern side of the town; the only side of the veil that they hadn't tackled yet. The other three Asters followed silently. When they reached the veil, they each placed a hand against it and spoke the words that should take it down.

There was a slight tingle in Sky's hand as he finished the spell. But the veil hadn't vanished yet. The four Asters moved up along the eastern side of town. Matu and Lian went into the opposite direction to Nathan and Sky. On the other side of the veil Sky could see the Amazon Rainforest. It was a surreal thing, having something so impressive rise up in front of him like that. Sky looked to his left towards Nathan. He had placed his hand against the veil again, but he was whispering the spell quite absently. His eyes were fixed on the Rainforest on the other side.

"What is it about that jungle?" Sky asked him.

Nathan turned to him. "There is no jungle like it in the world."

"So?"

The two of them moved along, placing their hands against the veil again and reciting the spell. When they were finished and the veil remained, they moved up again.

"It's like it's alive," Nathan told him.

"You say that about every jungle we go into," Sky pointed out.

Nathan shook his head. "Not like this one."

"What makes this one so different?"

Nathan thought for a moment, staring out towards the darkened jungle that was so incredibly close to them.

"It's just the immensity of it. My magic is stronger when the nature is stronger. And no place is stronger than this Rainforest."

"No wonder you feel drawn to it," Sky murmured.

"Yeah, no wonder," Nathan said softly.

The two of them placed their hands against the veil again. They whispered the spell once again. This time, when Sky finished, there wasn't the same prickling in his hand like before. Suddenly the cold of the veil swept all the way through him, chilling his bones and making him snatch his hand back instinctively. Next to him, Nathan did exactly the same. Sky stared at the veil. The darkened sheet started moving now, and not just in the breeze. And it was changing colour; instead of a dark blue, the veil was getting brighter. The blue started turning to purple, and then lighter still.

All of a sudden there was a bright flash. Sky protected his eyes with his hand and turned away from the sudden light.

When he took his hand away and opened his eyes, the veil had vanished. There was no dark sheet; there was nothing swaying in the wind. He looked around. It was gone; there was nothing surrounding the entire town anymore.

"Sophie was right," Sky muttered. "A bright flash but no explosion."

Lian and Matu came and joined them.

"All right, nice work," Matu said.

"So, we're done here?" Lian asked.

Matu nodded. "We're done."

Sky stared at the town behind them. There was nothing more they could do here. Or were supposed to do here. All they had to do was get their belongings from the gym and shimmer back to Saluverus. And then they'd probably never come back here again. They were now one step closer to leaving Gayle behind them.

Maybe one day the world would forget that the second Queen had been born in their generation. Maybe it was better that they all forgot. To act as though she'd never existed at all. And focus on the future.

Chapter 6

Even though the boys arrived back on Saluverus around five o'clock in the morning, local time, and just wanted to go to bed, they first had to explain in *a lot* of detail to Axel about what had happened in Brazil. Sky didn't think his decision to go into the Mendosa's house alone was such a big deal, but to Sky's annoyance, the Ambassador did think so, and took his sweet time in telling Sky off. Even more to Sky's annoyance, Matu backed Axel up completely. Lian did his best to mediate the situation, but couldn't quite hide the fact that he thought Sky should have alerted the others as well. Nathan was still in his silent, cold mission-state, and was no help at all to either side.

After they had completed their recap of the mission, with Sky taking a last opportunity to mention that they were successful in what they had been sent there to do, Axel updated them on everything that the Asters had missed on Saluverus.

The Memorial was tomorrow. What they also already knew was that the Memorial wouldn't be the traditional burning pyres on the courtyard in front of the castle, but without pyres in the Throne Room instead. Sky didn't particularly care about this piece of information, but he did care about what came next.

The decision on what to do with Gayle's magic no longer mattered. A final spell cast had made it very clear that neither Gayle nor her magic existed in this world anymore. Not even her bones could be found. So the Queen's Case would focus exclusively on determining the exact way the King had killed Gayle. The team would search the area around the town, each week splitting in half as they ventured further into the Amazon Rainforest in search of clues. When they reached teams of four, more researchers and soldiers would be sent in with the help of Madeleine's shimmer so they could go further into the Rainforest if necessary and split off again, to cover the most ground. Sky doubted the Asters would hear much about the investigation. Axel made it clear the Asters were on stand-by for the possible uprising in North America and therefore would have nothing more to do with South America.

Affinites had also been returning to their homes on the continents. Now that Gayle was dead and Disciples no longer had a reason to go after Affinites, the Small Council considered the Surface safe to return to. Many families, however, still remained, wanting to pay their respects at the Memorial. A few Affinites and their families weren't staying specifically for the Memorial. They were still on the island because certain members were to be part of the Queen's Case or Bone Recovery. Sky happened to know that one of those families was the Amsel family, consisting of Nadine Amsel and her five children.

Which brought Axel to the last piece of information. Supposedly there had been no further developments on the Disciples roaming around in North America, which meant that the Asters were grounded on Saluverus for the time being. Sky didn't mind it for now. He'd had a good, if short, fight, back in Brazil. The itch under his skin to do *something* had disappeared. He knew it would be back, but he could relax a little for now.

Sky slept long and deep that night. It was almost noon before he got out of his bed to get dressed. He was still half-pulling the blue sweater over his head as he pushed open his bedroom door. When he stepped onto the narrow balcony, Sophie's bedroom door opened up on the floor below. Sky watched and, not believing his eyes, saw Jacob bloody

Henderson step out of Sophie's bedroom. The English boy with wet blonde hair turned his head back to Sophie's room and said something that Sky couldn't quite catch, before turning to the door that led out of the Asters' common room and into the castle beyond.

Sky hadn't realised his breathing had turned sharper. He could feel his blood boiling. Before he knew it, he had literally flown down the stairs and right into his sister's bedroom.

"Jeez, Sky!" Sophie exclaimed at his sudden appearance.

It only then occurred to Sky that he perhaps should have knocked first. Sophie was standing in front of him, only half dressed. She was already wearing jeans, but as for her upper body... she was only wearing a bra. In her hands she was holding the shirt she was just about to pull on.

The sight of her didn't faze Sky in the slightest, and Sophie didn't seem to care either. They were brother and sister, or as close as they could be. And Sky had seen his sister with less than this on before.

"What the hell is wrong with you?" Sky exclaimed.

"Okay, I'm going to need more information," Sophie responded mildly. Her tone surprised him. There was a lightness about her that he hadn't seen in a while; that he hadn't seen since Gayle Mendosa died.

"Jacob? *Jacob?* Are you kidding me?"

"*That's* what this is about? How about, hey Soph, good to see you again. We missed you in Brazil, since we apparently can't think of any spell without you," Sophie said sarcastically as she pulled the black t-shirt on over her head and pulled her long blonde hair out of the neckline. Much to Sky's disgust, her hair was wet. Just like Jacob's had been. The thought of the two of them showering together made him want to throw up.

"Don't change the subject," Sky snapped.

Sophie rolled her eyes and sighed. "Fine. What about Jacob?"

"The guy is a nightmare! How could this possibly have happened?"

"He's only a nightmare to you," Sophie pointed out.

Sky narrowed his eyes. "That doesn't answer my question."

"What do you want me to say?"

"I want you to tell me if he's taking advantage of you," Sky demanded.

Sophie looked at him incredulously. "You're joking, right?"

Sky stared her down. He was going to pummel that son of a bitch into the ground if he was doing what Sky suspected him of.

Sophie straightened, her grey eyes starting to boil with anger, reminding him of a looming thunderstorm. "You're not joking. I really hoped you were joking."

"And I really hoped you were smarter than this," Sky snapped. A distant voice in the back of his head was telling him that he was going too far. But there was a roaring in his ears that blocked out any voice of reason. This was his sister. *His sister.* If that guy did *anything* to hurt her...

"You did not just say that," Sophie growled. "You think I can't take care of myself? Jake *is not* taking advantage of me."

"Oh, so it's *Jake* now?" Sky spat.

"Don't be childish," Sophie snapped. She went over to the chest of drawers near the door and pulled one of the drawers open.

"You know how he is. You know what he wants more than anything. He could be manipulating you without you even realising it!"

Sophie shot Sky a look over her shoulder as she pulled a jumper out of the drawers. "If you're just going to shout at me like I'm some stupid girl, then you might as well leave."

"I don't want to be shouting at you like you're—"

"Then don't!" she interrupted. "Just get out if you have nothing else to say."

Sky took a deep breath. "You've been through a lot," he said, forcing his voice to be calm. "I don't want to see him using you like this."

"And that's what you think is happening?" Sophie asked angrily.

"Yes! I think he's using you. I think he's buttering you up so he can get whatever information he wants so he has a better chance of becoming an Aster, *especially* now that there are two spaces that need to be filled!"

Sophie literally growled at Sky. "Stop treating me like some broken puppet that can be manipulated to anyone's will!"

"Then stop acting like one!"

The words were out of his mouth before he could stop them.

"GET OUT!"

"Soph..." Sky began, and then stopped. It was slowly dawning on him that Sophie had changed since the last time he had been with her. She wasn't a puppet. She hadn't been acting like she was being manipulated. She had looked happy, or like something close to that. There was more colour in her cheeks than there had been for the past week. Whether Jacob was manipulating her or not, he knew deep down that she wasn't stupid enough to fall for it.

"Get. The Hell. Out."

"Sophie, I didn't—"

But she wasn't paying attention to him anymore. She pulled on her jumper and headed for the small bathroom that was connected to her bedroom. She didn't even wait to see whether Sky had left before she slammed the door behind her.

A day had gone by and Sophie had not spoken a word to Sky since their fight. When the five of them were at breakfast on the morning of the Memorial, Sophie was still clearly angry at him. Sky didn't blame her, but he still didn't trust the boy she had chosen to be with. The way Jacob swaggered around like he owned the place, even more so since he was with Sophie, just didn't sit right with Sky.

The two of them had spent last night together as well. Sky put in a lot of effort not to run into Jacob in the common room, or anywhere else for that matter. He knew that if he did, there would be a confrontation. Sky knew it was better to just stay out of the way.

The other Asters knew of the relationship now, too. None of them seemed too thrilled about it either, but they still couldn't deny that Sophie looked more alive than she had done since Gayle's death. The therapy was helping, too. Sky overheard Sophie telling Nathan about it the night before; how it was refreshing talking to someone about her life who wasn't an Aster, but who had seen practically everything and who had worked with almost everyone on the island at some point.

The door to the dining hall opened and Diallo Madaki and Rose Radbourne entered. The two Ceders smiled at the five Asters before heading over to the breakfast buffet.

Nathan turned to Matu after waving at his mother and asked, "Have you spoken to your father lately?"

Matu looked up from his toast and shook his head. "No, why?"

"Because he and Madeleine are going to be leaving for a mission tomorrow," Nathan said.

Sky frowned at his brother. "What are you talking about?"

"My mother told me yesterday that your parents are going to investigate the situation in North America," Nathan revealed.

Sky dropped his knife; it clattered onto his plate. "*We* are on stand-by for anything that happens in North America. Why are they going?"

Nathan shook his head.

"Your mother didn't say anything else?" Lian asked.

"Not about that, no. But there's something else. According to Axel, not all the Disciples we ran into in Brazil were detected by our sensors."

"What does that matter as long as a few are detected?" Matu asked.

"The Small Council will send in the wrong number of reinforcements if they don't know how large the threat is," Sophie said. "Our sensors should pick every one of them up. Have the local Affinites had any more run-ins since you came back?"

Nathan shook his head again. "Not that my mother knew of, but Axel is definitely on edge. The mission to find the bones has been entrusted to Katherine and Mum to handle while Percy is responsible for the investigation into Gayle's death, but apparently Axel is worried because they might be facing more Disciples than the Small Council can detect."

"Do we even know yet why those Disciples were in the Mendosa's house?" Matu asked.

Nathan shrugged.

"Why is your mother telling you all of this?" Sophie asked Nathan.

"More importantly, why aren't *we* being told any of this?" Sky snapped. Sophie glared at him before turning back to her breakfast.

Nathan gave them a look that said he didn't know that either.

"I think it's time to ask our dear Ambassador a few questions," Sky said, starting to get up from the table.

"Do you really think that's a good idea?" Lian asked doubtfully.

"Undetectable Disciples in Brazil, and two of our parents are going to investigate something that we were supposed to be on stand-by for, and we know *nothing* of this? Yeah, I kind of want to know why. Don't any of you?" Sky got up from the table and looked around the group. Both Lian and Nathan nodded, but remained where they were.

"You don't need all of us to storm the Board Room," Lian said as an explanation.

Matu got up from his chair and said, "I'll go with you."

Then Sky's eyes found Sophie's. She just glowered at him. "You tell me, since I'm so easily manipulated these days."

Sky rolled his eyes and marched away. Matu caught up with him outside of the dining hall.

"What was that all about?" Matu asked.

"I told her I think Jacob is either taking advantage of her or manipulating her."

Matu let out a long sigh.

"What?" Sky asked irritably.

Matu glanced sideways at Sky. "You really are an idiot."

"Call me what you like," Sky muttered. They were heading along the corridor and down a flight of stairs that led to the Board Room.

"I'm calling you an idiot. Anyone can see he's not manipulating her."

They rounded a corner and passed a few Affinites who were on their way to breakfast.

"I just don't trust the guy," Sky declared.

"You don't have to trust him. You just have to trust her. Saying that she's being manipulated and too stupid to notice won't help. You might want to apologise for that."

"When she stops sleeping with the guy, I will."

"Oh please, Sky, don't be an arse as well as an idiot. Just apologise and move on. Maybe not be a complete hypocrite."

They turned down another corridor. This one was much quieter. The Board Room was all the way on the other side of the castle, and it would take them at least another few minutes to get there.

"How can you possibly be okay with it?" Sky asked Matu. Sky was not the only one Jacob was a complete jerk to. There had been plenty of times where the boy had belittled and annoyed the brother standing next to him.

Matu snorted. "Oh, believe me, I can't stand the guy. But it's not about me. Sophie seems to be doing fine. Better even."

"How do you know?"

"*Sky*. She can take care of herself, you know."

"*Can she?*" Sky interjected.

Matu let out another one of his exasperated sighs. It got on Sky's nerves. "You can't possibly be comparing her being with Jacob with her over-using her magic. I just told you *not* to be an idiot."

"I'm not... I'm just—"

"You're worried about her. I am too. But you have to let her make her own decisions. She seems to be doing better now that she's seeing Doctor Masalis, and being with Jacob doesn't seem to be making anything any worse. You're just going to have to accept it, whether you like it or not."

"I just don't know if she can deal with another loss," Sky murmured, chewing his bottom lip.

"Jacob Henderson is not going to die," Matu replied, irritation now edging into his voice.

"He might if I kill him," Sky muttered.

Matu chuckled at this. "And why would you kill him?

"I don't know. Could be anything. He gets on my nerves."

Matu looked at him, his expression one of annoyance. "Okay, if this is where this conversation is heading, then I'm out. Just accept her choice, Sky. It's all we can do."

"It better not last," Sky grumbled.

"It might not," Matu said. "You don't have to like the guy, but if she's okay, then that's really all you need to be worrying about."

Sky rolled his eyes. "Why are you always so rational?"

"It's a gift," Matu said proudly, a twinkle in his eyes.

"It's annoying is what it is," Sky muttered.

"Yeah, well, you might want to hide that annoyance for the next few minutes, all right?" They had arrived at the Board Room.

"I can't promise anything."

"You never do." Matu sighed. He knocked and pushed the door open.

Axel and Sylvia were already in the Board Room. It hadn't occurred to Sky that they could've found it empty, since it was only eight-thirty in the morning. But the Ambassador and Consul were there nonetheless. Both of them were sitting at the table, which was covered in papers and files.

"Sky, Matu," Sylvia said as the two of them entered. "What can we do for you?"

"We want to know what is going on in North America and what is happening in Brazil," Sky declared. His voice was steadier than he had expected it to be; he was glad he didn't sound like some whining child who had been left out of playing a game.

"What has brought this on?" Sylvia asked.

"We know that my mother and his father are going to North America for an investigation, and that you hadn't detected half of the Disciples I fought off in Brazil," Sky explained.

Matu cut a sideways look at him and said under his breath. "Fought off. Really?"

Sky shushed him with the shake of his head.

Axel Reed and Sylvia Allen exchanged looks.

"That doesn't concern you at the moment," Axel claimed.

Sky felt like his head was about to explode. "It *does* concern us actually. Percy said we were on stand-by for North America, and the next thing we hear is that two of our parents are being sent there for an investigation. How does that not concern us?"

"All right," Sylvia said after a pause, seeking to keep the peace. Axel shot her a look, but the Consul continued anyway. "We are still monitoring the situation in North America like we have done ever since we last spoke. There have been developments, but—"

"What kind of developments?" Sky interrupted.

Sylvia glared at him. "*But,* you will be informed of those *after* the Memorial, since that is where your attention should be. You've experienced a great loss and you each need to say goodbye and have closure before we send you anywhere else. As for Brazil: since your work on the veil and the street, that place is no longer your concern. Nicholas and Felix are working on why we couldn't detect some of the Disciples as we speak, and we will not be divulging any information on that matter with you until needed."

"And the developments in North America?" Matu asked calmly.

"If they are in need of our attention then you need to send us there now," Sky urged.

"The only developments are that there are more Disciples on the Surface of North America than when we last spoke—" Sylvia started.

"*Sylvia*," Axel warned.

The Consul cleared her throat and shot Axel an apologetic look. "If there was a dire need to send you, we would. However, there is not, so we won't. You will get an update after the Memorial, all right?"

Beside him, Matu nodded slowly. "All right, thank you."

Sky cast Matu an angry glance. How was this enough of an explanation for his brother? Why wait until after the Memorial? They were here now, just tell them now.

Matu shook his head minimally, telling Sky to leave it alone. He turned around and headed for the door.

Sky gritted his teeth, and managed to get out a "Fine," before following Matu out. Something was happening in North America. It might not be dire enough for them to go there now, but Sky had a bad feeling. News must be spreading in all seven territories of the Underworld that the Queen was dead, and North America was making its move; Sky could feel it. He just hoped they weren't one step behind *again*, and this time would be able to stop whatever that particular King was planning before it was too late.

Chapter 7

The Memorial for the Mendosa family was different from any other Sky had witnessed before. Memorials normally took place on the courtyard in front of the castle. Wooden logs would be stacked on top of each other in the form of a pyramid, but with enough of a flat slab at the top for a body to be laid out on. The courtyard was also a big enough space for a large number of people to gather to watch as the bonfires were lit and the bodies were burnt.

The Mendosa Memorial wasn't outside.

And there were no bodies to burn.

It was being held in the Throne Room on the top floor of the castle. It was the largest enclosed space in the entire castle. Two beautifully carved oak doors opened up at one short end of the large rectangular room. The long sides of the room were lined with benches, each slightly higher than the one in front, so everyone had an unobstructed view of the centre. High along the long walls and above the oak doors were balconies, each also with benches as well as room to stand at the back. The high vaulted ceiling was made completely of multi-coloured glass, and when the sun shone through it, a beautiful kaleidoscope effect with greens, blues and oranges would light up the dark wooden floor. But those magnificent colours weren't the most impressive thing in the Throne Room. At the other end of the room was the throne itself. It was made entirely out of green and brown vines, roots and branches, and dotted with red and orange flowers. The twisting and curling nature covered the entire wall, leaving space in the middle near the floor in the form of a single seat. Three wide steps led up to the dais. Before the steps was a large wooden altar, on top of which stood two black cauldrons. An ancient-looking book lay in between them.

Sky stepped into the room and stared at the throne. He felt his heart ache. None of this seemed real. It was like there had always been a part of him that had hoped that it was all a lie. That the Mendosas weren't really dead. That Gayle was still alive somewhere, and that she was coming—coming to sit on that throne.

It was useless to think that way. This Memorial would make sure they would never think that way again.

Sky moved up to the front of the Throne Room and took a seat on the highest bench on the right. Extra benches had been brought in, and the walkway in between was so narrow that two people couldn't walk side-by-side.

The Memorial would begin in under ten minutes, and Affinites from all over were filing into the room. Nathan walked in and took a seat next to Sky.

Sky scanned the packed room and found Matu sitting near the middle of the lowest bench next to Josephine. Sky wondered if any of the other Affinites they had rescued from the South American Underworld would be here. He knew Reth Okoth, a Kenyan Affinite and a close friend of Matu's father, was still in the hospital recovering from his injuries. Sky did spot his wife, Eidi, and his son, Yaro, standing on the balcony across from him.

The room was now near bursting with people. Sky scanned the room further. Lian was standing on the balcony over the entry doors with Anna, and to Sky's disgust, he found Sophie and Jacob close together on one of the higher benches across from him. Sophie felt his gaze the moment he looked at her. She stared him down for a moment before resuming whatever conversation she was having with Jacob.

Sky turned to Nathan and found that his brother was also looking towards Sophie and Jacob. There was something in Nathan's eyes that Sky couldn't quite place as he looked at the couple.

"You might want to stop staring," Sky said, nudging his brother.

Nathan shook himself out of his stare and turned to Sky. "She seems happy," he murmured. "She's doing okay, right?"

Sky shrugged. "Don't ask me. I haven't spoken to her since I found out."

Nathan sighed. "As long as—"

"As she's happy, yeah, yeah," Sky interrupted, dismissing Nathan's attempt to defend Sophie just like Matu had done the day before.

"I was going to say, *as long as it doesn't last*," Nathan muttered through gritted teeth.

Sky raised his eyebrows, surprised at the hostility his brother was presenting. He wanted to ask why Nathan seemed to be even more against the relationship than he was. But before he could, the entire room fell silent in an instant.

Sky turned his head and saw that Diana Griffiths, the last female Elder and Sophie's grandmother, was standing in the doorway to the Throne Room.

Diana Griffiths was wearing a long black dress, and a black cloak fell down from her shoulders. It pooled around her as she stood, monitoring the Throne Room. She had the same blonde hair as her daughter, but it was streaked with grey. It was whisked up in an elegant bun on the top of her head.

For minutes, it seemed, the room was silent as Diana remained still where she stood. Sky didn't know what cue she was waiting for, but from one moment to the next, Diana started walking towards the altar at the far end of the room. Then Sky understood. The doors didn't close behind Diana. The other two Elders stepped into the Throne Room behind her. They were both dressed in black as well, and they walked in single file behind Diana in complete silence.

When Diana reached the altar, she walked around to stand directly behind it. Harrison Mayne, Sky's grandfather, moved to the right and stopped to stand to the right of the altar. Nathan's grandfather did the same on the left. They both turned to face the room. Sky met his grandfather's gaze only for a moment. Harrison gave Sky such a small nod that Sky doubted anyone else would've seen it, before turning his attention forward.

Diana reached for the ancient-looking book in the middle of the altar, and opened it. Dust particles flew up as she turned the pages. The sound of rustling paper was the only thing that could be heard in the vast room.

Diana paused on a particular page and looked up. The lively twinkle Sky always saw in her eyes wasn't there today. Sadness shrouded her features as she began to speak.

"We come together today in memory," she began. Her voice wasn't amplified, but in the utter silence of the room, everyone could hear every word she spoke, loud and clear.

"Three lives were taken before their time. Not many people in this room knew them, but you have all come here to remember them. From wherever they are, I am sure that they are grateful."

Sky looked around the room. He wondered *how many* of the people here had known the Mendosas. He thought quite a few must have. Not in recent years, but Tomas was born an Aster and had lived on Saluverus all throughout his youth and young adult life. Not many people knew Cara, though, Sky did know that. She only came to Saluverus after marrying Tomas. And they left shortly before Gayle was born.

"Tomas Mendosa was an Aster by blood. He grew to be a fine man." Diana smiled softly, as if remembering some memory of Tomas as she spoke. "In the war twenty-five years ago, he was the one to free us of the horror that was Astaroth, the strongest of the Original Higher Kings. He was a great man."

Diana paused, letting the words sink in before continuing.

"Cara was not an Aster by blood, but an Aster she became nonetheless. She provided the most valuable information during the war, without which we would not have won. She was a great woman."

Diana paused again.

"We are here to remember two incredible people. When they birthed the most miraculous child, they cast everything aside to protect their daughter. And they did so until their final breaths were taken from them."

Diana stopped and waited once again. Nathan's grandfather stepped forward and placed his right hand on the rim of the cauldron on Diana's right. The entire room remained quiet as the Elder of Flora started whispering a spell. A few moments later a fire burst from the cauldron. Yet it didn't burn the hand that was still on the rim. Nathan's grandfather slowly retracted his hand and took a step back.

"Let the fire symbolise a cleansing. Let the flames burn away your sorrow, and let only a memory remain. Remember the greatness of the lives we have lost. And give thanks, for the lives they have lived," Diana said.

Sky stared into the flames. They shone brightly in the ever-darkening Throne Room. Dusk was settling over the island, and soon the moon would shine brightly through the coloured glass ceiling.

"Gayle Mendosa was a brilliant girl," Diana Griffiths continued. Sky felt his heart contract at where the Memorial was headed now. The hope—the salvation. That was what Gayle had signified for every Affinite and Aster alive. "Nobody here knew her personally, but she meant a great deal to all of us. She was supposed to come to us in these weeks, but she did not get that chance. Her death is a terrible loss, not just to those closest to her, but to us all. She would have been a great woman." Diana paused, and then added, "She would have been a great Queen."

Someone was sobbing near Sky. He didn't dare take his eyes off Diana to see who it was. He heard Nathan suck in a breath beside him.

"We could not protect her. That is a great regret we all will live with for as long as we are alive. But we will not let her have died in vain. She was taken from this world too soon, and I promise you all—" Diana paused to look around the room. There was a steely determination in her expression as she looked into the eyes of as many people as possible before continuing. "—Gayle Mendosa, and her parents, will be avenged."

A murmur went through the crowd. Sky balled his fists at his sides. Yes, they will be avenged, he thought to himself. He had no doubt that every Affinite around him believed the same. No Disciple, no *King*, would ever get away with hurting their world as badly as they had done a week ago. It didn't matter how long it took. It didn't matter that the Asters would first have to deal with the uprising in North America. The unknown King in South America would pay for what he did. One day... one day he would learn what happens to those who challenged the Asters. He would learn what happens to he who killed the Queen.

The murmurs in the crowd died the second Harrison Mayne stepped closer to the altar and placed his hand on the rim of the cauldron to Diana's left. He, too, started whispering, and within a few moments the second cauldron blazed up and a fire crackled within.

Sky's grandfather stepped back once more. It was nearing the end of the ceremonial-part of the Memorial. Sky knew what was coming next. Diana would recite the words spoken at the end of every Affinite and Aster funeral when the death was at the hand of Dark magic.

Diana closed the book in front of her. She placed her hands on top and looked up at the coloured glass ceiling.

"Tomas... Cara... Gayle..." she spoke. She lowered her head and looked at all the people in front of her.

"*May you be free*," she spoke.

"May you be free," repeated every single person in the Throne Room.

"*May you feel no pain.*"

"May you feel no pain," rang through the room.

"*May you find peace.*"

"May you find peace."

"*May your deaths not be in vain.*"

"May your deaths not be in vain."

Diana waited one moment longer. She stared out in front of her, her expression solemn but with a sense of strong conviction. Sky believed every single word as Diana finally said, "*You will be avenged.*"

"You will be avenged," rang through the room.

Sky could feel the buzz in his veins, the strength that filled him when he spoke those final words. He could feel the truth in them as he said them. He knew all the other Asters felt the same. They might not have been able to prevent Gayle's death, but they would do everything in their power to make sure it wasn't for nothing. She would be avenged. Whether it was tomorrow, next month, or next year. It didn't matter. Gayle Mendosa would be avenged. The South American King would pay.

Diana Griffiths looked around the crowd in the Throne Room one last time, and said, "From this moon to the next, these fires will burn. And we will remember, even once the final embers have been extinguished. We will avenge you. And we will never forget you."

After the Memorial there were drinks and food in the dining hall. The long tables had been moved to the walls of the hall and were now filled with so, so many snacks, half of which Lian didn't even recognise. Anna had just introduced him to Jaffa cakes, and Lian was still not sure what to make of them. They were delicious—that much he knew for sure. Anna was laughing at the way he had smelt the cake before daring to put it in his mouth, and now he had already lost count of how many he'd eaten.

The Memorial had been sad, extremely sad; especially when Diana had spoken about Gayle Mendosa and how nothing could've been done to save her, Lian felt like his heart was being ripped out of his body. He knew the other Asters felt the same. They all wanted to believe that there was more they could've done, but all evidence pointed to the contrary.

Even though Diana had used the fires just as a metaphor, it did seem like some of the sadness had burnt away. The dining hall was filled with light chatter; lighter than Lian had heard in days. It was nice to see, and even nicer to hear after the deathly quiet of the last few days. Even though there were no bodies yet to burn, it had been a good idea to have the Memorial. Everyone seemed to have got some form of closure.

Lian looked across the dining hall. He spotted Sky standing over at the bar. It didn't surprise Lian whatsoever that Sky was there. The drink in his hand was probably at least his second. Sky was talking animatedly with Kemal Malas and Ashu Bekele, two of the Asters' closest friends. Kemal had been transferred to Saluverus from his hometown in Turkey a few years back when he'd shown potential to become a great soldier. He had a round face, with dark eyes, bushy black hair and thick eyebrows. For a guy his size, the fluidity of his movements had surprised everyone during his first week of training on the island. Ashu's experience had been practically the same. In fact, Ashu arrived from Ethiopia on the same day as Kemal had from

Turkey, though Ashu hadn't been scouted for his fighting skills, but for his affinity for stealth. His skin tone was an even darker shade than Matu's and he had short, thick, black curls. Even though they came from completely different countries and backgrounds, Kemal and Ashu bonded immediately upon arrival and had been inseparable ever since.

Lian looked further around the hall. He couldn't see Sophie or Matu anywhere, but he found Nathan by one of the higher tables that had been placed in the centre of the dining hall, talking to Moroccan twins, Asmae and Marwa Kadiri. They, too, had been scouted and brought to Saluverus when they were fifteen. They were identically short, with medium-length, dark hair, and brown eyes which were magnified by their black-rimmed glasses. You couldn't tell by the looks of them, but they were deadly. Even more so when fighting side by side.

The Asters sometimes trained with the highly skilled Affinites who were in the soldier-programme. In those sessions the Asters weren't allowed to use magic, so they'd be equals, though for Lian that was always a problem. He couldn't help it; his magic always kicked in whenever he got hurt, without him even thinking about it, and he would be called out to stop fighting further. It was during those trainings that the Asters had met Ashu, Kemal and the Kadiri twins and had become good friends.

Lian's eyes drifted further and found Nora Amsel, the oldest of the five Amsel children, leaning on one of the other higher tables. Lian couldn't spot any of her siblings or her mother anywhere near her. Nora had a drink in her hand and she smiled and nodded to a second girl Lian didn't recognise. He just about made out the words "thank you" on Nora's lips when the second girl walked away from the table to meet up with some friends near the entrance.

"Do you know her?" Anna asked, following Lian's gaze and realising who he was looking at.

Lian continued to look at the German Affinite, whose mother would soon be off to Brazil to be part of the Queen's Case. Nora's flaming red hair stood out amongst the crowd.

"No," Lian said. Then he realised something, and added, "Do you?"

"Not well," Anna answered. "I've spoken to her a few times, but she's usually busy taking care of her brothers and sisters. She's actually really nice."

It didn't surprise Lian one bit that Anna had already spoken to Nora. Even though his friend was constantly busy with her studies to become a surgeon, she always seemed to have time to talk to everyone in the castle. Somehow, she knew a little bit about absolutely everyone. How she found the time, Lian would never know.

"Her mother will be sent on some kind of mission for Percy Kelly soon. You know? Jackson Kelly's brother. Well, of course you know," Anna was saying.

Lian tried to hide his smile, and Anna punched his arm for it.

"Ow!" Lian exclaimed.

"Stop laughing. It's unfair you know so much stuff and can't tell me," Anna exclaimed, her eyes sparkling with amusement.

"Considering how easily you gossip, I would think it's very smart that I can keep my mouth shut," Lian teased, grinning.

Anna narrowed her eyes at him and shook her head. "Come on, she's standing there all alone. Let's go over there," she said.

Lian followed as Anna led him through the crowd towards Nora Amsel. While he walked something caught his eye. Sophie had just entered the dining hall and was searching the crowd. When her eyes met his, she beckoned him. Lian nodded to her and reached out to grab Anna's wrist. They hadn't made it to the high table Nora was standing at yet.

"What?" Anna asked.

"You go on ahead. Sophie needs me for something. I'll catch up, all right?" Lian said.

"Sure thing." She gave him a kind smile before turning away from him and vanishing into the crowd.

Lian changed direction and headed for the entrance to the dining hall. Once out in the hallway he found Sophie waiting for him. Nathan was at her side.

"What's going on?" Lian asked.

"Axel wants to see us," Sophie replied. Both she and Nathan turned away and headed down the corridor. Lian followed.

"I hate always having to leave so suddenly," Lian admitted.

Sophie looked up at him. "It comes with the job, I'm afraid. Anna understands it, though, right?"

"Yeah, she does. It still sucks, though," Lian mumbled.

The three of them rounded a corner and Sophie led them into a room along the corridor. Lian had never been there before. It was like a small office, with a desk on one side and a few filing cabinets on the other, though none of it seemed to be in use.

Sky was already there, sitting on the desk, while Matu was sitting on the chair. Axel was standing near the narrow, tall window at the back of the small room. Lian closed the door behind him and turned to face the Ambassador.

"Thank you for coming, I won't keep you here long," Axel said.

"What's going on?" Lian asked.

Axel cleared his throat. "After you left Brazil, Karla and the other local Affinites finished preserving the scene. They are done changing the memories of the other inhabitants concerning the night of the disappearance and what has happened since then. They will not remember the Mendosas ever lived there."

The Asters remained quiet as the Ambassador continued. Axel was never one for pleasantries; he always dove right into what he wanted to discuss. Apparently, the Asters were being updated on everything that was happening in Brazil and North America right now.

"The Affinites involved in both the Queen's Case and the Bone

Recovery missions will leave tomorrow. Katherine and Rose are leading the Bone Recovery teams. Because the events in Brazil no longer concern you, you will be kept out of any developments concerning that matter. Now, as for Diallo and Madeleine's mission that you came to hear of—" Axel looked pointedly at Nathan, "they are to travel to North America and talk to some of the local Watchers. There are as many Disciples in North America as when we spoke last. However, they are moving around quite a lot, which is uncharacteristic. We're having Diallo and Madeleine go there in person, not only to talk to the Watchers, but also to get a sense of the latest developments on the continent itself."

"We are on stand-by for North America. Why aren't we being sent to do this?" Sky challenged. There was an edge to his voice. Sky, Lian knew, was itching to get off the island again. The fight against the Disciples in the Mendosa's house had calmed him down for about two days, but he was now back to being as irritable as he was since they'd been played so easily by the South American King.

"Diallo and Madeleine are there just to gather information. You are still on stand-by for if and when the North American King makes his move, but for now we'd rather keep you here on the island until Sophie is cleared for missions by Doctor Masalis. You should also take this time to regain your strength. Don't underestimate the effect the spells you cast in Brazil had on you."

Lian glanced at Sophie. She caught his gaze and gave him a reassuring nod. "It won't be long," she promised. She did seem to be doing much better since the night she almost died. Almost better even than before Gayle Mendosa had been killed. She always seemed refreshed when she came back from her therapy sessions.

"You could easily send in two of us to North America. Not all of us need healing," Sky asserted.

Lian caught Sophie shift on her feet. Her fists were clenched at her sides, but she said nothing. Nathan looked slightly uncomfortable, and Matu seemed to force himself to stay quiet. Lian wanted to snap at Sky that he could at least *try* to be more sensitive, but Axel spoke before he could do so.

"Do not underestimate the extra time you can now take to prepare, Mayne. An uprising is nothing to be taken lightly," he told Sky. "There is no arguing this point with me; the Small Council has made its decision. We will keep an eye on the developments in North America, and you will be updated, or even called into action when needed. Do I make myself clear?"

The Asters nodded and sounded their agreement. Axel stared at each and every one of them before saying, "Good. Take this seriously. You don't know what might await you in North America, and we're expecting you to be at your highest level of mental and physical strength. So, take the next weeks to make sure of that."

The Asters silently stared after him as the Ambassador left the small office and disappeared down the hall.

Chapter 8

A month after the Memorial things had settled back down on Saluverus. Despite what Axel had originally said, the Asters had received a few updates on the two separate missions in Brazil. The Queen's Case had split up so many times now that the Affinites were currently doing research in teams of four. Soon, Madeleine would shimmer in with more soldiers, researchers and scientists to broaden the search further into the Amazon Rainforest.

Another thing they were told was that dead Disciples had been found in the Rainforest, all with horrific animal wounds. They were covered in deep lacerations and lethal bite marks, indicating that their wounds were fatal, and not *post mortem* scavenger damage.

Sophie knew from legends that wild animals recognised Queen Aiyana as their queen as well, because of the magic she possessed. It was as if the animals in the Rainforest hadn't taken kindly to their new queen being attacked and killed, either. Whether this was proof that Gayle had actually managed to get to the Amazon while wild animals were trying to aid her escape, the investigators weren't sure of yet. The dead Disciples were quite scattered; the Affinites couldn't yet detect a clear path that Gayle might have taken the night she died. The investigation was still ongoing.

Diallo and Madeleine had returned from their mission in North America. The Disciple activity had settled down since the Memorial.

Only around the Grand Canyon National Park were the number of Disciples increasing and decreasing at fast inter-changeable rates, which was unusual to say the least. Disciples from all over the country seemed to be heading there, only to vanish. There were various entrances to the North American Underworld in the Grand Canyon, so when Disciples disappeared, it could only mean that they'd entered the Underworld. As long as the Disciples stayed there, it was nothing to be concerned about. Having more underground than on the Surface was never a bad thing. Still, Felix had his Watchers very much on the look-out for if suddenly the Disciples would be streaming out onto the Surface in higher numbers.

Sophie stepped into the girl's changing rooms in the arena. That morning the Asters were to train with ten Affinites under Jackson Kelly's supervision. The five female Affinites chosen were already in the room when Sophie entered. Sophie hadn't known before that morning which Affinites she and her brothers would be training with; there were many Affinites around their age with battle-advantageous affinities. Who the Asters trained with, changed each week.

It didn't surprise Sophie that Jillian Kelly, Percy Kelly's daughter, was standing at the mirror tying her hair up into a pony tail, and that the Moroccan twins, Asmae and Marwa were at their lockers, trading their thick black glasses for contact lenses. Sophie recognised the other two Affinites as well, and greeted both of them as she walked over to her own locker and took off her jacket. Finnish Affinite Elyn and Belgian Affinite Leonie both greeted her in return.

As Sophie hung up her jacket, Jillian came up beside her and leaned back against the locker next to Sophie's. "Did you hear about Brazil?"

Sophie turned to her friend, frowning. There were a number of developments Jillian could be referring to. "What about Brazil?"

"One team of the Queen's Case hasn't been in contact for two days, and everyone has been called back to base camp until they know why,"

Jillian said.

"How do you know that?" Sophie asked. Axel had told the Asters precisely this piece of information the evening before.

Jillian Kelly shrugged. "My dad told me. They're planning on sending in a rescue team. My mum will be part of it."

"Are you worried?"

"Not just yet. There are plenty of reasons why their communication could have broken down," Jillian said lightly.

Sophie nodded. "That's true."

"Hey," Jillian said, changing the subject and patting Sophie on the shoulder. "I hear congratulations are in order."

Sophie smiled at her friend. "Your dad tell you that, too?"

Jillian grinned. "You bet."

"Told you what?" Asmae asked from the other side of the room.

"I've been cleared for missions," Sophie revealed.

"Congratulations!" the twins both said in unison. Sophie grinned at their identical enthusiasm. People who didn't know Asmae and Marwa would not be able to tell them apart.

"I'm glad you're training with us again, now that your hand has finally healed," Jillian said happily. She turned on her heel and headed for the door.

Sophie looked down at her hand. The scars were thick and uneven, but finally painless. It might take a while before she could work a sword with that hand as well as before, but thankfully it wasn't her dominant hand. Most of the time all that was needed of her left hand was for the thumb to press the button on the side of her miniature wrist crossbow.

Sophie and the other four Affinites followed Jillian out through the door and onto the grounds of the arena. The nine boys were already there, standing beside a single table near the official entrance. On the ground near the table was a large circle, drawn in chalk. Nathan was talking to Arthur Kelly, Jackson's son and Jillian's cousin. Sky, Lian and

Matu were standing behind the single table together with Affinites Ashu and Kemal. Finally, to the right were Jake and the fifth male Affinite, Nils Forsberg.

Sophie and the five female Affinites gathered around the table. Upon it, Sophie counted fifteen daggers. There was nothing else. She moved to stand by Jake. He kissed her on the cheek and whispered, "You know what we're doing?"

"No," Sophie answered softly. She eyed the daggers once more when the main doors to the arena opened and Jackson and Percy Kelly stepped through.

"Is he now officially part of the Small Council?" Jake asked, looking at Jackson's twin brother.

"No idea," Sophie whispered.

"I don't think he minds being in a position with that much control."

Sophie chuckled softly, looking at the ex-soldier standing proudly next to his brother as if he were definitely not second to him.

"Today will be short," Jackson began. "One fight, one against one. No magic, one dagger each."

Beside her, Nils cracked his knuckles, chuckling softly to himself. If there was ever a challenge best suited to the massive Swedish Affinite with the affinity for agility, it was this one. At six foot six, Nils was faster than he looked, and it was almost impossible to bring him down without magic. Whoever was chosen to fight him today was going to have a hard time of it.

"Up first," Jackson continued. "Lian and Arthur. Grab a dagger and go and stand in the ring. One step outside and you lose."

Both Lian and Arthur took a dagger from the table and stepped inside the circle of chalk drawn on the floor. If Sophie had to guess, it had the diameter of about fifteen feet. It reminded her of a ring used for sumo wrestling. As the two boys stepped into the ring, the rest of them gathered around it, a few feet back from the edge. Lian and Arthur stood a few feet away from each other. Lian was jogging on the spot, while Arthur was rolling his shoulders and stretching his neck.

Jackson and Percy stood next to each other on one side of the ring. Jackson looked from Lian, to Arthur, to the watch on his right wrist. In his left hand he held a small whistle. "Ready?"

"Yes," Arthur said.

"Ready," Lian said.

Jackson brought the whistle up to his lips and blew.

The fight was exciting right off the bat. On paper, Lian should be the better fighter, but he often relied on his magic to sustain himself through injuries to surprise his opponents. Sophie could tell that Lian was concentrating harder to avoid Arthur's dagger, because without his magic, his injuries would affect him like it would anybody else.

Sophie watched as Lian skipped nimbly around Arthur. Arthur, in turn, was trying to block Lian's dagger-wielding hand with his free one, so he was free to wield his own dagger. But Lian was fast. He was the fastest of all the Asters, faster even than Sky when unable to use his magic of Speed. Any time Arthur came swinging with his dagger, Lian was long gone; jumping to the side or dropping to the ground.

The Affinites and Asters watching cheered and gasped as the two revolved around each other. To his credit, Arthur was not cowed by fighting an Aster. With his affinity for bravery, the same as his father, not even fighting an Aster who was allowed to use magic would stop him from attacking and taking his chances. Sophie knew he was trained personally by his father; it was Arthur's dream to follow in his father's footsteps and become the next Commanding Chief. And the Commanding Chief had to be able to hold his own against an Aster.

At one point Arthur had to jump back to make sure he didn't get stabbed in the leg, after Lian purposefully fell to the ground and rolled towards him. It was so unexpected that Arthur's jump back was more of a stumble. He was so far back already that he was now right on the edge of the ring, balancing on one foot to make sure he stayed inside. And Lian came at him again. With great strength from the one leg he was still balancing on, Arthur threw himself to the side just as Lian was about to deliver the blow that would make him the victor.

The onlookers gasped as Arthur threw his knife behind him as he fell, towards Lian. It was a blind throw; he wasn't even looking at Lian as he hit the ground just inside the chalk circle. As Arthur turned around on the ground to see what had become of his opponent, Lian jumped on top of him. There was nothing Arthur could do as Lian held the dagger to his throat with his left hand.

Sophie smirked as she saw Arthur's disappointment and Lian's elation. She doubted many of the onlookers noticed what she had, but she was sure Jackson had.

The Commanding Chief blew his whistle. "Arthur wins," he barked.

The look on Arthur's face was enough to make Sophie burst out laughing. The other onlookers started clapping. Lian dropped his head, but the smile didn't leave his lips. He leaned back from where he was still crouched over Arthur, revealing his right hand. It was covering up a nasty gash in his belly, and the Band on his wrist was glowing silver. His magic was working.

Arthur looked from the wound he'd inflicted with his blind shot, up to Lian's face. Lian shrugged and got to his feet, offering his hand to Arthur. "I thought maybe he wouldn't notice," he said with his crooked grin, cocking his head towards Jackson.

Arthur still looked slightly alarmed as Lian casually walked over to Sophie and lifted his shirt. Sophie forgot sometimes that many Affinites had never seen Lian's magic at work. Sophie doubted Lian had even thought of using it; his magic worked more instinctively than the magic of the other Asters. Most of the time Lian didn't even have to do anything; his magic would start working the second he got hurt.

As Sophie assessed the bleeding gash in Lian's abdomen, Jackson moved over to his son. Sophie couldn't hear everything that was being said, but she knew Arthur wasn't getting much positive feedback. Lian was the better fighter; he was faster and smarter. The shot that caught him in the abdomen was a lucky shot. Sophie overheard Jackson say precisely that.

Lian's blood was warm on her skin as she held her hand against his injury. Less than a second later she could feel the sizzle of her magic course through her body and culminate in her right hand. Her healing magic flowed into Lian and worked its way through every bit of damaged blood vessel, muscle and intestine.

When Sophie pulled her hand away, not even a scar remained. Sophie looked at her hand and sighed. It was coated in blood. Before Lian could move away, she was wiping her hand on his shirt.

Lian looked down at his shirt. "Was that really necessary?"

Sophie gave him a pointed look. "I could ask you the same thing."

Sky came over and clapped his hand on Lian's back. "It was a good throw. Tough to survive that one."

"I would've survived it." Lian grinned over his shoulder.

"Without magic?" Sophie remarked.

Sky laughed and threw an arm around his brother.

Lian opened his mouth to answer Sophie, but Jackson cleared his throat. "Up next. Nathan and Nils."

Sophie looked up at that. Those two boys had never been paired up against each other before. Nathan was tall and muscular, sure. But he was nothing compared to Nils. Only Matu came close to the Swedish Affinite's tall and broad stature. It wasn't like Sophie was worried about Nathan's safety. The Asters had been taught how to fight an opponent stronger than them. Those lessons usually revolved around when they'd finally come face to face with a King. But without magic, Nils was definitely stronger than Nathan. It would be interesting to see what Nathan would do to counter Nils' strength.

The two boys each took a single dagger and stepped into the ring. Nils stood nonchalantly to one side, twirling the dagger in his fingers. He had the same cocky air about him that Jake had whenever he fought. It didn't surprise Sophie that Nils and Jake were good friends. They were two of the strongest Affinites on Saluverus, and, right now, Nils wasn't afraid to show it.

Nathan moved to the opposite side of the ring. His movements were studied, precise. There was nothing nonchalant about the Aster of Flora. Sophie recognised the frozen calm that descended upon Nathan before every mission and training. As he turned around, Sophie saw nothing of the kindness she knew was in there. Any sort of emotion was buried deep beneath the surface now.

Nils tossed the dagger from one hand to the other, twirling it between his fingers each time. He smirked at Nathan, trying to rile the Aster of Flora, and did a few more tricks with the dagger. Nathan stared at him coolly, holding his dagger simply in his hands.

The corner of Sophie's mouth twitched up slightly. She knew there was very little that could affect Nathan when he was in this state. Sophie doubted Nils was impressing anyone with his tricks. Everyone here knew showy moves meant nothing. It doesn't matter how you kill. In war, theatrics mean nothing to the living, nor to the dead.

Jackson Kelly took his place next to his twin brother again and looked at the boys in the ring. "Ready?"

"Of course," Nils said smugly.

Nathan simply said, "Yes."

Jackson brought the whistle to his lips and blew.

Faster than a man of his stature should be able to move, Nils pounced, his affinity for agility clear for everyone to see. It made him particularly dangerous, because, at six foot six and with the physique of a bodybuilder, he wasn't just strong and powerful; he was also lightning fast.

Nathan saw the initial attack coming and dodged it easily. Then Nils came again. Their daggers clashed once before the two boys jumped back away from each other again.

They engaged a few more times after that, but always jumped back out of each other's range. Each time they came close, Nils tried to grab Nathan's dagger-wielding hand. But even with his agility, it was too predictable, and Nathan managed to avoid being caught time and time again.

The battle wove on. Without his magic and his broadswords, Nathan was less confident, though Sophie doubted anyone aside from her and the other Asters would be able to see it. They knew what Nathan was like if he had access to his signature weapons. He liked the broadswords because it kept his enemies at a distance. To injure his opponent with a dagger he'd have to get up closer. He was attacking less frequently than Sophie was used to. He was waiting for Nils to make a mistake in an attack, so that his defensive strike would make him the victor. Nathan would rather do that than take a risk and go full on the offensive. Especially with resources he was less comfortable with.

It was a good tactic in theory. But Nils was fit and strong and fast. Each punch the Affinite got in took more out of Nathan than the other way around. Nathan was fit too, but he lacked the strength his opponent had. He needed to do something different; something unexpected, to get Nils on the wrong foot. Nils needed to be surprised to be defeated. Sophie was sure Nathan knew this, and she wondered what he was planning.

"This could go on for a while," Jake whispered in her ear.

Sophie nodded. Neither of the boys seemed to be tiring. Nils might be more agile than the average Affinite or human, but it still took more effort to lug that mass of a body around; yet he showed no signs of slowing down.

After Nils got another punch in, which caused Nathan to stumble slightly, the Affinite chuckled. "Tiring yet, *Aster?*" he mocked. "Nothing special without your magic, ey?"

Nathan said nothing. It took less than a second after his stumble for him to regain his footing. There was no emotion on his face; nothing that would indicate that the mockery had any effect on him. Nothing that anyone else would detect anyway. Only Sophie could see the slightly raised lip that could form a snarl if only Nathan would allow himself to do so.

"Nils is getting frustrated," Jake whispered. "He wouldn't be trying to bait Nathan if he was still confident. Nathan's reading his moves."

Sophie watched Nils come at Nathan again. Nils jogged a little on the spot before suddenly lunging forward, swinging his left hand with the dagger towards Nathan's exposed right side.

Sophie narrowed her eyes as Nathan didn't move away quickly enough, and Nils' dagger cut through the fabric of his sleeve. Something was wrong. Sophie had never known Nathan to leave his right side exposed like that before. It was his strong side; he was right-handed.

Then Sophie noticed that Nathan had switched his dagger from his right hand to his left. And that he'd exposed his right side again. Nils lunged again, and Nathan only just avoided the blade, stumbling back a few steps in the process. Something flashed in Nils' eyes. He knew he was getting close. Nathan was slowing down.

Nathan held his hands close to him, making fists. But his right hand was higher, once again leaving the right-hand side of his waist exposed. Nils readied himself again. He tightened his grip on his dagger with his left hand and lunged again.

He missed Nathan completely. With incredible precision, Nathan pushed Nils' dagger-wielding hand away from him with his right hand. A split-second later Nathan threw his left hand with the dagger forward, towards Nils' right shoulder. Nils, seeing the attack coming just in time moved away to his left, avoiding the dagger.

But Nathan was never planning to beat Nils with his dagger, Sophie knew. Why would he do it with his weak hand? He'd planned it all. He'd planned for Nils' arrogance; for Nils to think Nathan was tiring and leaving his right side exposed as a result.

As Nils moved aside to avoid Nathan's dagger, he stepped directly in front of Nathan. It was in that moment that Nathan's right fist, strong and fast, cut from underneath, swinging upwards, hitting Nils right under his chin.

The sound of the impact echoed through the arena. Sophie knew Nathan had broken bone. Nils fell backwards. All six foot six of him crashed to the ground in a great thump.

A hush fell over the onlookers. Nathan was strong, but he wasn't strong enough to do this. Everyone stared at Nathan, Jackson and Percy included. Nils lay unconscious on his back.

Nathan, in turn, stared at Nils. His right hand was still in a fist, hovering in front of him. Not even he seemed to understand where that level of strength had come from. Sophie couldn't even begin to contemplate how it was possible for Nathan to bring down the bulk that was Nils.

Sky was the first to break the silence. He started laughing. "Oh... my... God... Nate!" he said as he ran into the ring and jumped up onto Nathan's shoulders. "Where the hell did that come from?"

Nathan stumbled slightly under Sky's weight. He didn't take his eyes off the Swedish Affinite, still unconscious at his feet.

Lian joined in Sky's enthusiasm, whooping loudly, and even Matu said, "That was incredible."

Jackson blew his whistle and pointed to Nathan. "Nathan wins," he said. The other Affinites broke into applause. Even Jake clapped, though he stared at Nils, frowning, also trying to make sense of what he was seeing.

Sophie stepped forward and knelt down at Nils' head. She traced her fingers over his jawline and felt an unnatural crunch underneath the skin.

"Well, Soph?" Sky asked, still laughing and patting Nathan on the back. Nathan in turn still looked dazed.

"Broken," Sophie replied without looking up.

Sky laughed even louder. "That's insane!"

Sophie put her magic to work and healed Nils' broken jaw quickly. But when she finished, Nils remained unconscious. She could only heal physical ailments. She couldn't wake him up if his body didn't want to yet.

When she looked up from Nils' body, she shook her head towards Jackson, telling him she couldn't wake Nils. He would have to do that on his own accord, when his body was ready. The force of Nathan's uppercut must have been even stronger than any of them had realised.

Sophie looked over to Nathan. His gaze was still distant, but he'd stopped looking at Nils. Sky was still jumping up and down next to him. Matu and Lian were there, too. And so were the other Affinites. The frozen focus had gone, and his insecurities had returned. Awkwardly he received the praise for a battle no one had really expected him to win, and certainly not in the way that he had. While everyone else was celebrating his strength, Nathan caught Sophie's eye. Perhaps only the two of them were questioning where that power had actually come from.

And even though she was the Aster of Knowledge, Sophie found herself without a single answer.

Chapter 9

One evening, a few days later, Sky, Lian and Nathan opted for the village café instead of going to their beds early. As long as they didn't drink and they'd be fit enough for anything they could be summoned for in the next twenty-four hours, the Small Council had nothing against them relaxing every once in a while. Though there was nothing on the tracking screens in the Board Room that suggested the Asters would be going anywhere any time soon.

Lian was sitting at one of the lower round tables, and playing poker with Nathan, the Kadiri twins, Asmae and Marwa, and Jillian and Arthur Kelly. He saw that Sky was up at the bar with Ashu and Kemal, drinking a beer. Only Sky would be drinking while on stand-by. Then again, only Sky could drink multiple glasses without having any trouble the following day. The only reason he was sticking to just a single drink now, Lian knew, was because in theory they could also be summoned somewhen in the night. And even though Sky rarely woke with a hangover, in the middle of the night he would still be tipsy. Jackson Kelly had been furious the first time he found out Sky was drinking while on call, but that day Sky had trained as well as he always did, so the Commanding Chief had no foot to stand on. Jackson now knew Sky wasn't stupid enough to drink more than he could handle.

"Dealer takes two," Asmae was saying.

Lian turned his attention back to the game.

"How is it having your father back on the island?" Marwa asked Jillian.

"It's strange," Jillian answered. "I know this is supposed to be normal, but him being away and only popping in every now and again used to be my normal, you know?"

Lian looked up at Jillian. She didn't look much like Percy, or his twin brother Jackson. The colour of their hair was the same, and she had the same eyes, but the rest of her features she must've inherited from her mother. It had always been strange to Lian how Jillian's family functioned. For the past twelve years Percy Kelly had been living almost permanently in Brazil. He travelled back to Saluverus no more than four times a year, and only stayed a couple of weeks. And in those weeks, he spent most of his time training with the best members of his battalion from the war against Astaroth; some of whom now made up part of both teams on the two missions currently in Brazil.

"Is it different now that he's here permanently?" Nathan was asking.

Jillian shrugged as she took the card Asmae dealt her. "Quite the same. It is strange now that Mum's gone, though."

"Why, where's your mother?" Lian asked. "I raise ten."

"Call," everyone except for Jillian said in turn around the table. They slid some of their chips to the centre of the table.

"She's part of the five-man rescue team my dad's sending in to look for the four people from the Queen's Case that the Small Council hasn't been able to make contact with for the past few days," Jillian explained. "I fold."

She placed her cards face down on the table and pushed them away from her.

"Seriously?" Lian said, surprised.

"Strange that he would send his own wife," Nathan commented quietly, perhaps more to himself than to the others around the table.

Arthur Kelly snorted beside him. Jillian looked over to her cousin and chuckled. Even though Jillian was Percy's daughter and Arthur was Jackson's son, they were so close that practically everyone mistook them for brother and sister instead of cousins. Nathan looked from one Kelly to the other with a question in his eyes.

"Is it funny?" he asked.

"I'm sorry, it's not," Jillian giggled, her eyes dancing with amusement.

"We just forget that our family isn't like others," Arthur began.

"That still doesn't explain—" Marwa started.

"Mum only had one condition when Dad proposed to her," Jillian interrupted. "No matter what, their marriage would never get in the way of her work. She has the same bravery affinity as Dad. She is one of the best soldiers on the island. They met when she saved his life, though he will never admit that." Jillian chuckled again, shaking her head. "They've trained together ever since, and she became one of his best soldiers. She told him she'd leave him if he ever chose someone else less suited for a job, just because he didn't want her to get hurt."

"He seems to have remembered," Asmae mused.

"Yeah, well, she meant it," Jillian said.

They were an interesting family. Arthur Kelly had inherited his father's affinity for bravery as well. He had dedicated his entire life training to become his father's successor one day. He made the Small Council take his name off the Transfer list because he never wanted to become an Aster. Becoming Commanding Chief was his dream, and it was either that or nothing.

Jillian had inherited the affinity for bravery as well, but she wasn't following in her father's footsteps. She got additional combat training like Arthur and other Affinites with battle-worthy affinities, but she chose not to have it be the focus of her life. In school Jillian excelled in chemistry, physics, maths and biology. Only Sophie got the same grades she did. For as long as Lian could remember, Jillian wanted to become a scientist. Her battle-minded parents never had a problem with that.

"Where are Sophie and Matu? They're usually up for a night out," Arthur asked.

"Sophie's off with Jacob somewhere—" Lian started. There were a few groans around the table, followed by a few laughs at each other's similar reactions. For everyone here, Jacob wasn't their favourite person. "And Matu is off having dinner with his father. Supposedly, he might be leaving the island soon."

"Why? Where's he going?" Asmae asked.

"You know that one team hasn't been in contact with the Small Council for a while? Well, apparently one of the Affinites in that team was one of the top soldiers in his regiment in the war. If the rescue team finds evidence of a struggle or battle with Disciples, Matu's father said he'll have Madeleine send him in immediately so he can help look for her," Lian explained.

"Who's the Affinite?" Asmae asked.

"Nadine Amsel," Lian replied.

Silence fell around the table for a moment. There were plenty of reasons that communication could break down on a mission, especially one so remote as deep in the jungles of Brazil. Still, everyone around the table knew that if Nadine weren't to return, there would be five children on Saluverus left as orphans.

The door to the café opened, breaking the silence around Lian and Nathan's table. Everyone around the table looked up to see four Affinites walk in, Nils leading the way. He cast his eyes over everyone in the café before heading over to a table near the back. His three friends followed him.

Lian sniggered the second Nils turned his back on their table. Sophie might have healed his broken jaw, but she hadn't taken away the injury completely. Even though it had been a few days since the incident, there was still some swelling and some significant blue and purple bruising.

"You know he's still upset that Sophie didn't heal his jaw completely," Jillian said.

Lian snorted. At the back of the café, Nils was rubbing his bruised jaw absently with his hand.

"He should be glad she healed him at all after his mockery during the battle," Arthur said.

"Didn't seem to affect Nate though, did it?" Lian said, slapping his brother on the shoulder.

"Doesn't matter," Asmae said. "You can't expect help from one Aster after coming at another, that's just not smart."

"Who ever said Nils was smart?" Lian pointed out. "Didn't even see the upper cut coming!"

"It was a brilliant move," Jillian commended.

"And the power on that thing; I didn't even know you could hit that hard," Arthur added.

Nathan smiled awkwardly as Lian patted him on the shoulder again and ruffled his hair. Lian could laugh at his brother. He was always the quiet one. Even when he pulled off a magnificent move like he had, Nate still couldn't boast about it.

"All right, all right," Asmae tried to calm the group down. "Back to the game."

Jillian leaned across the table towards Nathan and whispered, "How *did* you get so much power behind it?"

Nathan shook his head and opened his mouth to speak, but Asmae cut in before he could say anything. "Jill!"

Jillian chuckled and sat back down into her chair, shooting an apologetic look towards Asmae. Everyone except for Jillian, who had already folded, picked their cards back up again and the game continued.

"Where's Anna?" Marwa asked at some point. "I fold."

"Night shift with Marlena," Lian replied. "Fold."

"Fold," Nathan said.

Only Marwa and Arthur were left in the game. They weren't playing for anything, but especially these two took games extremely seriously. Asmae was the more outspoken of the twins, while Marwa was the quieter, more cunning of the two.

Arthur and Marwa eyed each other up and down, holding their cards up in front of them protectively.

"Show your cards," Asmae ordered.

Marwa gestured to Arthur. "You first."

Arthur looked round the table and placed his cards down in front of him. The five cards were three tens and two eights. "Full house," he spoke proudly.

Everyone around the table turned to look at Marwa, whose eyes were glittering mischievously.

"Come on then, what've you got?" Arthur asked.

Marwa placed the cards out in front of her.

All four jacks and a seven.

Arthur swore.

"Four of a kind," Marwa said triumphantly. She reached across the table and pulled the pile of chips towards her.

"I thought I had it," Arthur grumbled.

"Tough hand to beat," Lian admitted, clapping Arthur on the back.

"Never underestimate a beauty behind glasses," Jillian said.

Arthur rolled his eyes and turned his head away, standing up from his chair. Lian swore he saw the boy flush for a moment. And Marwa seemed to be very focused on separating the chips she'd collected.

"I'm getting another drink," Arthur announced, getting a hold on his composure again.

"You doing a whole round?" Jillian asked, looking up at her cousin.

Arthur narrowed his eyes at her. "Only for the winner this time," he replied, winking at Marwa. "Same as before?"

The Moroccan Affinite looked up through her dark lashes only for a moment and nodded quickly, before turning her gaze back to the chips in front of her.

"All right, new game," Asmae said, collecting all the cards out on the table. She started shuffling them, and then dealt out a new hand to everyone. Arthur returned again with two drinks. He offered one to Marwa.

"Non-alcoholic lime daiquiri, just as the lady likes it," Arthur said.

Marwa thanked him and then turned back to the game. Over at the bar, Sky and Ashu burst out laughing. The sound echoed through the café. Lian smiled to himself as he picked up the cards he was dealt. Even with the pending threat in North America, and the other, greater unknown threat that Gayle's birth had foretold, he was glad they could still have moments like this.

"All right, here we go again," Asmae said. "Everybody in."

Less than a week passed without any further updates. The Asters did know that Matu's father left for Brazil yesterday, but none of them knew the details of why.

All the Affinites who had come to Saluverus as a result of the Affinite kidnappings or for the Memorial had returned home. Sky's mother had joined her good friend and now widow, Orla Brown, and her son in their return to Perth to help move them into a new house, since their old townhouse had been completely destroyed.

Things on the island seemed to be completely back to normal. The masses of Disciples in North America were still coming and going in waves but nothing of significance was happening yet that would indicate an uprising. The Asters were back in the swing of their full-time trainings with Jackson Kelly. Percy was also still forever present, but Sky didn't mind the ex-soldier so much.

Sky was glad to have the trainings. By being able to use his magic on a more frequent basis again, he no longer walked around with his body aching to use it. The roaring in his ears had gone away and his blood was no longer humming with the need for the magic to be released. His anger at what had happened to Gayle and her parents hadn't disappeared, but at least his magic had settled down.

Sky wasn't the only one for whom the trainings had been a healthy release. Nathan seemed to be stronger than ever before. The one-on-one against Nils wasn't a stroke of luck. The blows Nate landed with his broadsword were harder than Sky ever remembered them to be. It was like his muscles had realised they were capable of delivering more strength. Sky didn't question it; they were all training better.

Sophie included; she seemed to be back to her regular self again, and she was stronger and fitter than ever before.

Sky had also managed to make amends with his sister. It was a strained conversation during which he told her that he *sort of* accepted that she was seeing Jacob. Because, annoyingly, that relationship was still a thing.

Sophie had laughed at him, but said that she appreciated the effort. "Thank you," she said. "I haven't felt lighter in weeks, so just... let it be, all right? I'm doing just fine."

Sky had narrowed his eyes at her. "Does this mean I have to try and like him?"

Sophie had looped her arm through his and told him, laughing, "I would never ask that of you, you think I'm a monster?"

And that was that.

At the dining hall buffet, Sky took a filled bowl of stew from Grace, one of the chefs in the castle's kitchens, and headed over to where Lian and Matu were already having dinner. He'd barely sat down when Sophie entered the dining hall.

"Where've you been?" Matu asked her. They hadn't seen Sophie all afternoon.

"The childcare centre," Sophie revealed.

"Again?" Sky asked. She'd been there a lot, hanging out with seven-year-old Banyu, whom she found in the false bottom in his bed when his house was overrun by Disciples in Indonesia. His mother and sister were on the island somewhere, too, but they often had other obligations which left Banyu alone in the centre for a few hours each day.

"He's leaving tomorrow."

"He's finally going home, is he?" Lian said.

Sophie smiled. "He finally gets used to European food, and now he goes back."

Matu chuckled. "Maybe he'll miss it so much, he'll come back."

Sophie snorted. "Doubtful." She looked at Sky's stew. "That looks good, though, I'm going to get me some." She set off towards the dining buffet, her long blonde hair swinging loosely as she went.

Sky looked around the dining hall. There were no more new faces on the island. He saw Nora Amsel sitting at one of the other long tables. She was surrounded by her two brothers and two sisters. Nora was spoon feeding her youngest three-year-old sister Amelie. They were smiling and chatting as if nothing was wrong. As if their single mother wasn't part of a research team that hadn't been heard of for as long as a week now. As far as the Asters knew, anyway. It was odd to see how calm the Amsel children seemed under the circumstances.

The doors to the dining hall opened again, and Nathan hurried in. He reached the spot where they were sitting just as Sophie returned with her own bowl of stew.

"There's something you need to know," he said in a hushed tone.

"About what?" Sophie asked as she sat down next to Matu.

"My grandfather told me something about the Affinites in Brazil," Nathan announced.

Sky dropped his spoon a bit too heavily in his stew. "Why does your family tell you everything? First your mother, now your grandfather. Why do mine always keep their mouths shut?"

"What did he say?" Matu asked, ignoring Sky's comment.

And Nathan told them, in that quiet, restful way he said everything, "The rescue team found two members of the research team. They were both killed."

"Do they know which two?" Sky asked, glancing over to Nora Amsel and her four siblings. He saw the older of the two brothers say something that made the entire family laugh.

Nathan shook his head. "Just that it's two men. They haven't identified them yet."

Sky let out an unintentional sigh of relief, and cursed himself for it. There were still two deaths; even though neither of them was Nadine Amsel, it wasn't something to be relieved about.

"What about the other two?" Sophie asked.

"I don't know. All my grandfather knew is that they weren't at the scene where the two bodies were found."

"What does that mean?" Lian asked.

"It means something is happening, but no one knows what. It's like they just vanished. No contact, no signals, nothing," Nathan said.

"Are we going to be told any of this?" Sky grumbled. And right then, as he spoke the last word, the chip in his arm started vibrating. He looked around the table and knew that his hadn't been the only one.

"I think we are about to," Matu said.

Sky started getting up. "Okay, hold on."

"Uhg, I haven't even had dinner yet," Sophie muttered. The five of them held on to each other in a circle. Sky's Band flared up and blue light filled their vision. Seconds later they were no longer sitting at a table in the dining hall, but standing near the oak table in the middle of the Board Room. Only Axel Reed was there. The lack of weapons on the table told them they hadn't been summoned to be sent straight out on a mission. This call must be just to inform them.

"Thank you for coming so quickly," Axel said. "Take a seat."

The Asters sat down around the oak table and waited for the Ambassador to update them on what they had already heard from Nathan.

"First things first. The Bone Recovery, led by Katherine and Rose, has not yet found a single bone that belonged to either Cara or Tomas. They are getting suspicious and wondering whether there is anything to be found at all. They think something in the Amazon tampered with the tracking spell. They will remain there for another few weeks to be one hundred per cent sure there is nothing to be found. We do not want to lose two forms of Aster magic forever, unless we are sure we have no other choice," Axel paused briefly, then jumped right into what the Asters had been summoned for.

"Now on to the next point of business. The investigation by the Queen's Case teams has led us to believe that Gayle managed to get into the Rainforest before she was killed. As the teams continued to split, they got quite deep into the jungle. About two weeks ago we lost contact with one of the teams of four. A rescue mission was instigated to go in search of them."

Most of this they already knew. Sky found himself once again impressed by Gayle's fight for survival and her attempt to escape. How she managed to get so deep into the rainforest without knowledge of her magic and while being hunted by Disciples was still a mystery to him.

Axel Reed swallowed once before continuing. "Three days ago, two bodies were found. They have been identified as Portuguese brothers Afonso and Danilo Borges. Because Nadine Amsel, one of the two missing Affinites, is a personal friend of your father, Matu, he was quite adamant to help look for her. He left yesterday with Madeleine and two scientists. Madeleine has returned with the bodies of the Borges' brothers, and, as you probably know, has since left for Perth with Orla Brown and her son."

"Do you know how they died?" Sophie asked.

"We think it was a Disciple ambush. A knife that can be tracked back to the Underworld was found near the bodies. The pathology lab is yet to confirm it as the murder weapon, but we are quite sure it is," Axel explained.

"Do they know what happened to Nadine and the other Affinite?" Matu asked.

"They are not sure yet. The reason the two scientists travelled with Diallo is because blood was found at the scene where the two bodies were found, and we're hoping they belong to either Nadine or Zangar. The scientists are testing the blood today, and if they do belong to the two missing Affinites, Diallo can cast a spell to see if they are still alive or not, and in what general direction they can be found," Axel explained.

Sky's heart sank. If the blood found at the scene was Nadine's, and Disciples were involved... He didn't like the odds of whether she would still be alive. He also didn't like the fact that Jillian's mother was part of Nadine and Zangar's rescue team. Even after the Queen's death, Brazil remained a dangerous place...

"So, what happens now?" Sophie asked.

"First, we wait and see what the bloodwork comes back with. That, and the *post mortem* reports on the Borges' brothers. But what seems most likely is that the team assembled there at the moment, including Diallo, will be tasked to find Nadine and Zangar," Axel said.

"What about us?" Sky asked.

"Diallo knows that he can call upon the five of you if they run into trouble. The Small Council has no reason to believe they will. The attack has all the indicators of a few rogue Disciples taking their chance to kill a few Affinites. With even one Ceder there we don't believe they will try again."

Sky just about accepted this as a reason. Now that Sophie was cleared by her therapist, there was no real reason to keep the Asters on the side lines. Even with what Axel said next, Sky didn't see a reason not to have them help in South America.

"Then, something else. As you can see," the Ambassador said, turning to the screen and switching it on with the remote he was holding, "the mass of Disciples in North America seems to have accumulated around the Grand Canyon National Park. We believe the North American King, Mitrik, will be making his move soon, which is why you will remain here until he does. Be ready, for at any time you could be summoned to go. Continue with your training, but do nothing that would weaken yourselves too much to jeopardise a mission. Understood?"

The Asters nodded and murmured their responses.

Sky assumed Axel had nothing more to say. His final words seemed dismissive enough. The man was probably about to tell them to leave when his phone started to ring. Axel picked up and listened to whatever the person on the other end of the line had to say. Sky and the other Asters watched as the Ambassador closed his eyes while the other person talked. Sky noticed that Axel's free hand was clenched by his side. Axel was definitely upset by whatever he was being told.

"All right, thank you. We will get back to you as soon as possible," Axel said eventually, and he hung up the phone.

"What's happened?" Sophie asked quietly, having noticed the change in Axel's demeanour, too. Sky could tell that Axel's mind was whirling by the way that his eyes remained distant. He was dreading something; that much was clear.

"That was Diallo. The blood that was found did belong to Nadine and Zangar. He cast the spell... Neither one of them is still alive," Axel said. He then seemed to realise that he didn't have to tell them this. He shook himself and said, "There are no further updates for you all. Now if you will excuse me, I have to find Nora Amsel and tell her that she and her four siblings will stay on Saluverus permanently. They are orphans now."

Chapter 10

On a Sunday morning, after yet another workout, Sky left the arena and headed for one of the castle's side entrances. In the past few weeks the weather had become colder, but today was an exception. The sun was out and there were no clouds in the sky. There was still a brisk wind, and Sky needed a coat to keep warm.

Because both the arena and the castle were built high into the cliffs, he had a view over most of the island. Many Affinites had taken advantage of their free day and were doing all kinds of activities out in the winter sunshine. Some were out on the castle courtyard having a picnic, while others were riding their horses up into the North Forest that covered the northern corner of the island. Many more were just strolling in the balmy conditions.

Sky was glad he didn't have anything else to do that day. Sophie had convinced Sylvia that it was a good idea to refresh the Asters' memory on various spells that might come in handy during their mission in North America. She wasn't wrong, the boys only ever did remember the most important spells. With her magic of Health and Knowledge, Sophie knew practically every spell ever invented, but she still wanted the boys to know their fair share for if they were separated. The logic was there, but Sky still didn't like being cooped up in a classroom again, having finished school two years ago.

Sky made it to the side of the castle and pushed the door open. He walked along the corridor towards the dining hall; he was starving. The castle was completely deserted. In the distance, however, Sky heard voices. He decided to ignore them, the grumble in his stomach too much to bear. But then the voices started getting louder; not because they were coming closer but because whoever they belonged to had started shouting. Curiosity tugged at Sky and eventually he found himself walking in the opposite direction of the dining hall and towards the raised voices.

As Sky came closer, he realised that the voices were coming from the Board Room. This was not just a fight between two random Affinites. If the voices came from this room then it was definitely something Sky would want to know about. He knew Matu would condemn him for eavesdropping, but he didn't care. Sky crept up to the door and placed his ear against the wood.

He recognised the voices immediately. It was Percy Kelly and Axel Reed.

"They were sent there on my orders!" Percy shouted.

The Affinites. In Brazil. It had to be about them.

"That is not news to me!" thundered Axel. Sky rolled his eyes. The Ambassador could be so unarguable in his answers sometimes. It didn't surprise Sky one bit that Percy was enraged.

"I sent them in. It is my duty to make sure they are all right!" Percy bellowed.

"No, it is not. We gave you permission to handle this. It is not your duty to go flying in there without any knowledge of the situation!"

"Those are my men and women out there! My wife is out there!"

Sky's heart stilled.

Percy's *wife*.

Sky had almost forgotten.

It still seemed so unusual to him that Percy would send his own wife into a situation where Affinites had already been killed with no clear explanation of why or how. Then again, if she was one of the best soldiers, then could Percy really tell her *not* to go on this mission? He was only going to send the best of the best, and from what Sky knew, Eva Kelly was one of the best.

From what Sky had heard, the tracking spell Diallo cast on the little blood he had, only gave him a vague direction as to where Nadine and Zangar's bodies were. Apparently, they were in completely opposite directions and the team present had split into two groups of eight to go and find them. One group was headed up by Diallo, the other by Eva. That was about a week ago.

"It is not unusual to receive little to no information from your soldiers when they are working, you know this," Axel said in an attempt to calm Percy down. Sky could tell he was trying to keep his voice under control.

"I know more than you think, Axel," Percy growled. "I haven't heard anything from any of her team for too long! None of this is normal. I gave them specific orders on when to contact me, given the message it would send if they didn't. *Especially* considering what has happened to the first research team we lost contact with! They would only fail to send something back if they really weren't able to. They are my soldiers and I will find out what happened to them and I will find a way to assist them. I have been behind a desk for far too long. I will go, and you won't stop me."

Her team... That meant the Small Council was still in contact with Diallo's team, which meant Matu's father was still all right. Sky dreaded what the break in contact implied for the eight members of Eva Kelly's rescue team. What the hell was going on in Brazil? Sky held his breath for Axel's response.

"You honestly believe you should've heard something by now?" Axel questioned tautly.

"Yes," Percy snapped.

"You're sure?"

"Are you doubting my soldiers' ability to follow orders?" Percy snarled. "I know exactly what they do and how they work. There is nothing they can do to surprise me, *except for this*. I'm going in. Do not stop me."

There was a silence. Axel was thinking.

"Spell me if you like. Or send the Asters in after me if that will make this an easier decision for you," Percy added. "But know that whatever decision you make, I will go either way. Even if you send in the Asters; I will go with them. My wife is in there. You will not keep me from finding out what happened to her."

Another silence.

Then finally: "I don't want you going alone. No matter how good you think you are."

Percy muttered something Sky couldn't hear through the door. He wondered what Percy meant by *spell me*. Sophie would know immediately. Sky was trying to think of a spell that could be cast on an Affinite. Of course, there were plenty, but Sky had never spelled an Affinite before. Axel obviously knew what the soldier was talking about, otherwise he would've asked about it by now.

"You will take two soldiers with you. Not Jackson; we need him here for the Asters. But any two others of your choosing."

Another grumble from Percy. Then he heard footsteps, and he realised that at least one of the two men inside the Board Room was heading right for the door. Sky shimmered out just as he heard the door click open. He knew the men wouldn't have known that he was there. He vanished before the door would have revealed him standing on the other side.

When the blue light left his vision, Sky looked around. He was in another part of the castle. He realised that he hadn't actually thought of a place to shimmer to after vanishing from the hallway outside of the Board Room.

He was in a long hallway. Doors with numbers on them lined the walls, and Sky realised he was in the residential wing of the castle. He doubted there would be many Affinites here anymore. These rooms – he recognised – were for visiting Affinites; not ones who lived in the castle permanently.

Sky headed along the corridor and down a flight of stairs. He was about to turn a corner that led to the main entry hall when something caught his eye. Sky stopped and headed back.

In a side-corridor stood a girl. She was looking around with a puzzled look on her face. Sky walked towards her. As he neared, he saw that she couldn't have been more than ten years old. Her flaming red her told Sky exactly to which family the girl belonged.

"Are you all right?" Sky asked. He hoped that the German girl had already been taught a bit of English. All Affinites were expected to learn the language. It varied per family and per city how early the teaching started.

The girl's pale brown eyes shifted to Sky. She had a very frightened look on her face.

"Are you lost?" Sky asked.

The girl nodded. Her bottom lip trembled slightly.

"Where do you need to go?" Sky asked.

"Out... outside," the girl stammered. So she did know English. Sky let out a sigh of relief. This would've been a whole lot harder if she had no idea what he was saying.

"I can take you," Sky suggested, offering his hand.

The girl's eyes filled with hope and she took Sky's hand. It didn't escape him that the Band around his wrist caught her eye. Sky smiled down at the girl as he led her back to the main corridor and towards the entry hall.

"What's your name?" Sky asked.

"Lena," the girl answered. She had obviously got some of her energy back. There was no hesitation in her voice as she spoke.

"That's a pretty name. I'm Sky," Sky said. They were at the entry hall now. If Lena had walked any further, she probably would have found her way there herself.

"I know," Lena breathed, her face reddening. "You're an Aster."

Sky laughed and looked down at Lena. "Yes, that's right."

"The greatest, yes?" The girl's English was impeccable. There was a German accent, sure, but this level of English was surprising coming from a ten-year-old girl.

Sky gave the girl a mischievous grin. "You bet."

Lena giggled.

The two of them made it to the entry doors and they stepped out into the fresh winter air.

"There!" Lena pointed. Sky looked over the stone railing that stood along the platform outside of the entry doors. Two sets of stairs on either side led down to the courtyard in front of the castle. Nora Amsel was sitting on a picnic blanket on the courtyard. She was holding her three-year-old sister in her arms. A boy who looked about fifteen was lying on his back and holding a book up above his face, reading, while another boy, who looked slightly younger than Lena, was running around the blanket like an idiot.

Sky was about to let go of Lena's hand, since she didn't need help finding her way anymore, but Lena held on tightly and pulled Sky along behind her. As they neared the Amsel family, Nora looked up from her youngest sister.

"I see you've made a friend," she said in English.

"I got lost," Lena admitted. Then she said something in German to her sister.

Nora nodded once and then said something back in German as well. Sky frowned, recognising none of the sounds the girls made as actual words. Lena in turn responded again in her native language. She had quite a shocked look on her face. Sky looked from one sister to the other, trying to understand what the hell they were talking about. Then suddenly Lena burst out laughing and pointed at Sky.

Sky frowned again, and realised they had been making fun of him. Sky looked over to Nora, clearly offended. He even noticed the oldest brother trying to hide his smirk behind his book. The oldest Amsel smiled at him apologetically, before turning to her sister and saying, "Go and play with your brother."

Lena rolled her eyes, but obeyed. She let go of Sky's hand and ran over to where her younger brother was still running around.

"You don't have to be offended. You're not the first to fall for it," Nora chuckled.

Sky raised his eyebrows. "You mean this happens more often?"

Nora smiled. "Yes. Making these jokes seems to be Lena's way of coping."

Silence fell between them. Sky looked down, not quite sure what to say.

"Thank you," Nora said, breaking the silence. When Sky frowned, she added, "For bringing Lena here."

"Oh, yeah, of course," Sky stuttered. "Anyway, I will uhm…"

"You can sit if you like," Nora offered.

Sky sank to the ground gratefully. He hadn't wanted to leave awkwardly, and was glad that Nora had given him the option to stay or go. He hadn't really been in this kind of situation before. When orphans came to Saluverus they mostly kept to themselves, and it had never occurred to Sky to introduce himself in those desperate early days after an orphan lost their parents and had to leave their home and move to Saluverus. But here he was, sitting next to a girl who had just lost her mother and was now responsible for her four younger brothers and sisters.

"I'm sorry," he said quickly. "About your mother."

"Thank you," Nora replied. She looked down at her youngest sister. The three-year-old had fallen asleep in her arms.

"Are you all right?" Sky asked.

Nora looked at him. There was a sadness in her pale brown eyes; they were exactly the same colour as Lena's. Sky wondered how long it would take before they would liven up with joy again. "She died doing what she believed in. Though they won't tell me what she was doing, precisely."

Sky bit his lip. He knew he shouldn't, but he divulged, "She was sent to Brazil to find out exactly how Gayle Mendosa was killed so we know how that King works and thinks."

Nora stared at him for a moment, obviously surprised that he told her all that. "A noble cause. She would have been proud to die for that."

Sky closed his eyes. "You aren't supposed to know that."

"No one does," Nora promised. "Right, Stefan?"

Sky could punch himself. He had completely forgotten that her oldest brother was lying a few feet away reading his book. The fourteen-year-old boy lowered his book and made the movement of zipping his mouth and throwing away the key with his hand, before turning back to his book.

Nora chuckled slightly. "He won't tell," she assured him.

Sky let out a low breath. "Well, I hope not."

"Thank you," Nora said. "For telling me. It brings us more peace knowing how she died. She died doing what she believed in. And with honour."

Sky frowned. He hadn't told her exactly how her mother died. Sky didn't think even the Small Council knew that yet. As far as Sky knew, Diallo's team hadn't found her body yet.

"What was her affinity?" Sky asked.

Nora thought for a moment, probably translating in her mind. "Aim and preci-zion," Nora answered, her German accent thicker as she tried to pronounce the last word.

Sky looked at the girl for a moment. She could only be a few years younger than him. There was too much calm wisdom in her eyes for her young age.

"Do you have the same affinity?" he asked.

Nora shook her head. "None of us do. Maybe Amelie," she said, looking down at her youngest sister, asleep in her arms. "We all have *calm* from our father. We are never fazed and can always think under pressure."

It made sense now. All of them. How they were handling their mother's death. Sure, the youngest brother was running around like an idiot, but it was better than breaking down and crying. They had all just lost their mother, and somehow, they seemed calm and composed through the whole situation. There was a sadness in their eyes; it wasn't like they didn't feel anything at all. They were grieving, but they would go about it in their own way; their affinity helping them along.

"Do you like it? Your affinity?" Sky asked. He realised he'd never had a conversation like this before. He'd never really shown much interest in Affinites, with the exception of Ashu, Kemal and the Moroccan twins. And his interest in the girls he slept with was never more than physical. He had one great female Affinite friend: Camille. She worked in a café somewhere in Canada; Sky always forgot what the place was called. She was one of Felix's Watchers. She hadn't come to Saluverus during the emergency or for the Memorial. From her Sky had learnt most of what he knew about Affinites. But it was interesting hearing about them from someone else.

It was nice talking to Nora; she didn't ogle him like many of the other girls on the island did. Truth be told he didn't mind the ogling one bit, but it was nice to have an interesting conversation with someone just this once.

Nora looked towards Lena and her other brother. "I want to be a soldier like my mother," she admitted. "I will never be one with my affinity. I find that sad."

She was right. Affinites whose affinity had nothing to do with combat only got the bare minimum of combat training. Nora, with her affinity, would never be a soldier. It surprised Sky that, even with everything that had happened to her mother, she still wanted to be one.

Sky was about to ask her more about it when a voice behind him stopped him.

"Miss Amsel."

When Sky turned around at the same time Nora did, Sylvia had a great look of surprise on her face. "Sky," she said, bewildered. She then turned her attention back to Nora and said, "We have to talk about your family's permanent move to Saluverus."

"Yes, of course," Nora agreed.

"I'll leave," Sky said. He stood up.

"Thank you again," Nora said once again. Sky looked down at her. He knew she was talking about him revealing what her mother had been doing before she was killed. But when Sylvia asked them what she was thankful for Nora only mentioned Sky leading Lena back here when she got lost.

Sky bade both Nora and Lena one last goodbye before leaving Sylvia to whatever the Consul needed to discuss with the German Affinite. As Sky walked away, he wondered how long the Amsel family would stay on Saluverus. If Nora turned eighteen soon, it would be her decision whether to move her family elsewhere. If she could find a way to earn a living, there was nothing to stop her from moving back to her mother's home in Berlin. Sky doubted that she would. She had four younger brothers and sisters to care for. She wouldn't be able to do that without some help; and Saluverus would help for as long as necessary.

She was a nice girl. Sky felt bad for her that she had been left to take care of her siblings all by herself. Maybe she needed some support. He wondered if Nathan would be interested in her. His brother was always such a romantic that he never really got the courage to ask a girl out. Maybe Nora would be someone for him.

Sky grinned to himself as he finally headed for the dining hall.

Chapter 11

The days wore on. Percy Kelly sent back reports as his investigation in Brazil moved forward. Sky had recognised the two soldiers he had taken with him to South America. Female Affinite Yua Tanaka had portalled in from Japan especially for the job, while Icelander Kristjan Stefansson had been on Saluverus already. Both of them had been part of Percy's battalion back in the war against Astaroth.

There was a collective sigh of relief when Percy Kelly confirmed that Eva's rescue team appeared to still be alive; they had left clues behind in the camp that had been their last known location. For some unknown reason, their communication systems had been smashed.

One of the clues was found within a detailed report of their investigation, left at a smaller camp they'd set up before heading deeper into the jungle, and setting up a camp there. The report ended with the information that Eva and her team would be spending the next few days finding out everything they could about Zangar's death before returning to the home base. The report included coordinates for where they had found Zangar's body. Percy, with the two Affinite soldiers accompanying him, had decided to set off to find them, rather than wait around at base camp for their return.

In the five days that followed Percy's departure, Sky was bored out of his mind. There was the constant worry that something might be happening in North America, so he had to stay alert in case they would suddenly be called in. But as the days wound on, nothing seemed to be changing. Yes, there were many more Disciples on the Surface, but as long as they weren't attacking Affinites or holding humans hostage there wasn't anything the Asters needed to do. They didn't even need to be sent out to investigate; there were enough of Felix's Watchers amongst the Affinites living in North America to get enough information on what the Disciples were doing.

Shockingly little, apparently. Which only irritated Sky further.

Before Percy's departure, Sky had found out what Percy had meant by *spell me*. Axel had informed Sky that a spell had been placed upon Percy that he could call for Sky if something were to go wrong, or if he got terribly injured. Only people possessing magic themselves could call for an Aster or Ceder of Speed and Flight, but with this spell, so could Percy, temporarily. For this spell, perhaps in response to Sky's frequent complaint about the Asters being side-lined, or the fact that Madeleine was busy in Perth, Sky had been chosen. Although Sky was aware of the spell, he had never experienced it himself before. However, now that Eva's rescue team was believed to still be alive, and Percy was days away from catching up to them, even that piece of action didn't seem to be happening either.

Annoying Nathan about Nora Amsel had also become boring. Sky guessed that his brother probably had eyes for another girl – that was the only reason Sky could think of for Nathan not giving things a go.

Nathan had joked about why Sky hadn't gone after Nora himself; he seemed to go after literally everybody else. Sky had been offended. First of all, he was three years older than the German Affinite, while Nathan was only one year older. And also, why would he hook up with someone who had just lost their mother? That was just cruel. It wasn't cruel if he was actually interested in more than that; but the whole world knew that he wasn't. Nathan on the other hand...

None of it really mattered. Sky needed to find other ways to keep himself occupied until the Asters were sent back out into the field. He was itching to get into action. But as the days wore on, it didn't seem to be happening any time soon.

When Sky had wanted action, he hadn't expected this. Just less than a week after Percy Kelly had left Saluverus with Yua Tanaka and Kristjan Stefansson, a scream shattered through Sky's body in the middle of the night.

For a moment, Sky lay paralysed in his bed. The scream had come so suddenly that for a moment he hadn't known what came over him. The scream had been in his head. It was a desperate call for help; as if someone had called his name so that he would shimmer towards him.

Sky clutched his head. There was a ringing in his ears as the echo of the scream faded away to the back of his mind. Sky got out of bed and headed for the chest of drawers next to his bedroom door. He hurried; he didn't understand what had happened, but he knew he would either have to leave the island fast, or quickly let Axel know that something was going on. Someone was trying to contact him, or was contacting him by accident. Someone with magic, or spelled with the magic for an emergency call.

Just as he pulled a shirt over his head another scream ripped through his mind. It was so loud that Sky instinctively placed his hands over his ears, as if that would've made a difference. This time, instead of being frozen to the spot like he had been in his bed, Sky quickly pulled open the bottom drawer of his dresser and took out a belt and two short swords that lay in between his socks and underwear. He put the simple weapons belt on and attached the short swords to it. And with the scream still very much alive and echoing in his brain, Sky set his magic to work. The Band on his wrist started pulsing and he let his magic follow the scream, searching for where it came from.

The blue light enveloped him and he shimmered from his room.

When the light vanished, Sky was no longer standing on the hardwood floor of his bedroom. No; the ground underneath his feet was softer and... damp? Sky opened his eyes slowly, blinking in the sudden brightness of sunlight. He was still looking down, and he realised that he was standing on earth; brown, muddy earth. Sky lifted his head and gaped at the sight around him. He was nowhere near Saluverus; he knew that much for sure. He was almost one hundred per cent certain that he wasn't even in Europe anymore either, for he was surrounded by trees the height of skyscrapers and the width of some of the smaller towers of Saluverus' castle. There were lush bushes everywhere. Green... it was so green. Sky looked around him. Nathan would go mad with envy when Sky told him about this.

There were trees with fuzzy branches; there were trees growing out of other trees. Vines hung all around him, and shrubs covered the forest floor. Sky could barely see his feet in the dense shrubbery. And it was humid beyond belief; his clothes were already damp and clinging to his body.

Sky looked at the ground near his feet. Wherever he could see through the large green leaves he could see the dark ground underneath. But there was something a few feet away from him that wasn't brown like everywhere else. What he saw there was something lighter, something beige, something...

Sky's heart froze. He was looking at human skin.

He rushed closer and dropped down to the ground. With his bare hands he pushed away the leaves blocking his view. Gradually a torso was revealed. Sky ripped a few plants from the ground to get a better look. As Sky's gaze moved up the arm and shoulder and reached the face, his hands slowed; he recognised the man immediately.

Kristjan Stefansson, one of the two soldiers Percy Kelly had taken with him on his investigation to Brazil.

Brazil... Sky was in Brazil...

He placed his hands quickly under Kristjan's jawline and found no pulse. Kristjan's skin was cold. The man had been dead a while. He couldn't have been the one who called for Sky with his scream.

Sky got up and scanned the forest floor. He moved slowly, his eyes flitting in every direction, just trying to spot something that was unnatural for a jungle. Something man made. And then he saw it.

The dense and grown-together plants on the jungle floor just up ahead of him were flattened and torn. Sky hurried forward and followed the path of destruction. He tried to make as little noise as possible. Whoever killed Kristjan could still be here somewhere, and if he were strong enough to take on the Icelandic soldier, then he was someone to contend with. Even with magic.

Though as Sky moved through the jungle, he quickly came to the conclusion that whoever it had been, wasn't there anymore. Sky had learnt from Sophie that if the birds started singing again, and many of them were doing so, that that was nature's way of saying whatever danger there had been, was there no longer.

Sky's search led him to spot a tree, to the right of which he could distinctly see a pair of legs lying on the ground. It was quite a bit further up ahead, and Sky used his magic to get closer faster. The other side of the tree led to a small clearing, but Sky had no eyes for the open space as he dropped down next to the Affinite Sky recognised as Percy Kelly's wife.

He'd seen her plenty of times before; there was no mistaking her. Eva Kelly was a very bland woman, with dull brown hair and not a very pretty face. Even in death her lips were pursed in such a way that made her look like she was harshly judging everyone around her, when she was probably just curiously and calmly looking around. Her brown eyes looked blankly up at the canopy above her.

Sky reached out and closed her eyes. While he did this, he took in the rest of her body to see how she died. A wave of nausea swept through him as he looked. Kristjan had a single stab wound in his chest; the blade must have punctured his heart. Sky hadn't seen any other injuries beyond that; the single attack had been excellently placed. Sky had almost been impressed if he briefly forgot it had been Disciples who had done this.

Eva Kelly's death was nothing like Kristjan's. Her entire chest had been ripped open. Sky could see her broken ribs and shredded organs underneath. From his anatomy classes Sky could just about distinguish what remained of her heart and lungs. Her torso was so horrendously ripped to pieces that Sky could even see part of the woman's spine underneath. And the smell...

Sky felt bile rise in his throat and closed his eyes for a moment. He raised his head so that when he opened them again, he would see the clearing and no longer the butchered woman beneath him. For a moment he thought of Jillian. He remembered how she'd been laughing in the café down in Saluverus' village. How was she going to react when she heard that her mother was dead? Would she want to see the body? Would Axel even tell her how horrendous the injuries were? Sky would make sure Jillian didn't know. No one should see their mother like this.

Sky swallowed once and opened his eyes.

What he saw in the clearing wasn't much better.

Two more bodies lay lifelessly about thirty feet away from him. Sky was about to get up and go towards them when something caught his eye. On the other side of the two bodies, something was moving, and it didn't look like an animal...

A human leg. It was twitching.

Sky was beside it in seconds, his Band glowing fiercely on his wrist. He reached the leg first, and only then looked up to see who it belonged to.

"Percy!" Sky exclaimed as he recognised the soldier. Percy's eyes were distant and he didn't look at Sky when his name was called. His shirt had been ripped and was drenched with blood. His leg looked shattered; Sky could see bone. But that wasn't the worst of it. Foam was coming out of Percy's mouth. Instinct made Sky push Percy on his side. He felt a crunch underneath his fingers and realised that the top part of Percy's arm must also be broken.

But it helped; the second Percy was on his side the man retched. Bile and foam and blood spewed out of the man's mouth and onto the jungle ground beside him. When Sky figured everything had come out, he pulled the soldier back onto his back to assess him for further injuries.

Percy's face was bloodied too; there was a gash from above his right eye down to under his cheekbone, and from there blood was spreading all across his face.

"Percy! Can you hear me? It's Sky. Sky Mayne!" He leant over the man, trying to get his attention. Suddenly, Percy's eyes became alert, and started darting every which way. When they finally met Sky's, the soldier began to struggle. He brought his hands up beside him and started pushing himself away from Sky. Blood bubbled in his chest and bone crunched in his arm as Percy tried to move.

"Hey, hey, hey," Sky soothed, reaching the man. "Don't move, all right? I'm going to get you out of here. We'll get you all healed up, all right?"

Percy's eyes flitted wildly around. His head was shaking from side to side and the rest of his body started trembling. Sky placed his hands on Percy's shoulders and was about to shimmer the both of them to the Medical Bay on Saluverus, when Percy let out a scream. An echo of the scream immediately blasted through Sky's head. It completely threw the Aster off guard. So much so that when the soldier lurched upright and pushed against Sky, bones crunching again, Sky tumbled backwards onto the ground. A second later, Sky was back on top of Percy. He didn't care that the man didn't want to be shimmered. There was a wild look in Percy's eyes that Sky had never seen before. They were darting in every direction like some terrified rabbit expecting a fox to jump out of nowhere. But Sky wasn't a fox trying to kill a rabbit. He was trying to help the soldier; and with his magic he'd be able to.

Sky reached for Percy's shoulders one more time and dug his nails into the soldier's skin. Before Percy could struggle and push him off again, Sky put his magic to work, and blue light filled his vision.

A second later, the two of them landed on the floor of the Medical Bay, in the exact same spot as when Sky had appeared there with Sophie all those weeks ago. To Sky's surprise, the exact same woman from that night was again standing at the patient's desk. Sky knew her name now: Dagmara. She was Polish, like Bianka and Marlena.

To Sky's great relief, Bianka Mazur was standing next to Dagmara.

The second he could, Percy swung his good arm across himself, smacking Sky on the side of his head. Sky was so glad that he made it to the Medical Bay and that the Chief Medical Officer happened to be working the night shift, that he didn't seen the blow coming. He was in the middle of shouting "I need help!" when the blow came and Sky toppled to the side.

Bianka and Dagmara were there in seconds. The bleeding of Percy's chest had got worse since the two of them shimmered. Bubbles were appearing through the sheet of blood covering his ripped clothes, and Sky knew that it must be air escaping one of his torn lungs.

"Mum, get me Katherine and Sophie now! And Jackson, too!" Sky shouted to the ceiling. He crouched beside Percy just as Bianka commanded Dagmara to do something in Polish. Bianka then crouched down on the other side of Percy and met Sky's gaze.

"He needs to be on a stretcher," she explained, her accent thick through her English. She then pointed down the hall to where a stretcher was mounted on the wall.

Using his magic, Sky got the stretcher from the wall and was back beside Percy in less than two seconds. Percy seemed to have calmed down slightly, and with the help of two male nurses who had come running, Sky and Bianka managed to get Percy onto the stretcher. The male nurses had arrived with a bed on wheels, and the four of them lifted the stretcher, with Percy on it, onto the bed.

"Let's get him to the operating room," Bianka ordered.

Sky ran alongside the rolling bed and said, "But Sophie and Katherine can heal him."

"Sophie and Katherine aren't here yet!" Bianka snapped. "And I don't know his injuries until we see what's in there. Some cannot be healed with magic."

Right as she said the word *magic*, Percy, who had calmed down considerably, suddenly spasmed and frantically tried to move around and sit up straight. Sky leaned over the bed and forced the soldier back down. He was much stronger than his injuries made him look. One of the male nurses walking behind Bianka reached in and helped keep Percy lying down in his bed.

"He must stop struggling!" Bianka demanded.

Sky was using all the strength he had to do what she said. It took a few moments before the man finally gave in and leant back in the bed. As the four of them rolled the bed down the corridor, Dagmara suddenly appeared from a side corridor. She passed Bianka a small piece of paper and then took a place in between the Chief Medical Officer and the male nurse beside the rolling bed and reached over Percy's body. She had two small white towels in her hands, and she was pressing them against the open wound on Percy's chest to try and slow the bleeding.

At the end of the corridor, they turned left and headed for the lift at the end that led down to the operating rooms in the basement. As they neared it, there was a sudden flash of blue light, and four people stood blocking their way.

Madeleine stood in the middle, with Sophie and her mother on one side, and Jackson Kelly on the other. Bianka, Sky and the two male nurses stopped moving the bed. Dagmara kept the white towels firmly pressed on Percy's chest.

Jackson Kelly was the first to move. "Percy!" he shouted, recognising his brother. Percy, however, didn't reciprocate. The wildness in his eyes hadn't gone and they were still shooting around the room in panic. Then he started spluttering, and more foam started coming out of his mouth.

"On his side!" Bianka commanded. Sky and the male nurse on the opposite side of the bed worked together to move the soldier. Dagmara tried her best to keep the towels in place so no more blood would escape the open chest wound. Sophie and Katherine came up on either side, while Jackson remained at the foot of the bed, looking over at his injured brother.

The moment Percy lay on his side, he coughed, and more blood, foam and bile came out of his mouth. Part of it landed on Dagmara's forearms; the nurse didn't flinch. She kept her hands firmly on the towels on Percy's chest. Once all that was blocking Percy's airway was out, the soldier breathed in once more. Sky and the male nurse were starting to turn him back onto his back, when suddenly Percy's wild and shifting eyes found Katherine's. The split second Percy recognised Katherine, he started moving himself away from that side of the bed. Pushing off with his one good leg and one good arm and moaning something none of them understood. Dagmara tried, but she couldn't keep her hands firm on Percy's chest as he struggled. Blood stained the white sheets red.

"Percy! Percy!" Katherine called. "I'm here to help you, just let me help you!"

She reached out her arms, and the Band on her wrist started glowing golden. Instead of calming him down, this only seemed to make Percy want to get away from her more. Violently he started flaying his arms about him, preventing Katherine from finding a clear place on his body where she could rest her hands and let her magic work.

"Katherine, move back!" Bianka ordered.

Sky and the male nurse on the other side were trying their best to hold Percy down by his shoulders and legs, but it was only through the soldier's own will that he finally settled down again. It seemed to coincide with the moment Katherine left his field of vision. She had moved up behind his head. The second she could, Dagmara was there again, pressing the towels to the soldier's open wound.

Everyone kept still as they watched Percy calm down again. There was so much blood on the bed and the floor underneath now. Sky knew they needed to get him healed or to an operating room *fast*. The soldier was bleeding out right in front of them.

Bianka looked up at Sophie, who had come up beside Sky. Even though Percy was barely moving in his bed, his eyes were still actively scanning the space around him and his breathing was extremely shallow. Bianka nodded at Sophie, and she leaned over the bed, her hands outstretched, her Band glowing golden.

Percy's reaction was instantaneous. Shouting gibberish he frantically started pushing himself away from Sophie's outstretched hands.

"Hold him steady!" Katherine commanded, coming back around from Percy's head and to Bianka's side. Sky and the male nurse opposite him reached over and clamped down on Percy's shoulders. The other male nurse, who was now beside Sophie, practically threw himself over the bed to pin down Percy's legs.

But the man didn't stop struggling. In fact, he squirmed and spasmed harder than he did before. Especially once Katherine leaned over the bed as well.

"Steadier!" Katherine snapped.

But it was impossible. The more people came in to help keep Percy steady, the more distressed the soldier became. Blood was bubbling even more fiercely from his chest wound now and Percy was even using his shattered leg and his broken arm to try and manoeuvre himself away from being touched by Sophie and Katherine's magic.

"They're trying to help you, Percy, stop!" Jackson yelled, panic stark in his voice.

A bone snapped.

The sound seemed to reverberate through the corridor. Percy Kelly was willing to break his own bones to get away from the magic.

"Everybody STOP!" Bianka ordered. "Katherine, Sophie, move back NOW!"

The Aster and Ceder of Health stepped back, shocked both by Bianka's sharp tone and Percy's reaction to them. Percy continued to struggle, but less so now.

"Let him go and step back," Bianka commanded. The two male nurses stood back up straight and stepped away from the bed. Sky still had his hands firmly on Percy's shoulders. His struggles were slowing, but he hadn't stopped trying to get away yet.

"You too," Bianka told Sky pointedly.

Sky looked up at Bianka; the Chief Medical Officer stared him down fiercely until Sky reluctantly lifted his hands from Percy's shoulders. Only Dagmara was still there, holding the now red-stained towels against Percy's open chest wound. Sky still didn't dare to take a step back; he was ready to jump on top of the soldier again if he tried to get away and make his injuries worse. But to his great surprise, Percy stopped moving altogether, and slumped down, his head resting against the blood-soaked pillow.

"Take this," Bianka told Madeleine, passing her the note that Dagmara had given her a few minutes ago. "The locations of the best surgeons on the island. Dagmara has already notified them. Send them to Operating Room *One*."

Madeleine nodded once, looked down at the note and shimmered out of the corridor.

Bianka motioned to the people around the bed that she was planning on moving Percy Kelly towards the lift again.

"No!" Jackson exclaimed urgently, blocking their path. "You're not taking him to surgery. How will he survive it? Heal him! Use magic!"

Katherine made to move back to Percy's side, but no sooner had Jackson spoken the word *magic*, than Percy spasmed and started struggling again.

Sky and the two male nurses jumped back in and tried to keep Percy as still as they could so as to not make his injuries any worse than they already were, but it was well-nigh impossible.

"Katherine, keep your distance. This patient wants no magical care, that much is clear," Bianka stated baldly. "If he wants none, then he gets none."

"He doesn't know what he wants. He is obviously distressed. You don't know if he will survive long enough to even undergo surgery! You have to force him to get healed. Sedate him first if you have to." Jackson had turned from shouting at the Chief Medical Officer, to pleading with her.

"That is against the rights and the wishes of the patient. You have seen it. It will only make things worse. He will not stay still long enough for them to work and he will create new injuries if he struggles further during their healing. I have my best surgeons coming in. They are his best chance now. Now *please*, move aside." Bianka's voice was strong, her tone resolute. She pushed the bed forward and didn't wait for the Commanding Chief to step to the side.

The lift doors opened and the entire company, except for Jackson,

Sophie and Katherine, stepped inside. As the lift doors closed Bianka called, "Inform Axel!"

The lift began to move. When the doors opened again, Sky's mother and two women Sky didn't recognise were waiting on the other side. The two women were already prepped and ready for the surgery and took the places of Dagmara and Bianka. Madeleine moved out of the way, keeping out of Percy's line of sight, as Dagmara and Bianka slipped off to the side and started washing their hands and prepping themselves. The two male nurses followed suit. Through the glass, Sky could see another five people in the operating room.

Sky watched as a mask was dropped over Percy's nose and mouth. A few moments later, Bianka and Dagmara entered the operating room from a side door. Gowns and gloves were given to them once they stepped in. Bianka moved to Percy's side and gestured with her hand. Dagmara took one of the scalpels from a tray at Percy's feet and handed it to the Chief Medical Officer.

"Sky."

Sky turned to his mother. Her eyes were bright and alert.

"Were there any others?"

Sky realised she was talking about the Affinites in Brazil.

"There were three dead. I don't know if there were any others. Or if they could be alive," Sky answered.

"But there is a possibility?" Madeleine pushed.

Sky nodded. There could be. Percy was still alive. And there were more Affinites still unaccounted for.

"Then let's go." She held out her hand. Sky took it. His mother didn't know where to go. But Sky did. Once he'd been somewhere, he could shimmer there again without someone calling him.

Sky put his magic to work and shimmered himself and his mother back to the Amazon Rainforest, wondering even in that split second of flight, what awaited them there.

Chapter 12

When Sky had spotted Percy across the clearing, he hadn't looked around much further. When he went back with his mother, he realised how blind he'd been. Aside from Percy's personal soldier, Kristjan Stefansson, and Percy's wife, Eva, Sky and Madeleine found another four Affinites. To his own disgust, Sky found himself relieved that they had been dead a while. Even if it had dawned on Sky to return the second the two male nurses had arrived to hold Percy still, he wouldn't have found any alive.

Of the four of them, Sky only recognised Yua Tanaka, Percy's other personal soldier. He could tell these four were Affinites by their clothing and their weapons lying close by. He hadn't expected to have to make that distinction, but in his rush and panic to keep Percy alive, Sky had completely missed the fact that there were not only Affinites there.

As Sky and Madeleine moved through the clearing, they found Disciples as well. Five of them, in fact. And they were all dead, too. Some kind of battle between them and the Affinites had taken place.

"Eva's rescue team had eight, Percy's had three," Madeleine was saying. The two of them were making their way through the clearing, sending the bodies back to Saluverus' morgue in the basement of the castle with their shimmers. "That makes eleven in total."

"Kristjan, Yua and those three make five," Sky added.

"This one makes six," Madeleine said. She crouched down next to the Affinite. Sky leaned in and closed the eyes of the female soldier. She had multiple stab wounds to the abdomen. She wouldn't have survived long with that amount of bleeding, but it seemed strange to Sky that such a well-trained soldier – one of Percy's best – could have sustained such injuries in a fight. It didn't fit in with the picture of a battle. Sky shook off a feeling of unease and used his magic to shimmer the woman home. He couldn't begin to imagine what had happened here. She might have been tortured and left to die before others came in to fight. Still, something didn't seem to fit.

Sky followed his mother across the clearing to where they knew another two Affinites were. Sky and his mother had flown over the clearing and the nearby area to note where all the casualties were before dropping down and sending them home. They wanted to make sure there were no other surprises and especially no Disciples lurking around for a final ambush.

Sky broke away from his mother and headed for the Affinite next to a great tree. Sky had seen this one before. It was Eva Kelly. Her injuries were more severe than any of them. She must have been killed by the wrong kind of Disciple; one who revelled in his kill. Her injuries looked just as shocking on second viewing. And the smell hadn't improved, with the body lying out in the Brazilian heat like this. Sky closed his eyes for a moment before using his magic to send her back home. As Sky's Band pulsed and a blue light appeared, his mother came up behind him. Sky stood up and looked at her.

"Including those two we get to eight," she said, and walked towards where they had seen the last two bodies from the sky. Sky followed her in silence.

The two final bodies were of two male Affinites. They were lying on top of each other. The Affinites looked nothing alike. One had dark skin and bushy black hair, while the other was pale with faded red hair.

Madeleine crouched down and moved her arm over the two bodies, her Band glowing. Her shimmer appeared and enveloped both bodies completely. When the blue light vanished, the bodies had disappeared.

"Those make ten. So, we are missing..." she trailed off, looking around the clearing.

"None. Eleven went in. Ten dead and Percy is in surgery," Sky finished. He stared at the nature around him. Nathan would love to be in one of the most beautiful stretches of nature the world had to offer. His brother had been in the Amazon Rainforest twice now in a short space of time, but never for pleasure. Maybe one day it could be.

Madeleine Mayne placed a hand on her son's shoulder. "You did good," she commended.

Sky shook his head and brushed away his mother's hand. "*Good?* How is this good? They're all dead! We should've been able to avoid this!"

"It was not your responsibility to save them," Madeleine replied tensely.

"No, it wasn't. It was yours!" Sky shouted, stepping away from his mother. He stared at her, and she stared back. She knew he wasn't talking about the Affinites anymore. She should've been able to save them. Save *her*. The Queen to come. They should've been able to...

Sky sighed and shook his head. "I'm sorry. I just... I wish there was something we could've done. That *I* could've done." He closed his eyes and sighed again. "She should be alive."

Madeleine let out a breath. "I know you do. I do, too. I replay that night in my head every second of every day, trying to find something that I could've done differently. That I could've detected something, *anything*. But there was nothing that could be done."

"Like there's nothing to be done here?" Sky asked, gesturing to the torn and destroyed nature as a result of the battle. It wasn't an accusation. But these deaths, just like the deaths of the Mendosa family—it all seemed so unnecessary. All of it.

"Only Percy Kelly can answer that question. He is the only one who can tell us what happened here," Madeleine said.

"But it might be weeks before he recovers," Sky sighed.

"It won't take weeks for him to be able to speak. He will be able to tell us."

"And what if he doesn't survive the operation? What then?"

"It won't be your job to find out what happened here, son," Madeleine said quietly.

"It will be. Percy told Axel that if he didn't come back or if something happened to him, that he had to send in the Asters," Sky told her, remembering the conversation he overheard between Axel and Percy Kelly.

"Even so. You won't be the Asters he will send in," Madeleine replied.

Sky whipped his head around to his mother. "We are perfectly capable of—" His voice trailed off. There was something in his mother's eyes that stopped him. He stared at them. At those dark, infinite blue eyes that were identical to his own. "What do you know that I don't?"

His mother looked at him for a while. She radiated strength. Nothing seemed to faze her. The second they shimmered into the clearing, Sky had expected her to at least *react* to the sight, and if not to the sight then to the *smell*. But she had been cool and composed; had treated every Affinite with respect and with no trace of revulsion towards the mangled bodies and the horrific smell. It was a quality Sky had most wanted to inherit, but just didn't have. All this battle site did to Sky was fuel his anger. He wanted nothing more than to avenge these deaths. The only thing he knew for sure was that Disciples were responsible, which meant that the South American King was once again responsible. All seven Kings used to be so abstract to Sky; he'd never faced one before. But his anger towards this one was very, very real. And one day he would make sure he'd come face to face with him...

"I got a call," Madeleine began eventually.

"From who?" Sky asked.

Madeleine looked at him, telling him with her eyes that she wouldn't answer that question. Sky groaned his frustration. Because she travelled widely for the Small Council, his mother had contact with Affinites all over the world and they fed her the same information they passed on to the Small Council. Madeleine never did anything with the information, while Sky obviously would, given half the chance. She just wanted to be informed. Axel had a tendency to leave out pieces of information for the good and success of a mission, but she preferred to know the whole story.

"Mitrik is days away from making his move," Madeleine divulged.

Mitrik. The Higher King of the North American Underworld.

"Is your informant sure?" Sky asked.

Madeleine chuckled. "Very sure. Otherwise, he wouldn't have told me what he told Axel. You won't be finding out what happened here. I suspect you will be sent to North America."

Sky nodded slowly. "Will Rose and Katherine's Bone Recovery team be pulled back?"

"Possibly. But it won't matter."

"Why won't it matter?"

Madeleine let out a long sigh. "Because they suspect the bones can never be found."

Sky stared at her and said quietly, "What?"

"Each area where the spell implied a bone could be found has come up empty. Rose and Katherine already suspected nothing could be found a few weeks ago, but Axel wanted them to be sure."

"And what does that mean?"

Madeleine looked at her son. Just for a moment the strength left her eyes, and she allowed him to see the sadness underneath. Cara and Tomas had been her Aster family. In all her radiating strength, it was easy to forget that she'd lost people, too. Probably only Sky's father would be able to see what she was hiding underneath.

"Cara and Tomas' magic are lost forever. There will only be five Asters from your generation onwards. You five are all the world has left," she said.

"How bad is that?" Sky asked tentatively. He would never ask that question to anyone else in any other situation. No one would ever get to see his vulnerability or worry.

Madeleine smiled slightly. "Not bad. You have proven your worth with just the five of you so far. A King and a few Disciples are nothing you haven't handled before."

"We've never faced a King before," Sky admitted.

Madeleine turned to face her son completely. She placed her hands on his shoulders and stared into his eyes. "You are my son. You have trained well to become as strong as you can be. You can handle Mitrik. I wouldn't say that if I didn't believe it."

Sky looked into those deep blue eyes. "What about the South American King? Can we handle him?"

Madeleine's features hardened. Whatever emotions she had openly shown him had disappeared once again. "He took something from all of us. If you come to face him, you will have every living, breathing Affinite and Aster there beside you. Sooner or later, he will pay for what he has done."

Sky stared at his mother. He believed every word she said.

"Come on," she said, offering Sky her hand. "Let's go home. You need to prepare yourself for what Axel will have you do next."

Chapter 13

The operation had gone on for hours. And hours and hours. And somehow Percy Kelly survived. Even with all the blood loss from his open chest and his shattered leg and his double-broken arm. And then there had been the internal bleeding.

That the man was still alive was a medical miracle.

How he managed to survive all those injuries without any magical assistance, Sophie would never understand. She had tried to convince her mother for either one of them to step into that operating room when things seemed to be going south. Just to give the surgeons a little extra assistance. But her mother had refused. Sophie knew why, though she hadn't wanted to accept it.

Sophie didn't get it. Percy had never had anything against the Asters. Or magic of any kind. He and his brother had been the best soldiers, fighting right alongside the Asters on the front lines in the war against Astaroth. Why was he so against it now? It didn't make any sense.

Sophie leaned against the doorway of Percy Kelly's room in the Medical Bay. He looked better than he had done when he came in. Just. A bruising had appeared on his face around where it had been cut open. His skin was purple and blue and throbbing. His leg was in a gigantic cast and so was his arm. His struggles had made his injuries in his leg and arm worse than when he was brought in. The crack that they heard in his final struggle to stay away from both Sophie and her mother had been the sound of his *humerus* snapping. That bone in his upper arm must have already been damaged when he came in, but it fully broke while in his most frantic state. One of the two bones in his lower arm was already broken.

Sophie couldn't imagine the kind of rehabilitation and physical therapy this man would have to go through before he could move properly again, let alone join his brother again in training Affinites.

Even after Percy had been put under anaesthesia, Bianka had not allowed Katherine or Sophie to go near him. Sophie knew that if a patient didn't want to be healed with magic, it was absolutely forbidden for her to do so, but it took all her effort not to walk into the room and even just heal that one cut on his face.

Why didn't he want to be healed by magic?

The question spun around in Sophie's mind.

"Here you are," came a voice behind her.

Sophie turned her head to find Jake standing there. He stepped forward and wrapped his arms around her. Sophie leaned back against his chest.

"How did you know where I was?" she asked.

"I thought I might find you here," Jake mused.

Sophie chuckled. "Liar."

"Fine. I went to the library first. I overheard a studying nurse say Percy Kelly had come back, severely injured. Then I figured you'd be here," Jake kissed her neck once and then looked past her at the man in the bed. "How is he doing?"

"He survived the operation, miraculously."

Sophie could feel Jake's arms tighten around her ever so slightly. "Have you been here all day after being here all night?" he wondered.

"I couldn't leave... I had to know," Sophie whispered. "I need to know."

"Why not heal him? Don't you need to know what happened out

there?"

"He won't let me. I'm not allowed to if he doesn't want it."

Jake let out a sigh. "You should get some rest. You know they'll notify you if there are any changes."

Sophie tightened her hands on the arms around her. The strength of him was comforting. He was right, of course. Standing here day and night wouldn't help Percy. And it wouldn't help her. And still, she couldn't leave.

"Just a little while longer," Sophie said softly.

Jake kissed her neck again, but made no move to leave her to it. "All right," he whispered in her ear. He would stay, Sophie realised. For however long she would stand there he would stay. Even if he thought doing something else would be better for her. He wouldn't force her to do anything, he wouldn't talk down to her or tell her she wasn't thinking straight. He would never treat her like she needed someone else to make her decisions for her because she was still broken in some way.

"Thank you," she whispered.

A slight tightening of his arms around her was his only response. And the two of them stood in the door opening for a while. They didn't say anything because there was nothing to say. Sophie stared at Percy's body and his beaten, broken face. He was the best soldier Saluverus had ever seen. And yet some Disciple had managed to do this to him. None of it made any sense. Even with the element of surprise, Percy would've been able to defend himself better than this.

Sophie stared at the cast around his leg, and the bandages around his head for a long time.

Movement from the bed triggered her to step into the room. Sophie broke away from Jake's hold immediately and walked forward.

"Soph, are you sure?" Jake was saying. Sophie ignored him. Jake came up close to the bed, but remained at the foot of the bed.

Percy Kelly's eyelids fluttered open and his eyes immediately darted around the room. His gaze quickly found Sophie, and panic flared in his eyes.

"No, no, no, no, it's okay. I'm not using magic, okay? No magic," Sophie assured Percy quickly, as he immediately tried to move away from her. Sophie held up her hands and revealed the Band on her skin. It was just the black lines wrapping around her wrist like a bracelet. It was not glowing like it would if she were using her magic.

"No magic," Sophie repeated. Percy's wild eyes stared at Sophie's hands. His entire body trembled, but he seemed to believe her. A few moments later the soldier's body stilled, but his eyes remained wild and alert.

"Dar... dark..." Percy whispered. Sophie could barely make out what he was saying, he spoke so quietly.

"I'm sorry, I don't understand you," Sophie said. She kept her hands up where Percy could see them. She didn't want him to panic and ruin all of Bianka's hard work.

"Dark... creation... my dark..." Percy rasped. Pain covered his features. "Eva... mine... creation destroyed..."

Sophie tried to make sense of what he was saying. She was about to ask him again, but he suddenly clenched his eyes closed and started screaming. The monitors around Percy's bed started beeping and flashing, and Percy screamed even louder. It was as if he was finally feeling all the pain from all his injuries.

"Nurse!" Sophie yelled.

"We need a nurse in here now!" Jake shouted.

She stepped back from Percy. It took every bit of effort for her to step away from the patient instead of towards him. Her magic hummed in her ears. Her fingers itched to be pressed against Percy's chest so the magic could flow through them.

Dagmara, the nurse who had been on call the night Percy came in, dashed into the room, followed by a male nurse Sophie didn't recognise, and Marlena. Dagmara was talking so fast that Sophie couldn't follow what she was saying.

Dagmara took a syringe and emptied the contents into Percy's upper arm. It seemed to calm him down enough for Marlena to lower a mask over Percy's mouth, which sent him into a deep sleep.

It was the vibrating of the chip in Sophie's upper arm that finally made her walk out of the room. She wanted to stay; she needed to know whether Percy would be all right, and if it was her presence that had triggered all this, or if this was bound to have happened the moment he woke up.

But she forced herself to walk out of the room and call for Sky. It would take her at least thirty minutes to get up to the castle, from the Medical Bay down in the village. Since she didn't know what this summoning was about, it was better that her brother could shimmer the two of them up there. That was protocol. No more than five minutes, or you shimmer.

"What's going on?" Jake asked.

Sophie looked at the boy apologetically. "They're calling me. I have to go."

Blue light appeared, and before either of them could say anything else, Sky had taken a hold of her arm and shimmered the two of them to the Board Room.

Mitrik was making his move. Or so it seemed.

Lian stared at the map of North America that was displayed on the television screen above the corner desk in the Board Room. He was the first to get there; he'd been in his bedroom at the time and it took only a few minutes to get from there to here. Sky had gone off to get Sophie from wherever she was; Lian guessed the Medical Bay. He wondered if Sophie had been in the Medical Bay all day to see if she could be there when the soldier woke up. Sky had told them that the man hadn't wanted to be healed by magic; had fought vigorously against it, despite his horrific injuries. Percy also hadn't wanted to be shimmered back to Saluverus. None of them could make sense of it.

They needed to get information from the soldier. But that didn't seem to be why they were being summoned now. The television screen was focused on North America. After Lian sat down at the oak table, he took a good look at the screen.

There didn't seem to be any more Disciples in North America than there had been in the previous weeks. The only difference between then and now, was that they were all clustered in south-western America. It was too big of a coincidence to ignore that the Grand Canyon was where multiple entrances to the Underworld of North America existed. The King could gather his forces just inside his territory, and a second later spill out onto the Surface.

The doors to the Board Room opened again and Nathan and Matu stepped inside, followed by Jackson, who looked drawn and tired with concern for his twin brother. The two Asters were still wearing their training gear, and had obviously come from a training session in the arena.

A blue light appeared near the window, and Sophie and Sky appeared. They silently took a seat, like Nathan and Matu had just done.

"Good, now that you're all here," Axel said. He was standing at the head of the table, waiting for everyone to sit down before beginning to speak. The Spymaster, Felix Hauser, was leaning against the filing cabinets along the wall behind them, while Sylvia Allen was sitting on the desk chair near the door. There was no sign of Nicholas Nelson.

"Thanks to Sky's quick response, he was able to bring Percy back here alive. When the soldier has recovered enough, we should get a better idea of what is happening in Brazil," Axel began. He looked at Sky and gave him a complimentary nod.

"I still don't understand why he didn't call when he was being attacked? Since he could," Sky said.

It was true. Percy had been spelled to be able to call for Sky, or he could subconsciously call if he got severely injured. Somewhere during the fight he should have had the time to call Sky. He only needed to shout his name. Even whilst fighting, Percy should have been able to call the Aster of Speed and Flight.

"That is a question only Percy can answer for us," Axel said. "As Sophie and Sky have probably already told you, he has experienced not only physical trauma, but psychological trauma as well. We don't know if this was just from the shock of what he witnessed and therefore it will ebb away with time, or that his panic and fear for magic will stay. Doctor Masalis will be treating him, and hopefully we will get our answers soon."

Lian kept his face neutral. If anyone could help Percy Kelly it was her. There was also something to be said about the Small Council appointing her specifically to treat the soldier—just like they had appointed her specifically to treat Sophie. She truly was the best in the business.

"What about my father?" Matu asked. Lian looked at his brother. Matu seemed calm and composed, but it wouldn't surprise Lian if his mind was racing. His question might've seemed to come out of the blue, but it wasn't hard to know what he was thinking: his father was leading a rescue team just like Eva Kelly had done. Was it just pure luck that Diallo's team wasn't attacked? Or would they be next?

Axel inclined his head towards the Aster of Strength. "We have given him and the other Queen's Case teams the instruction to return to home base just on the edge of the Amazon Rainforest. We are pulling them all back until further notice. Your father's team should be back there in a few days, from where Madeleine will help shimmer everyone back here."

Matu shifted uncomfortably in his chair. After what happened to Eva Kelly's rescue team, Lian didn't blame him. Sure, her team was weaker because it wasn't led by an Aster, but that didn't automatically make Diallo's team any less of a target, despite what the Small Council might think. Lian knew what it was like to lose a parent – to lose both – and he didn't want that happening to anyone in this family he had here.

"That was all from South America," Axel continued. "Now if you turn to the screen, you will see that the Disciples have gathered in one particular spot in North America."

"The Grand Canyon," Sophie observed.

"Precisely. They are appearing as much as they are disappearing around one of the entrances to the Underworld there. We are expecting Mitrik to make the Canyon his base before spreading out further across the continent. We have received information that a group of human hikers has gone missing. This might be completely unrelated, but this is precisely why we are sending you now. We want you to go there and identify the Disciples from Mitrik's inner circle—we doubt Mitrik will be there in person, yet. Your mission will be to drive the higher-ranking Disciples back down into the Underworld; the lesser Disciples will follow suit, or at least will refrain from taking action on the Surface. If they cannot be driven down, you have clearance to kill them. Do what you need to do to put an end to this potential uprising. You will leave tomorrow afternoon. Make sure you get a good night's rest. Tomorrow, pack lightly. Jackson will arrange for your weapons to be ready for you and you will be fully briefed tomorrow before you leave. You are expected here at four o'clock. We will see you then."

The Asters got up and left the Board Room. No one spoke much as they headed for their bedrooms. They had been sent on multiple missions before, dealing with groups of Disciples that had gone rogue, or a small rebellion here and there. But never in the time that they'd been active as Asters had there been a full-scale uprising led by a King; an attempt to reclaim even part of the Surface of the earth.

And this was it. This would be the first time they'd be facing a King's Inner Circle. It would be the first time they'd be facing a King.

Chapter 14

The following afternoon, Axel, Jackson and Sylvia led the way to the static portals in the castle's basement. From Sky's perspective there didn't seem to be any reason why they were using these instead of his shimmer, but he was stared down angrily by Axel after making his feelings of offence very clear. There was a reason. Sky barely listened to the explanation. Something to do with how the location they were being transported to was already set up for teleportation.

Jackson was carrying two very large duffel bags filled with weapons, which clanked and clunked with every step he took. Matu offered to take one of the bags, but the Commanding Chief refused.

As they walked down the last flight of stairs Sky came up to Sylvia's side. "Any word on Percy?" he asked.

Sylvia Allen glanced at Jackson Kelly for a moment, but he was in a deep conversation with Matu at the time. They were talking about Matu's father, who would return to Saluverus in two days' time.

Sylvia shook her head. "They put him in a medically induced coma last night so his body has time to heal without him consciously feeling the pain," she replied. "We won't know if he'll actually wake from it when he is healed enough to do so. Olga has been at his bedside all this morning, and won't leave. She wants to be there to talk to him when he wakes up."

Sky was silent for a moment. At the bottom of the stairs, they turned left and headed down the corridor. The lowest floor of the castle wasn't decorated the way the rest of the castle was. There were no windows here; they were one level below the courtyard outside, and all the hallways and rooms were lit with artificial lighting. No paintings hung on the walls; there was no atmosphere to speak of. The place gave Sky the creeps. It, of course, had nothing to do with the fact that the morgue and pathology labs were down here, which now kept the bodies he and his mother had sent back to the island from the Rainforest.

"Sophie said he was speaking gibberish when he woke up. Is that normal?" Sky whispered to Sylvia, given that Jackson and Matu had ended their conversation. Sky didn't imagine Jackson would appreciate them talking about his brother.

Sylvia cast Sky a glance. "No, it is not," she answered worryingly.

Axel opened the door at the end of the corridor. Jackson was the first to step inside.

"Disorientation, yes," Sophie interjected, stepping beside Sky and waiting until the rest of the party had filed into the room. Sky raised his eyebrows at his sister. It shouldn't have surprised him that she'd been eavesdropping. "Mumbling happens, too. But this was... different. I can't explain it."

"Let's hope he gets over it," Sky said lightly. He saw something flicker in Sophie's eyes before he stepped into the room.

The Portal Room was a large, narrow, rectangular space, painted completely white. The door they'd just walked into was all the way at the end of one long wall. The other long wall opposite them had seven glass doors. Nothing could be seen through the glass but what looked like billowing clouds. Each door led to a different continent; the name of that continent was written in black calligraphic letters above each portal.

The Asters walked towards the glass door that had *North America* written above it, while Sylvia and Axel walked along the opposite wall to stand behind a single computer standing on top of a podium. Jackson stepped towards the Asters and gave Matu and Nathan each one of the weapons bags he was holding. A smaller backpack he shrugged off his shoulder and passed on to Sky, which contained spare vials of their blood. Sky always got this backpack when there was a possibility the Asters would have to separate during missions. It was mostly because it contained Sophie's blood, which could be used for healing, and because Sky could shimmer to anyone who might need it. The backpack could be fastened extremely tightly to his back and was so compact that it wouldn't bother him during a possible battle.

Jackson then stepped back to stand behind the Ambassador and the Consul. Sylvia Allen was busy typing away on the computer; probably filling in those super precise coordinates that Sky would supposedly have shimmered to in the wrong way. Sky forced himself not to roll his eyes. She looked up at Axel and nodded that she was ready.

They had received their full briefing back in the Board Room, but as Sylvia waited for the signal to start the transporting, Axel briefly went over their mission again. "You will be transported in to one of David Hughes' cabins. He will be waiting for you there and will update you on the developments in the Grand Canyon. If there are signs of an uprising, you must do whatever you can to stop it, but make sure there are no human or Affinite casualties before you make your stand to push the Disciples back down into the Underworld. Any questions?" Axel explained.

All five of them shook their heads. Axel nodded in return, and said, "All right." He turned to Sylvia. "All set then?"

"It's ready," Sylvia announced.

There was no sign that the portal behind the glass door was ready. It didn't change colour or consistency, so they would have to trust that Sylvia had entered the right coordinates.

"Good luck," Jackson said.

Only Sophie thanked him. Matu was already sliding the glass door open. He didn't look back. He stepped through the doorway and into the cloudy nothingness behind. The white clouds closed in behind him and Matu was gone. The thickness of the clouds of the portal shone brighter for a short moment before returning to its duller white. Nathan was next, and then Lian. Sophie followed a few seconds later.

Sky gritted his teeth. He definitely preferred his shimmer. The static portal made him feel like he was literally being tossed through time and space. With his shimmer there was only that short moment where there was no feeling of ground underneath his feet, and that feeling was gone almost as quickly as it came.

The second he stepped into the portal, it felt like he was making multiple summersaults. He was spinning through the whiteness until suddenly his body was pulled abruptly back upright, right before he was thrown down onto a very real and very hard wooden floor. Sky grunted as he fought to keep his footing during the landing.

All his siblings were already there.

"Next time I'm shimmering," Sky muttered.

Sophie cast him a *look*. "They had their reasons."

"Oh, I'm sure they did. Just next time, you all take the clouds, and then just call me, and I'll shimmer right to you."

Sophie rolled her eyes.

Sky looked around. They were standing in a tiny bedroom. There was barely enough space for all of them. There were two single beds against each wall, and high cupboards lining the wall near the ceiling. There were two bedside tables, and that was about it. Everything was made of wood. And it was dark. A weak lightbulb barely illuminated the space. The red curtains were tightly drawn across the single square window above the two bedside tables. Sky wondered what the chances were that someone would walk by when they portalled here, or if they were just being extremely cautious.

Sky was closest to the door of the bedroom, and opened it. He stepped into a room that was much more spacious. There was a small kitchen to his left, a rectangular table with six chairs in front of him, and to his right were two leather sofas. And a middle-aged man was sitting on one of them. He was quite tall and looked to be in good shape for his age. His dark brown hair was cut extremely short, and his eyes lit up the moment Sky stepped out of the bedroom.

"Ah, you've made it!" the man exclaimed.

The other four Asters filed into the living space behind Sky.

"David Hughes?" Sky asked.

"Oh, yes, yes, that's right," the man prattled, jumping off the sofa, walking over and extending a hand to Sky. "Yes, I am David Hughes, and you must be...?"

"Sky. Sky Mayne," Sky answered, extending his hand.

"Ah, yes, Aster of Speed and Flight. Very nice to meet you, very nice indeed," David said, shaking Sky's hand strongly before doing the same with the others. "Ah yes, and miss Sophie Griffiths you must be. Ah, and then of course Matu Madaki, heard great things about you, and your strength. And Lian Fai, no pain, ah yes, very interesting I've always found you. And then you must be... Nathan Radbourne. Oh, it's good to have you here, good indeed."

David stepped back and looked at them for a moment. "You all aren't very good at fitting in with humans, are you?"

Sky looked at the other Asters and then down at himself. They were wearing fighting gear; very light fabric for the warmer weather, but a good layer of protection in case they were to engage in battle while they were there. Then Sky looked at David. The man was wearing mountain shoes, khaki shorts and a red t-shirt, with a logo of a single brown triangle and a yellow sun around its tip.

"We're not here to fit in," Sky said shortly.

David laughed. "No, no. I suppose you're not. Now, come with me. You have heard most of what has been going on here from Axel, I assume." He gestured to the whole room with his hands. "This will be your cabin, by the way. There are three bedrooms with two single beds each. You can leave whatever you don't need to bring to the Canyon here. It will be under lock and key."

The Asters dropped their bags with their personal belongings, which mostly included a change of clothes, behind the sofa on the floor and indicated to David that they were ready to go. Nathan and Matu also dropped the weapons bags that Jackson had given them, and Sky did the same with the backpack.

"All right, come around here and I'll tell you all that I know," David said, gesturing to the rectangular table. The Asters walked over to the table and Sky noticed that one of the chairs had a bag slung over its back. David took the bag off and sat down. The Asters followed suit and all looked at David expectantly.

"Right," David said, suddenly becoming quite serious, the smile vanishing from his face. "There have been disappearances of human hikers in one particular area of the Grand Canyon."

David reached into the bag and pulled out a small tablet. He tapped the screen a few times and turned it to the Asters. The tablet screen showed a video of a news broadcast. A female newscaster was sitting at a large desk, and there was a picture of the Grand Canyon behind her. She was talking about the disappearances of a hiking group that had left for a three-day hike four days ago, and hadn't returned yet. The group was a German family of four; mother, father and two children.

"This is the only disappearance the local authorities know about. There are a few others, but we – and by 'we' I mean the hiking tour companies around the Canyon – have managed to keep them out of the news for now. It is not uncommon for radio signals to fall out sometimes. Signals are hard to come by in the Canyon. But I can tell you that there is more to it than that. There is Dark energy circulating where all the hikers have disappeared. And it is my company's priority to find them," David explained.

"Yours?" Lian asked.

Sky was watching the newscaster. She was saying something about the responsibilities of the rescue team of the Canyon Trekking Company. A logo popped up on the screen; a brown triangle with a yellow sun around its tip.

"Are you Canyon Trekking Company?" Sophie asked, stealing the words right out of Sky's mouth.

"I am indeed. We are the go-to rescue team if any hikers go missing in the Canyon for any period of time. We have an exemplary record, you see. The other companies that do tours here entrust us to also find any of their hikers. They know I have the men and women, the contacts, and the means to find whoever's missing – though they don't know, of course, that some of those means have a touch of Affinite power to them." He winked broadly. "And in cases like these, where I know Dark magic is at play, I can call you and we can keep it quiet from the human authorities long enough so that we only have to adjust the memories of those who have gone missing and have seen things they shouldn't remember," David said.

"That's very smart," Matu admitted.

David inclined his head momentarily. "I haven't gone in myself. I have an electronic map like yours in my study, which tells me more than enough about the Disciples coming in and out of the Canyon. Tomorrow, my sons will take us as close as possible to where one of the entrances to the Underworld is, and you will have to take it from there."

"Tomorrow?" Sky asked.

David looked at Sky. "Yes, tomorrow. I know you would rather go down there today, but I assumed you would want to go through all the information I have on the trail you will be going down, the humans that have gone missing, and the layout of the canyon floor and where the entrance to the Underworld is."

"He's right. We need to be optimally prepared," Sophie agreed.

Sky rolled his eyes and slumped back down into his chair. Another day of waiting... and studying.

"The trail itself takes at least a few hours to get down. Four if you're fast enough—"

"And we can't shimmer... why?" Sky wondered.

"Because you don't know what's waiting for you down there," David replied, frowning at him.

"He's right. Better for us to see what has been happening and make a plan, than to shimmer right into possible trouble," Matu concurred.

"That seems just about a good enough reason," Sky muttered. He wasn't looking forward to half a day's hike. That would tire them out more than a shimmer would. Then again, an unnecessary battle if they shimmered right in between Disciples would tire them out even more; if not injure them badly.

"Do you have all that information here?" Sophie asked.

David placed the bag onto the table and patted the top. "Everything you need is in here. I suggest you start on the trail early just before sunrise. Then you'll have most of the day to *do what you do best*, right?" David laughed.

The Asters had trouble laughing with him. It was as if the man didn't realise they were talking about a potential uprising from a King himself.

"Thank you," Matu said.

"How close is the trail?" Nathan asked.

"Oh, it's about half an hour's drive from here. We'll pick you up tomorrow morning in the truck and get you down there," David explained.

"*We?*" Sky asked.

"Yes. I'll have one of my sons drive us, then I can update you on whatever news might've come in today or overnight. Shall I leave you all to it, then? Don't want to stand in the way of the Asters saving the world." David laughed again.

Sky managed a tight smile.

"Yes, thank you," Sophie said politely.

"All right, then." David got up from his chair and headed for the door. "I will see you all tomorrow morning. There's plenty of food and drink in the fridge. Help yourself. My card with my number is on the coffee table if you need anything else. Good luck!"

The door closed behind him.

The five Asters stared at the door, momentarily speechless. *This* was one of Felix's best Watchers? Sky had to believe all sorts of people could be Watchers, but he had never expected one to be so chipper. So annoyingly chipper.

"We'd better get started," Sophie said. She turned the backpack towards her and started pulling out various maps of the Canyon floor and the trail they were going to descend the next morning. She handed these to Nathan and Matu. There was also a brown binder, which contained detailed profiles and pictures of the hikers that had disappeared. She handed one batch of these to Lian and kept the rest for herself.

Sky leaned over so he could join Lian in looking through the different profiles, and found himself impressed with the information David Hughes had gathered. He hated that they had to spend another day and night here. It might've been half past four when they stepped through the static portal on Saluverus, but because of the time difference, it was early in the morning here. Sky supposed it wasn't the worst thing in the world to spend a few more hours preparing as best they could for whatever they would face down in the Canyon.

He still groaned, however, when Sophie pulled out detailed reports of Disciple activity over the past few weeks. She passed the reports to him and told him to get started on them. Sky grumbled something he was sure she didn't hear. He got up from the table and made his way over to the sofa. He threw himself down on it and opened the report, hoping that whatever was in it, was relevant enough to make a difference once they went down into the Canyon tomorrow.

The following morning the Asters were all ready to go when there was a knock on the door. Sky finished fastening the straps of the small backpack with the vials of their blood, before sliding the last two short swords into their sheaths at his thighs.

They were all heavily armed. Sky spun his short spear in his hands with contained energy as the five of them filed out of the cabin and into the morning darkness. It was just before sunrise, and the sky was filled with beautiful shades of deep blue and purple. Sky looked around and couldn't believe how different this place was to Saluverus. There were no lush, green forests, and there was no freshly cut grass. There was sandy rock and highly dehydrated grass and a few trees that had seen better days. It reminded him of the Outback in Australia. His mother had taken him there a few times when he was younger and had come home for the holidays.

Just a few feet away from the cabin stood what looked like an army truck. Two boys who looked about five years older than Sky sat behind the wheel and in the passenger's seat. They turned to look at the Asters following David outside, smiled and waved.

"Those are my sons. Jason's behind the wheel. He's the oldest. And that's Wesley over there beside him. They will be driving us to the trail," David said proudly. The Watcher walked around the back of the army truck and pulled open the fabric flaps at the back. He jumped lithely up inside.

Sky was the first to follow him. Inside the back of the truck were two benches that had been screwed tightly to the floor. David sat on the right-hand bench and slid all the way up close to the front of the truck. Sky followed his lead, but did so on the bench opposite him. The other Asters followed suit, and as soon as they all sat down and had the bags of extra weapons and supplies dumped at their feet, David called, "We're in!", and the truck started to move.

As they hurtled uncomfortably down the rocky roads of south-western America, David turned and addressed the Asters.

"I hope you all slept well?" he queried.

The Asters murmured their responses. This was the morning of a mission. They had all spent the previous day and most of the night preparing themselves for what they were about to face once they got down the trail. None of them were in the mood for chit-chat.

David seemed to realise this, and decided to talk at them instead. "There have been no new developments since yesterday morning. The same thirteen tourists and two tour leaders are still missing," he revealed. "I do hope it's not as bad as Axel predicts it is. We were very sorry to hear of the Queen's death. A real shame that was, a real shame. As if you all don't have enough to deal with, and now you might have an uprising on your hands... Pff, well." David smiled broadly at them. "But the Ambassador tells me you are extremely good at what you do, and I have no doubt that you will be able to handle whatever is happening down there. There haven't been many Disciples on the Canyon floor; most seem to have entered the Underworld. I think it's better that you focus on getting through that entrance. It won't be hard. If you studied the maps I gave you, you should know where it is."

"We do know, yes," Matu replied.

"Good, yes. Very good indeed," David went on. He reached into his pocket and pulled out a pile of company cards. "If you need anything, just call the number on the back. If you need Affinites to help bring the humans out, just let me know and we will be there to lend a hand."

Matu thanked him, taking the cards and passing them out amongst the Asters so they each had one.

The truck started to slow.

"Ah, it looks like we're here. All right, out we go," David said as the truck ground to a halt.

The six of them piled out of the truck. The vehicle had stopped near the edge of the Canyon. The sky had turned from purple to a deep orange; the sun was barely peeking out above the edge of the Grand Canyon's rocky cliffs. The view was absolutely incredible. Sky could see all the way down to the bottom of the Canyon and the red and orange cliffs stretched out for miles and miles, in all different shapes and sizes. Some peaks stretched even higher than where they were standing, and all the way down in the valley, a narrow river snaked in between the ancient cliffs.

There was the beginning of a narrow path close to where Sky was standing. A wooden sign that read *Angel Trail,* painted in red, stood near the path, with an arrow pointing diagonally downwards. Two round wooden poles stood on either side of the trail, and there was red and white tape woven between them, blocking off the path.

"I closed this trail off three days ago," David explained. His older son, Jason, stepped past them and started untying the knots that tied the tape to the wooden poles. "The authorities and other hiking companies think I did it because of erosion. They believe the path is dangerous and could lead to a collapse. I'm supposedly having it checked out and secured before a next group of hikers is allowed to go down."

"And the truth?" Nathan asked. Sky could tell that the cold focus had taken a hold of his brother again. His brown eyes no longer had that warm and kind quality as he looked at the Affinite.

David grinned. "The truth? Towards the bottom of the way down this trail is one of the three entrances to the North American Underworld within the Grand Canyon. This is your fastest way to get there and I didn't think you would enjoy keeping your cover amongst clueless hikers."

Sky nodded appreciatively. David might talk a lot and speak very lightly about the impending danger so close to his business and his family, but the man was smart. He came to the Small Council with a problem, and before the Asters had even arrived, he'd made sure everything was laid out for them impeccably.

The younger of the two sons, Wesley, had started helping Jason with the unwrapping of the tape, and the two of them were just about finished. The Asters did a last check of the weapons that they would take with them, leaving the rest in the bags in the back of the truck. Sky looked at his brothers and sister and nodded; they were ready to go.

"This is where we part ways. Use that phone number if you need anything at all. If you do find the hikers, try and get them back up here; we will take them someplace safe while you deal with the *actual* problem. Be safe now. Good luck to y'all!"

Wesley and Jason moved out of the way, so that the Asters could step between the two wooden poles and start down the path. The Asters all turned around, raised a hand to the Affinite father and sons, and said their thankyou's before starting down the trail and disappearing out of sight.

Sky heard the engine of the truck being turned on again above him, and soon the sound faded into the distance, leaving the Asters alone to start their descent down into the Canyon and towards the entrance to the North American Underworld.

Chapter 15

For most of the trek the Asters walked in silence. David had failed to mention that this was one of the tougher trails in the Grand Canyon, and they had to focus all their attention on getting through the narrow pathways and down the steep steps. Matu wasn't particularly afraid of heights, but he was glad the trek required all of his concentration, which kept him from worrying about his father in Brazil. Diallo and his team were travelling back to Saluverus today. Matu knew his father should be fine; no rogue Disciples were stupid enough to try and take on the Ceder of Strength. Still, he didn't like how seemingly easily Eva and Percy's teams had been attacked and killed.

As Matu shimmied along a particularly narrow ledge, he couldn't help feel a little flutter in his stomach when he looked at the drop below. He was glad to have Sky with them; at least with his shimmer they wouldn't have to drag possibly wounded humans back up this trail, while also possibly being chased by Disciples.

Every now and again they would spot where the trail would continue some way further down, and Sky would shimmer them there to spare them some time and energy, and so that the hike wouldn't take the four hours that David Hughes had told them it would.

It was two hours after they had started out, and Matu scanned the Grand Canyon while they took a small break. He estimated that they were about an hour from the entrance to the Underworld. It surprised him that there was no one to be seen. From where he was standing, on quite a decent outlook point, he couldn't spot any other hikers. Or any Disciples for that matter, while the map back on Saluverus had said the Canyon was crawling with them, and David had confirmed the same thing.

So where were they all?

Matu took one last swig of his water bottle and turned back to the other Asters. When he stepped back down from the small platform, he saw they were all ready to go.

"Nothing?" Sophie asked.

Matu shook his head.

"They have to be here somewhere," Lian muttered.

Sophie voiced her agreement.

Nathan kept his usual silence.

"I could fly overhead?" Sky offered.

Matu shook his head again. "It wouldn't help. You'd have to fly a long way to see what I wouldn't have been able to. Better we stay together until we reach the entrance, and work from there."

Matu could see the annoyance on Sky's face, but his brother kept his mouth shut. Instead, Sky took the lead and led them further down the trail. Lian was behind him, followed by Sophie and Nathan, while Matu took up the rear.

The trek was going well. They had trained for this; they spent hours and hours on their fitness, so this physical exertion was next to nothing for them.

Another twenty minutes passed since their small break, when suddenly Sky halted with a grunt. Matu nearly bashed up against Nathan, who had stopped as suddenly as everyone else in front of him. The path had widened out and they could stand with three of them next to each other.

"What the hell," Sky muttered. He was staring out in front of him; as if he was seeing something none of the others could.

"What's going on?" Sophie asked, coming up beside him and looking in the same direction that her brother was.

"I can't get through," Sky grunted. He lifted his hand and brought it forward. And there it was: his hand met something hard. Matu could see it from the way Sky's hand suddenly stopped in mid-air. Sky hadn't paused his movement; something was blocking his way.

Lian was on Sky's other side and tried to walk through as well, holding his hands out in front of him when just as suddenly the same happened. Something invisible, but definitely physical, was stopping them from getting through. Matu checked the map. The entrance to the Underworld was about a hundred feet below them.

"Let me try," Matu said. Sky and Lian moved aside so that Matu could reach the invisible wall. He curled his right hand into a fist. His Band started glowing bronze and in one mighty sweep, he punched the invisible wall.

The whole thing shuddered. The ground underneath their feet grumbled for a second. Black lines, like ripples on the surface of a pond, spiralled out from where Matu had punched the wall.

"It's a dark veil," Sophie breathed. "Similar to the one our parents faced in Brazil."

"You mean this King and the one in South America are working together?" Sky asked.

Sophie studied the veil. "Unlikely. It's just a simple spell. Every King would know it."

"Just help me break the damn thing open," Matu said. His brothers immediately started forming a circle around him, ready to chant a spell that would grant Matu the strength of their magic and channel it through his own. Only Sophie didn't comply to his demand.

"Just try again by yourself," Sophie said.

"Why?" Matu asked.

"Just do it. I have a suspicion."

Matu took her word for it. He turned his attention back to the invisible wall in front of him. He could see the trail on the other side. The ground there looked exactly the same as it did where he was standing. And yet he couldn't just walk over to it.

Matu rallied his magic again, and punched. The ground around them shuddered again. Matu heard something rumble and crash behind him. He didn't want to know where it had come from. He also didn't have time to look around to see for himself, because enough was happening in front of him.

The veil was no longer invisible: it was now a cloudy sort of grey. Matu could no longer see through it the way he was able to before. Except for where he had punched twice now, because a hole had formed in the veil. The hole was about the size of his fist; it was big enough for Matu to put his hands in. He did so; each hand gripping a side of it, his knuckles touching as he put his magic to work again. His magic sizzled through his body as he tried to split the hole open further.

It happened faster than he thought. The moment he pulled at either side of the hole, two huge cracks appeared above and below it. The wall moaned as Matu pulled harder, the cracks becoming rips, and the rips eventually becoming one giant split in the wall.

Matu stopped the moment the split was wide enough for a single person to step through. It was still quite narrow, but it was enough.

Matu could hear Sophie suck in a breath behind him as he shimmied through the tear in the wall. He hadn't known what she had suspected as he stepped through, but he doubted she'd expected it to be as bad as what he saw once he took in the other side.

Matu's breath caught as he took in the Canyon now.

"That's not good..." Lian breathed the second he stepped through the veil.

Sophie looked over her brother's shoulder. "Yeah. I was afraid of that."

Matu could tell she was using a light voice just to keep them calm, but what they saw shocked them all to the core.

The invisible wall had concealed everything. Matu had estimated correctly; the Asters were standing on the trail a hundred feet above the entrance to the Underworld. Matu couldn't see the entrance from where they were standing, but if he looked down, he could see a group of Disciples vanishing underneath the rock overhang the Asters were standing on, and not returning.

Then there was the floor of the Canyon itself. All along the river that snaked in between the high cliffs were hundreds of tents and horses and carriages.

And Disciples.

So many of them.

Matu looked up. Everywhere above him, the sky had a cloudy, hazy look about it. The veil wasn't just a single wall. It was like a dome, concealing the massive camp from onlookers and Saluverus' sensors. The Disciples coming to the Canyon and disappearing weren't going into the Underworld; they were just going behind the veil.

"Get back," Matu hissed.

Another group of Disciples was heading for the entrance to the Underworld, and where the Asters were standing, they were incredibly exposed. All the Asters shot backwards and leaned against the cliffside of the trail; the Disciples jogged inside the entrance underneath the Asters, without spotting them.

Once the Disciples had gone, the five of them stepped back onto the middle of the trail to take in the full scope of the Disciple camp. Fires were lit all along the river. There were larger tents with smoke coming out of a hole in the top, which were probably used for production of some kind, while there were also smaller tents, which were probably just for residential purposes.

Matu risked leaning further out to study the trail near the entrance of the Underworld. There was a guard stationed on each side of the entrance, and then another guard every twenty feet along the trail all the way down to the floor of the Canyon. They were all dressed in stark black uniforms. White lines criss-crossed their armour and weapons; the colour of the North American Underworld.

"Over there," Sophie whispered.

Matu turned to see what Sophie was looking at. She was pointing towards the tent right at the bottom of the *Angel Trail*. This tent was bigger than any other tent on the entire Canyon floor. It reminded Matu of a circus tent, with multiple turrets and a great circumference.

A man had just stepped out of the front flaps. He was flanked by two heavily armed guards. Matu's breath hitched as he saw the man's hair that reminded him of liquid silver; from this distance Matu couldn't see much else. But the hair was enough to give away the man's identity.

It was Mitrik.

The North American King.

"What is he doing here?" Sky hissed. He had only ever seen the North American King in pictures and drawings. Never had he thought they'd see him the second they stepped through the veil. Kings were usually more protective of themselves than that. Sky would've expected Mitrik to be somewhere deep in his Underworld territory; probably on some throne some ancient predecessor had made before he was born.

"He's cocky," Lian muttered.

"That could work in our favour," Matu contemplated.

"Or not," Sophie warned. "He's doing this for a reason. He's been gathering these Disciples for the past two months. He knew we'd come sniffing eventually."

"Then why is he still here out in the open?" Lian asked. He freed the bow from his shoulder and reached to grab an arrow from his quiver. "I've got a clean shot."

Sophie reached out and placed a hand on Lian's bow. "Don't," she said.

"What? We're never going to get a better chance than this," Lian objected.

"Remember what Axel said? No human or Affinite casualties. Those human hikers are down there somewhere. They'll be dead the second we kill Mitrik. That's why he's out here. He knows exactly where we are, but that we can't do anything to him," Sophie whispered.

Sky's head whipped to his sister. "*What?* How could he possibly know that we're here?"

"That veil we just broke through? It's like a protective bubble. It was only ever meant to keep us out. Humans can walk right through it, but once they see the other side and want to come back, they can't. It only works one way," Sophie explained.

"But I just broke it," Matu said.

"You made a hole; you didn't break it," Sophie pointed out. Sky realised then that the veil still existed by the way the sky had a hazy look about it. "Which means we have a way out. But it also means that Mitrik would know the second we got here. We're the only ones it'd keep out, and so the only ones who would damage it."

Sky nodded slowly. "So he knows we're here. Why hasn't he raised the alarm yet?"

"Because he wants us to see something first," Sophie said softly, speaking her thoughts out loud.

"Like what?" Lian asked.

"What about that?" It was the first time Nathan had spoken since they stepped through the veil. While the others had been fixated on the King standing right below them, Nathan had apparently been looking around the Canyon.

Sky followed his brother's pointing finger. Just a bit further along the river, but heading towards the large circus tent, was a line of people in chains.

Humans. There was no mistaking them. They were all wearing similar shorts and t-shirts. And they were all wearing bulky boots that would've been perfect for hiking up and down the Grand Canyon trails. Some of the hikers had baseball caps on to shield their heads from the sun.

Sky counted seven of them. He knew a total of fifteen humans were missing. Sky looked around the Canyon floor, but saw no other prisoners. His gaze returned to the seven they'd spotted. Their wrists were in handcuffs and their ankles were shackled as well. They shuffled along the riverside. There were two Disciples leading the hikers, two Disciples on either side of the third hiker, and another two Disciples bringing up the rear.

The Asters watched as the seven hikers were brought up to Mitrik, who was still standing in front of the circus tent. He seemed to be speaking to them, but there was no way Sky would be able to hear what was being said. Not from this distance, anyway. And Sophie's whispering wasn't helping.

"Will you shush?" Sky snapped at her. But when he looked over, he saw that Sophie's Band was glowing and he realised she must be reciting a spell. When she was finished, she pulled back her hair from her right ear, and angled her head towards the Disciples and the King below them.

"What are they saying?" Matu whispered. He also realised that Sophie had cast a spell that would improve her hearing to such an extent that she would be able to hear what was being said far below.

Sophie didn't answer. Sky turned his attention back below and saw that the Disciples were herding the humans towards the beginning of the trail that led up to the entrance of the Underworld.

"They're being taken to the cells," Sophie told them. "Tonight, they'll be the first in the ring."

"*The ring?*" Matu repeated unbelievably.

Sky stared at the circus tent below them. It wasn't the King's quarters like he had assumed. No, the King was keeping something inside it, and it would be revealed tonight. Back in the Dark Ages, when the Kings each ruled a different continent of the Surface, humans were enslaved and Affinites were hunted for sport. Sky had heard that sentence about a thousand times in his history classes.

Humans enslaved, and Affinites hunted for sport.

But humans and Affinites had more uses: entertainment. The Kings' fighting rings had been legendary. Humans were put up against humans, or Affinites against Affinites, or Disciples against either humans or Affinites. Bets were placed, blood was shed and people were killed. All for entertainment.

It surprised Sky that Mitrik was busy resurrecting this tradition while also trying to reclaim the Surface of North America. The fighting rings were not the first thing that came to Sky's mind when he thought of a King's uprising. But here Mitrik was, having his first round of humans ready for this evening's entertainment. Perhaps it was a way for the King to show the Asters and Affinites how easy it had been for him to set this up. He was cocky. And extremely sure of himself.

Sophie turned to her brothers, her face a mask of worry. "We need to get them out."

"Well, obviously," Sky snorted.

Lian spoke before Sophie could snap something back. "What's the plan? We can't make a stand out here; there's too many eyes watching."

"We save them from the inside and work our way out," Matu decided.

Sky peered over the edge and could just about see the entrance to the Underworld. He could see the start of a dark corridor behind the two men standing guard. "I can shimmer us just inside."

"We still have the guards to worry about. They'll notice us the moment we appear," Matu said.

Sophie peered over the edge. "Those doors can close. If we're fast enough, we can lock them out."

"And lock ourselves in," Sky pointed out.

"Can't you shimmer us out?" Lian asked.

"I probably can. But each Underworld comes with its own surprises," Sky warned.

"I can get us out via a different route if we need to," Nathan said. "I can make a new corridor and doorway."

Sky nodded at his brother.

"They'll still come after us when we get out," Lian said thoughtfully. "If Sky's shimmer doesn't work, we'll need to create a diversion for Nate's way to work."

"Then we split up," Sophie said. "After we free the humans, we split up. One group to draw the Disciples away and the other to get the humans out." She was still peering over the edge. "The humans have gone through the entrance. There are no additional guards going with them."

Matu reached into his pocket and pulled out his phone. "I'll call David to be ready at the top." He held the phone to his ear and walked away from the group, whispering to David.

"We only need to get the humans to the veil," Sophie realised. "Inside, they are under Mitrik's protection. Those Disciples leading the humans, they're lower ranked. They won't dare follow us outside of their King's protective bubble."

"What if we're followed by higher-ranked Disciples?" Sky asked.

"I doubt they'll follow us further either. It's just another move in his chess game. He showed off the humans, and we're taking them back. Mitrik isn't a fighter himself; our parents found that out during the war against Astaroth. He likes violence, sure, but he doesn't fight himself. He's more strategic than that. He's just waiting for us to show our hand."

Nathan frowned. "Then those humans are a trap for us."

Sophie looked at him for a moment. The thought had crossed her mind, too. But they were humans. The Asters couldn't exactly leave them to be put up against each other or up against Disciples in Mitrik's fighting rings. They had to rescue them, and the Asters would have to deal with whatever trap was laid out for them afterwards.

"Are we ready to go?" Matu asked, re-joining them after his call with David Hughes.

Sky checked the fastenings of the backpack one last time, making sure they would not get in the way during a fight. Once he was sure, he exchanged looks with all of his siblings, to see if they were all ready and knew what the plan was. Each and every one of them was ready. Their eyes were alert, and they had their hands on the hilts of their signature weapons.

Sky grinned. The anticipation of a fight waiting to happen was humming through his body.

Matu nodded. "All right. Then let's go."

Chapter 16

Getting in wasn't the problem. In fact, it was even easier than they had anticipated. The second Sky shimmered the five of them in right behind the two Disciples standing guard, it was only a matter of seconds before Lian and Matu had killed both guards, pushed them forward and out onto the trail, and closed the doors behind them.

The doors just looked like two pieces of rock, but they fit perfectly in the space that was the doorway to the Underworld.

But there was no lock.

As easy as they had been to close, it would be as easy to open them again.

"Nate; reinforcements," Matu commanded.

Nathan came up close to where Lian and Matu were now leaning against the doors so that the Disciples on the other side couldn't break in. Their appearance, followed by the murder of the two guards, didn't go unnoticed. It had never been the plan to remain invisible. Mitrik knew they were there. It would only be a matter of time before everyone else knew, too.

Nathan's Band glowed green, and from the sand rock walls suddenly tiny green vines poked through. In a matter of seconds, the vines grew larger, longer and thicker. They grew all across the doors, until there was only a wall of green where before there had been the two large rocks that had filled up the entrance to the outside.

Nathan dropped his hands and nodded. They could hear the Disciples on the other side of the doors trying to bash their way in, but with a green wall like this, Sky had no doubt that they would be bashing and pushing for a long while. Sky didn't exactly know how strong Nathan's magic was, but by the way his brother had been training the past few weeks, Sky was pretty sure those Disciples would need a battering ram.

They hurried down the corridor. They were not long behind the seven chained humans who had been taken through the entrance into the Underworld. This wasn't like when they had gone into the South American Underworld with a tracker that led them right towards Josephine Stewart and the other captured Affinites. Here, the Asters had no way of tracking the humans, so the best they could do was to run quickly after them, and hope they wouldn't lose them.

The sound of chains clattering on the rocky ground helped them along. As softly as they could, the five Asters hurried through the corridors. As they turned one corner, they were suddenly faced with a group of five Disciples.

The Disciples were dead seconds after they recognised the Asters for who they were. The Asters were clinical and fast, and moved on very quickly, Sky leading the way.

The clanking of the metal chains around the humans' ankles came closer and closer. As soon as Sky felt they were only a few feet away, he slowed down. They had come to the end of a corridor and Sky made himself stop. He peered around the corner and saw what he had expected. The humans weren't guarded heavily. The six Disciples that had been around them before were now accompanied by only two more. The humans were standing still while one of the front two Disciples was busy opening a large metal door. Sky knew that they had to free the humans before that door was opened. He couldn't shimmer to a place he had never seen before, or didn't know the coordinates of. He couldn't shimmer to the other side of a locked door without knowing what the other side looked like. It didn't take a genius to figure out that these Disciples were going to lock the humans up inside. The Asters had to act now.

Sky turned his head and whispered, "Eight. Two in front, two back, four centre."

The other Asters nodded. Sky placed his hand on Sophie's shoulder, and readied himself for a shimmer. He waited for Nathan to unsheathe the second broadsword from his back, and for Lian to free the dagger from his wrist. Lian's bow and quiver were slung across his shoulder. In these close quarters the bow was useless.

Both boys nodded to Sky when they were ready. Matu didn't need to draw any weapons – he was already wearing his knuckle knives – and Sophie already had her hand on her rapier sword.

Sky nodded once, and shimmered. He and Sophie vanished, and appeared right in between the metal door and the Disciple trying to open it.

"Surprise," Sky said, grinning as utter shock appeared in the Disciple's eyes. He was dead before he could reach for his weapon. Sky trusted that Sophie finished off the other Disciple near the front. He used his magic of Speed and shot past the first two humans who looked absolutely bemused, and drove his short spear straight through the heart of one of the four Disciples. Lian was there too, his dagger slicing through a female Disciple's throat.

There was a crunch behind Sky and without looking he knew that Matu had taken on the two rear-Disciples by himself. Nathan was on the other side, and after a few swings of his two broadswords the final two Disciples were dead on the ground.

Sky smirked. There was blood on his face, but he didn't mind the stickiness of it. The five of them worked as a perfect fighting machine, and he loved it.

"Who are you people?" one of the humans gasped.

Sky turned and found a man, probably in his forties, staring at him. His skin was grey and his lips were dry and crusty. Sky didn't want to think about how long these humans had been kept without water or food. Even if Sophie healed all of them, she couldn't exactly fill their stomachs with food to give them energy. And somehow, they would have to get out of here while being chased by Disciples.

"Long story," Sky said dismissively. "Which you won't remember."

He turned to Sophie, who had picked up the keys that had been dropped by the Disciple in front of the metal door. There were only three keys on the ring, one large, presumably for the door, and two smaller ones. Sky walked towards her just as she tried the first of the small keys in the locks around the ankles of the human closest to her. The lock sprang open with a click.

Sophie then stood up and tried the other key on the handcuffs around the woman's wrists.

"Won't work," the woman rasped. Sky looked up and stared at her. Her dark hair was dusty and tangled. Her skin was pale like the man further back, and she looked tired, so very tired.

"Why not?" Sky snapped.

"He gave the keys for our wrists to the white-haired man with the weird eyes," explained the man who had spoken to Sky before. "Said they'd be taken off in the ring. What was he talking about?"

Sky stared at the man for a moment. "You don't want to know."

Sophie had turned her attention to the ankles of a younger woman, possibly in her thirties, who was the second in line.

"You're very cryptic in your answers," the man said pointedly.

Sky shot the man a dangerous look, but before he could say anything else to shut him up, Lian intervened.

"What's your name, sir?" Lian asked.

"It's John," the man answered. "You have to help my family—my family..."

Sky looked at the other humans in the group. There were a teenage boy and girl of about sixteen years old at the back. In front of them stood John and another two men of a similar age – one Caucasian and the other looked Chinese. And then at the front were two middle-aged women, also Caucasian and Chinese.

"All right, John, we will, all right? I'm Lian. And that's Matu and Nathan. This here is Sophie, and the pain in the arse over there, that's Sky," Lian said, pointing at his siblings. Sky rolled his eyes, but Lian's words had the desired effect. John, and a few of the other humans, chuckled slightly, despite everything. Then Lian continued, "These guys here were going to kill you. Or have you fight for survival. Or fight each other. However the story ends, you would've died. We're trying to avoid that. We're going to get you out, all right? So just listen to whatever we direct you to do, and don't question us, because we're your best and only shot at getting out of here alive."

John stared at Lian for a moment, and then nodded stiffly. Lian smiled and patted him on the back. "Good man," Lian said.

Sophie had made it to John's ankles and freed him from the shackles. "Thank you," he whispered.

Sophie didn't look up at him. She looked at Matu instead. "There is no key for their hands. Can you break the handcuffs?"

Matu stepped forward and placed his hands on the cuffs of the woman last in line. The Band on his wrist started glowing. The woman inhaled sharply. Matu's hands tightened around cuffs and he pulled.

Orange sparks jumped up from where Matu had touched the handcuffs. He shouted and retracted his hands immediately. He held his hands open so that they could all see that his palms had started blistering.

"What's wrong?" Nathan asked.

"They're magic-proof. I can't break them," Matu hissed, and muttered a few Swahili words afterwards, for good measure. Sophie was next to him in an instant, having passed the keys on to Sky. Sophie's Band glowed golden and the blisters on Matu's palms vanished into nothing.

Lian frowned at the group of humans. "But they're not magical."

"They're not. But we are." Sky unlocked the ankle shackles from the teenage girl at the back. "All right. I need everyone to gather around and take a hold of someone. We're getting out of here."

"Are you sure that's going to work?" Lian asked. "If Matu can't use his magic on those shackles, how are you sure you'll be able to shimmer them anywhere?"

Sky was busy herding all the humans closer together. "Because I'm not actually touching the shackles, now, am I?"

The seven humans now stood huddled closely together, the Asters around them. They were all holding on to someone else, making sure that no one would be left behind. Sky closed his eyes and pictured the platform where David and his sons had dropped them off. He could feel the Band on his wrist starting to pulse, and he could feel the blue light build up inside of him, ready to engulf anyone he was touching. As the blue light surrounded them all, Sky held on to the picture of the platform in his mind. But the picture was starting to fade. Something white and cloudy was blurring the image of his destination. It reminded him distinctly of the cloudy veil that Mitrik had put up around the Grand Canyon.

Sky felt the blue light drain away around him.

"No, no, no, no," Sky rambled, looking desperately around him. They were still in the damn Underworld corridor close to the metal door.

"What happened?" Sophie asked.

"Is it the handcuffs?" Matu added.

"It's not the handcuffs, it's the veil. I can't shimmer through it, only within it," Sky growled. He stepped away from the group and looked around the corner of the corridor. No Disciples were coming yet, but he knew they would be coming soon.

"But I put a hole in it. Are you sure?" Matu asked.

"Yes, I'm sure. See," Sky snapped. He put his magic to work and pointed at the human called John. Blue light appeared all around John and the man vanished momentarily. Then a second later the same blue light appeared right next to Sky, and John was standing there instead. John reached for his head, clearly dizzy, his eyes wide. He stumbled to the side in shock. Sky gave him no further attention.

"Crap," Lian muttered.

"What are the odds you can shimmer all of us somewhere within this veil where there are no Disciples but which is close enough to it that we can get through?" Matu asked.

At that moment a wailing siren shattered through the silent corridors. Sky strained his ears and could distinctly hear running footsteps in the distance.

"Zero," Sky sighed.

"All right, we don't have much time," Sophie said. She had come up beside Sky and was scanning the adjacent corridors. "We need to get them out of here and to the tear in the veil."

"I can make a narrow hallway in the walls close to the corridor leading back outside," Nathan said.

Matu nodded. "Good. How long will that take?"

Nathan shrugged. "Not sure."

"Then you need a distraction." Sky looked over to Lian and Sophie. "You two, you're with me. Matu, find a place to hide them while Nate makes a tunnel."

Matu turned to Sky. "Give me the keys."

Sky tossed the keys to his brother and looked around the corner again. The footsteps were growing louder by the second.

Matu ran past the humans and towards the large metal door. He fumbled with the keys momentarily before finding the right one and unlocking the door. He pulled it open with a creak, revealing a large oval room with absolutely nothing inside. He turned back to the group of huddling humans. "Get in."

"Woah, woah, woah, we're going in there? You just killed all of them to avoid us being put there!" John exclaimed.

"What did my brother just tell you about questioning us?" Sky snapped.

The other humans bowed their heads and followed Matu's instructions. John was the last to step in; he hesitated in the doorway and looked over his shoulder. "You've done this before?" he asked Sky.

Sky hadn't the faintest clue why the man was asking him in particular. He opted for a cocky grin and said, "Getting humans out of the North American Underworld while being surrounded by a dark veil that won't let us use our magic optimally while an alarm is going off and a murderous King is nearby? No. Getting out of tight situations alive with hundreds of Disciples coming after us at once? All the time."

"We're good at this, sir. This is what we do. We will get you and your family out," Matu assured.

"This is not my family."

Sky blinked at this news, and tried to not let the weight of his words sink in.

"They separated us down by the river. You have to save them, too."

Nathan jumped beside Matu and placed a hand on John's back, guiding him through the metal doorway. "One thing at a time."

Matu followed, but as he stepped through the doorway Sophie stopped him by placing a hand on his shoulder. She looked back to Sky as she said, "Take the backpack. If you run into trouble, you'll need my blood for healing."

Sky undid the straps of the backpack and handed it over to Matu. His brother took it and immediately slung it onto his back, first loosening the straps to accommodate his larger frame, and then fastening them tight. Before he stepped into the other room, he cast one last look at Sky.

Sky understood what Matu meant and nodded. "We'll find the other humans. Just get *them* out."

"All right, we need to move *now*," Sophie pushed.

Sky took one more look at Nathan and Matu. They were pulling the metal door closed. He met Nathan's frozen stare for a second before the door thudded shut. There was a distinct sound of a lock clicking into place.

Sky turned his attention to Lian and Sophie. They were waiting for his signal. Sky waited a few more seconds, listening to the footsteps that were coming closer and closer. When they were in perfect range, he gave a short nod, before dashing out into the adjacent corridor, where he knew the Disciples would see him, and then running further into the depths of the North American Underworld.

There was nothing for Matu to do but wait. Nathan had actually created a tunnel in the wall of the room they had hidden in, and he had vanished inside, closing the tunnel up behind him. Matu couldn't see what was happening in the corridor outside without opening up the metal door.

So Matu waited for Nathan to return. In the meantime, he'd put in the effort to learn the humans' names. He had to keep them calm throughout this horrible experience, and Matu found that being able to call them by their names settled them down a bit. John was a hiker from Canada, and he'd come here with his wife and older son, who were being kept somewhere else in the Disciple camp. Then there was the

German family, Frank and Karina and their twin children of sixteen, Otto and Ella. Ella had started shaking quite badly and her father had started talking soothingly to her in their native language; Matu couldn't understand a word of it. Finally, there was the Chinese man and woman; Niu and Lin. They had come to America on holiday with Niu's wife and Lin's husband. The husbands apparently were close friends and they had come here as a group of four. Their respective spouses were in the same other group of hostages as John's wife and son. Matu kept asking each of the humans all kinds of questions, just to keep them thinking of something else and to keep their breathing under control.

After a short while there were three knocks on the door, followed by a silence, and then another single knock. Matu jumped to his feet. The keys were still in his hands and he unlocked the metal door. He pulled the door back an inch and peered around it. Only Nathan was on the other side. Matu turned back to the seven humans and said, "This is it. We have to go."

Frank hauled his daughter up to her feet and kept a hold of her hand. They all came close to the metal door. When everyone was ready to come out, Matu opened the door completely. He looked at Nathan for a moment. The Band on his wrist was still glowing, though Matu couldn't see what he was using his magic for.

"Follow me," Nathan said. He turned away from the group and walked quietly to the end of the corridor, which led to another corridor running perpendicular to it. To get back to the entrance of the Underworld they would have had to turn left here and then the corridor would start to bend to the right. Nathan was careful to avoid treading on the Disciples the Asters had killed earlier. He stopped at the intersection and peered in both directions. Matu strained his ears and could detect the sounds of fighting to his right. That must be where Sky, Lian and Sophie were, keeping the Disciples distracted while they could make their escape. There were footsteps coming from their left, but not close enough for them to be at risk of detection.

Yet.

Nathan tiptoed across the corridor and placed his hand on the wall. A large oval shape on the wall started shimmering slightly, and then turned black. Matu realised that the wall hadn't changed colour, but that the tunnel inside was just so dark that it looked black. Nathan moved away from the opening of the tunnel that he had created, and grabbed one of the lanterns that hung on the wall. Matu did the same.

Nathan looked back at the group of humans. "There won't be more light. Please tell me none of you are claustrophobic." He scanned the group. Every one of them shook their heads. Even Ella, the sixteen-year-old German girl, was convinced she wasn't.

Nathan's eyes revealed no relief or any other emotion as he said, "Follow me."

He was the first to step inside the tunnel. Karina, the German woman, was next to step in, followed by her son, daughter and husband. Then came Niu and Lin, and finally John stepped inside.

Footsteps were getting closer. Matu scanned the corridor one more time before stepping in after the Canadian human.

"All in!" Matu called all the way to the front. He couldn't see Nathan; only the light of his lantern that he held above his head. There was a low moan, and next to him, Matu saw the corridor vanishing and turning back into sandy rock. The tunnel was no wider than a single person, and Nathan was basically creating it with every step he took.

Matu was extremely glad that none of the humans were claustrophobic. This was a brilliant way of getting out of the Underworld without much detection, and with the Disciples running after Lian, Sky and Sophie, hopefully, they could get these humans out without much of a hassle.

Up ahead, Nathan started to speed up. They didn't need to jog to keep up with him, but they had to keep a steady pace going.

"How is this possible? How can he do that?" John asked. Matu weighed his options. He decided not to be cryptic like Sky and tell John the truth.

"He has magic that connects him to the earth. He can manipulate it in any way he likes," Matu explained.

"And you?"

"I am strong, sir. I can make these tunnels, too, it would just make a hell of a lot more noise."

"And the other three?"

"They all have their own magic, too."

"How many of you are there?"

"Just us five. There are many others who have affinities for specific skills, but only the five of us have actual magic."

"How come no one knows about you?"

"We make it our business to remain undetected. These guys down here want nothing more than to have control of the Surface of the earth. To have control over humans and all of us, too. All we do is make sure that doesn't happen, and leave you humans to live in peace."

"And the other one—the arrogant one—he said we won't remember?"

"It's protocol to wipe the memory of any human who has seen this part of the world."

"And what will I remember then?"

"Probably something like you came here to hike, but all the trails were closed off so you never went down, and you opted for playing games in and around your cabin for the past few days, until your holiday resumes elsewhere."

John nodded in front of him. "Good. I don't think I want to remember any of this."

Matu chuckled at the lightness in John's voice. Somehow the man had managed to turn his fear into something calm and sensible. And almost humorous.

The light from the lantern in Nathan's hand stopped moving forward. Chains clattered as the humans didn't detect the sudden halt and bashed up against each other.

The lantern light bobbed as Nathan turned around. "We need to follow a left corridor, while the one we're trailing is heading even further right. Stay here while I check it out and create the next tunnel. Give me two minutes," he said. Nathan turned back around, there was a low moan and a rocky wall came up in between Nathan and Karina. Matu waited with the humans in the flickering light of his single lantern. He could hear one of the women crying softly, but Matu couldn't tell who it was in the near darkness.

Matu tried not to worry about Nathan. He glanced at his watch. Two minutes was all Nathan had given him. Supposedly if he wasn't back by then, he would've been found out. It would then be up to Matu alone to get these humans out. It wouldn't be hard for him to break out of this tunnel, but to get seven humans all the way out of the entrance and through the broken veil to where the Disciples wouldn't follow... That was another matter entirely.

Matu needn't have worried. There was a low grumble again, and the rock wall in front of Karina disappeared. Nathan was on the other side, motioning them to come. "Quickly, come on, come on," he was saying.

Karina jumped out into the corridor. Matu looked past John and the other humans ahead to see that Karina had already dashed across the width of the corridor and into the new tunnel entrance that Nathan had created in the wall opposite. This time Nathan didn't go in first. He was standing in between the two tunnel entries and ushered every one of the humans inside.

Matu stepped out into the corridor behind John, who immediately hurried into the tunnel on the other side. Nathan quickly followed. Matu glanced around him once, just to see where in the Underworld they were now. He estimated that they were about three quarters of the way to the entrance. If Matu remembered the path they took on the way in correctly, they wouldn't have to jump through open corridors again. He quickly followed Nathan into the tunnel. The second he was in, the tunnel closed behind him and they were once again engulfed in darkness, save for the two flickering lanterns.

The first part of this tunnel was slightly wider. Nathan stepped past the humans, taking up his place at the front of the party again. "This tunnel will lead us to the trail outside. There will be a few steps upwards in this one; I want to get onto the trail above the entrance, instead of come out through the entrance like they will all expect."

Nathan resumed his fast pace through the tunnels. The steps slowed them down a bit. The light from either lantern didn't reach far enough to show each step of the staircase that Nathan was creating. Carefully, each human followed in Nathan's wake, up the steps, until eventually each of them had reached the top. Then Nathan continued moving straight ahead. Matu knew that Nathan wasn't exactly sure where on the trail he'd end up. He could connect with the earth enough, but to know its layout exactly was difficult, even for Nathan. Before, he'd just been following the corridor right beside the tunnel. Now, he was making his own path through the rock of the Grand Canyon. Matu only hoped that the Disciples that were sent into the Underworld to find them were being kept nice and busy by their siblings.

Suddenly Nathan stopped and turned around. "The real entrance is about thirty-five feet below us, to our left. If there are any guards, they will see us and come immediately. The *second* you step out onto that trail you run to the right, do you all understand me? You will find a white wall with a crack in it. Go through there and you will be safe, but do not stop there. You keep going. There will be people at the top that will help you. Matu and I will take care of the Disciples. *None of you* look back and worry about us. Just get yourselves up to the top."

Matu smiled at his youngest brother's assertiveness, his strength. Nathan looked at every single one of the humans. There was such a cold focus in his eyes. Only in situations like these was Nathan all soldier. There was no kindness in his face, no compassion. Just the soldier, and just the job at hand.

Nathan looked at Matu and waited for him to be ready. Matu checked the straps on the backpack, and tightened them once more. When he was sure the backpack was fastened, he gave Nathan a small nod.

Nathan didn't even nod back. "All right, here we go."

He only waited for one second. A moment later the rock crumbled away in front of him, blinding all of them as sunlight burst into the tunnel. Nathan jumped out, practically pulling Karina out behind him.

The other three Germans followed quickly. Then the Chinese pair and finally John jumped out. Matu was out a second later, turning left when all the humans had turned right and were hurtling up the trail. Nathan already had a broadsword in one hand and a vine in the other. Matu had no idea where Nathan got the power from to have a vine appear so quickly. His magic should be getting depleted with the immense amount of effort it took to make the tunnels, but Matu detected none of that in Nathan's face or in his stance.

Matu's fears turned out to be well founded. There had been at least five Disciples still working on the entrance doors that Nathan had sealed shut with vines. It amazed Matu that they still hadn't found a way through that thing, but none of that mattered now. All five of them had noticed Nathan and the humans jumping onto the trail above them, and they were all heading towards them. They were shouting orders and Matu doubted it would be long before more would follow.

Nathan and Matu took a few steps back and rallied their magic. These five Disciples wouldn't be a problem. It was whoever they had called for back-up who would be the problem, especially with the parched, famished and sleep-deprived humans who would not be getting up to the top of the *Angel Trail* in good time.

The five Disciples were dead in seconds. Matu threw one against the Canyon wall, and used a second one to throw against a third. Nathan did nice work with his broadsword on the fourth, and used his vines to pull the fifth one off the trail and down to the Canyon floor below.

"More will be coming," Matu warned.

Nathan didn't answer.

The two of them turned around and raced up the trail. To Matu's surprise the humans had made it farther up than he had expected. The imminent threat of Disciples coming to kill them must have done wonders for their motivation and adrenaline. Even the chains around their wrists didn't seem to slow them down as much as Matu had feared.

They had almost made it to the veil when Nathan and Matu caught up with them. The veil was no longer a cloudy white colour. It was like glass: Matu could see through it completely, yet it was obvious there was something there. Once they made it to the crack in the veil Matu took a moment to lean over the edge of the trail and see what was coming up behind them.

What he saw wasn't comforting at all. At least twenty Disciples were now making their way up the trail. They had already reached the entrance to the Underworld, and they were all better armed than the ones Nathan and Matu had killed minutes earlier.

"You know how Sophie thought they wouldn't come after us after the veil?" Matu called over his shoulder. He had actually locked eyes with one of the Disciples at the front of the party for a moment. They knew they were at the veil, and still they were coming.

"What about it?"

Nathan was helping John get through the crack in the veil. The Canadian man was larger than any of them, and it was taking a bit of pushing from one side and pulling from the other to get the man through.

"Yeah, I think Sophie was wrong." Matu jumped back from the edge of the trail and followed Nathan through the veil. The German family had already run on ahead while Niu and Lin had waited to help get John through the crack. It didn't take long for the five of them to catch up, though, because the German family had come to a standstill.

"What's going on?" Matu asked.

Nathan pushed past John and the German children to see what was happening. Matu did the same, and he saw the problem. He looked back and saw that the twenty Disciples on their tail had increased in number, and they were getting dangerously close to the veil.

Meanwhile, up ahead there was no path left in front of the German parents. It had all crumbled away; the huge crash they had heard when Matu made a hole in the veil on their way down, must have shattered the entire rock wall.

Matu remembered this part of the trail. It had been a make-shift staircase of about two hundred feet in length. Matu looked up and saw that the trail resumed over a hundred feet diagonally above them. He looked at the rock wall beside them. Even if they had all been excellent climbers, and if they hadn't been cuffed, there still would've been no way to get to the next part of the trail.

"Can't you make another tunnel?" Frank, the German father, asked Nathan.

Nathan placed a hand on the wall near him. A few pieces of rock came free at his touch. "It's too unstable. The entire wall could collapse and kill us all."

Matu looked down. He could feel the immensity of the drop in his stomach as he saw the ground of the Canyon floor loom very far beneath them.

And then he looked back down the trail.

There were two Disciples who were farther up ahead than the others. There was quite a space between them and the other thirty-odd

Disciples running behind them. The front two Disciples had reached the veil, and ran right through it. Not through the hole Matu had made, no. They'd passed right through the veil, as if it was nothing more than a bit of fog. The second they did, there was a bright white flash, and the whole veil disappeared, exposing the Disciple activity down below. It made Matu's heart jump right into his throat. He had no idea how, but the veil was now gone completely. That small crack in the veil was supposed to buy them time. Matu had Sky's blood in the backpack, but at the speed the Disciples were running up, he wouldn't have time to get it out, drink it and shimmer all of them to the next platform in time. The Disciples would be upon them too soon. And there was nowhere for them to go.

Chapter 17

They hadn't run far. Just far enough to get to a slightly narrower side corridor that led to a closed door, so that they couldn't get attacked from three sides at the same time.

Disciples were mostly stupid, in Lian's experience. Lian sometimes believed they were nothing more than mindless robots, following some code that someone had activated in their brains. To their credit, these ones were slightly more than that. They weren't the worst fighters. Their ancestors had been Affinites once, before they corrupted their souls and chose to serve a Higher King. Each of these Disciples had an affinity, too, but there was no knowing what kind of affinity they possessed. Lian noticed it when he engaged with two Disciples at once. One of the two was dead in seconds, but the other... The other saw Lian's blows coming, with much better anticipation than any human soldier would've been able to. It still didn't help him much. Lian was a better fighter; he had made sure he was. Because even though magic helped him to keep fighting for longer than humanly possible, it didn't help him be better at one-to-one combat. Not like Sky's speed helped him act faster than any opponent would expect. Or like Matu, whose blows were so much stronger that even if an opponent was fast enough to block one, Matu would bash right through.

Lian spun around, faking one blow so that the Disciple would avoid it and leave his left side exposed. Lian jammed his dagger in between the Disciple's ribs and the blade sliced into his heart. Lian yanked the dagger back out and pushed the Disciple out of the way, for another one was already advancing.

He barely had time to see what Sophie and Sky were doing. The three of them were just buying time for Nathan and Matu to escape with, hopefully, only a few Disciples charging after them. Sophie had chosen their position tactically. If any Disciple decided to make a break for it and go back to the entrance and outside, they would know. That was their main priority: that no Disciples from in here, would join the Disciples outside in pursuit of the humans, Nathan and Matu. Nathan's vines blocking the entrance weren't going to hold forever.

Lian ran towards the Disciple advancing on him and dropped to his knees unexpectedly. He had a dagger in each hand and slashed the blades across the Disciple's thighs. The Disciple cried out as her legs buckled. She didn't have time to steady herself as Lian jumped back to his feet and cut her throat.

There was a blue light flashing through the small army of Disciples in front of them. Sky was darting through them so fast that he was a mere blue blur. Blood sprayed wherever he went, Disciples dropped to their knees with wounds to their chest and abdomen. Lian turned around and found Sophie fighting behind him.

More Disciples came in, but none of them were heading for the entrance anymore. Their tactical manoeuvring seemed to have worked.

Lian and Sophie were now fighting side by side. Every now and again Sophie would push off against him and throw herself towards her opponent. Then seconds later, Lian would feel that comforting weight of her shoulder against his again.

Lian pulled a sword from a sheath at his side, stepped away from Sophie and blocked a Disciple's attack with it. The Disciple swung one more time, but Lian had read his move. With one hand on his sword, and a dagger still in his other hand, Lian blocked the attack with his sword and used his dagger to quickly finish the Disciple off.

When the Disciple dropped to his knees in front of Lian, he suddenly spied a female Disciple standing quite a bit further away. There were others in between Lian and this Disciple, but her bow and arrow had caught his attention.

There were Affinites who had an affinity for aim and precision. If this Disciple had a similar affinity, then they were in danger.

Lian threw the dagger he still had in his hand straight towards the Disciple. He had never been the best at throwing daggers; this one, too, didn't hit the Disciple right in the heart like he'd wanted to. Lian darted out of the way of the arrow just in time to see the dagger catch the Disciple's stomach.

There was a scream behind him, and all other sounds of the battle vanished from his hearing.

Sophie.

Lian spun around.

He'd managed to avoid the arrow, but Sophie had been next to him, facing the other way. The Disciple hadn't aimed the arrow at Lian's chest, like he'd aimed the dagger at hers. It had been aimed lower.

Sophie was on the ground, having lost the strength in her right leg. The arrow was burried deep in the back of her upper right leg. Blood was staining her trousers. She had her hands braced on the ground, and was starting to push herself up, but she wasn't going to be in time to block the swinging sword of the Disciple she had been fighting.

Lian cried out in anguish; he couldn't get there in time.

There was another Disciple behind him who was about to cut him down. There was nothing he could do for his sister as she looked up and saw the blade coming down.

The blow didn't kill her. Sophie had managed to throw her body sideways far enough that the sword only caught the fabric of her right sleeve. Blood welled up where the blade had sliced through the top layer of skin, but Sophie didn't even seem to notice it. The Disciple pulled back his sword and was about to strike again. Even though she was on the floor, an arrow deep into her leg, Sophie steadily raised her left hand as he readied to swing his sword again.

A whiz and clicking sound told Lian she'd shot a bolt at her attacker from her wrist crossbow. For a brief moment, after he managed to push the Disciple he himself was fighting back a few steps, Lian stole a glance over his shoulder. In that short moment he saw the Disciple sink to his knees, clawing at the open wound in his throat. Sophie's aim was impeccable.

There was another whiz, followed by a click, and then another. So many Disciples were still coming from deeper inside the Underworld to join the fight. It wasn't every day that the Asters were in their territory, and Lian could see the adrenaline-fuelled excitement in their eyes as they came at them.

From her low position on the ground, Sophie fired bolts at every Disciple she could see. She couldn't get up; the arrow was buried so deep in her leg, Lian knew there'd be muscle damage. Even if she had possessed his magic, he doubted her leg would have the strength to carry her weight.

Lian tried to protect his sister as best he could. She was helping him too; her bolts slowing down every oncoming attacker, but it was only a matter of time before she'd run out of bolts.

And that time came sooner than he'd hoped for. Lian heard a couple of clicks, but no whiz followed. When he got the chance, he looked over his shoulder again. Sophie was crouched on the ground right behind him. She'd lowered her left hand with the crossbow, knowing it was useless now. A male Disciple rose up in front of her, a sword raised, ready to bring it down.

And Lian couldn't do anything. He couldn't turn around and help her; the Disciple he was fighting would kill him the second he turned.

Even in this incredibly vulnerable state, Sophie stared the Disciple down as he swung his sword.

And just then there was a blue flash, and Sky was there. He crashed right into the Disciple with his short spear, impaling him and pushing him back against the two Disciples standing behind him. Those were the only ones on Sophie's side at that moment, and once Sky had sliced through the three of them, he turned around and shot across the hallway and did almost the exact same thing to the Disciples in front of Lian.

Lian didn't hesitate. He spun around and dropped to his knees.

His sister had already turned slightly, and was now lying on her left hip. Her right leg was on top of her left and she had turned her upper body so that she could assess the damage for herself.

Lian assessed her, too. She had minimal other injuries. A few cuts along her arms, but nothing major. The slice in her left shoulder was deeper than Lian had initially thought, but Sophie was leaning on that arm as if she didn't even notice the wound was there.

Lian quickly reached towards one of the smaller cuts and let some of her blood drop onto his fingers. He brought his fingers to his lips. He would never get over the horrible taste of blood, but he had to do it to save Sophie.

"Lian!" Sophie caught his hand, stopping him in his tracks. She was looking at something behind him. Lian turned around and saw what she meant.

Two Disciples had broken away from the right-hand end of the corridor and were heading towards the entrance and back outside to where Nathan and Matu would be with the seven hikers.

Knowing Sophie would've wanted this instead of being healed right there, Lian turned away from her and hurled himself at the ankles of one of the Disciples. With all his might he pulled the Disciple down to his knees. The Disciple, holding a sword in his hands twisted on the ground and tried to swing it towards Lian. Lian spun away and the blade crashed into the rocky ground. He reached for his own sword and drove it home.

He then jumped to his feet and skipped to the side, narrowly missing the swinging sword of the second Disciple who had been moving towards the entrance. This one was harder to kill. Lian moved to the side and spun around, swinging his sword. But the Disciple jumped back, avoiding the blow Lian had expected would have killed him, giving a few other Disciples the time to run past and head for the entrance. By the time Lian finally delivered the killing blow, after receiving a slice to his thigh, five Disciples had vanished around the corner. The injury to his thigh wasn't deep and thanks to his magic he didn't feel the pain anyway.

Lian's gaze shot back towards Sophie. She was still lying on the ground, but Sky was in front of her, fighting off two more Disciples trying to get past him. A flash of blue light and Sky had vanished and appeared again behind them. It took less than two seconds before both Disciples dropped to the ground, dead.

Sky caught Lian's eye just for a second. There were still Disciples advancing upon them, separating them. Lian couldn't get back to Sophie. Both Lian and Sky managed to avoid a few blows long enough to exchange a few words.

"I've got her!" Sky called out. "Go help Matu and Nathan!" He vanished and appeared once more in front of Sophie.

"Are you sure?" Lian called back.

Sky reached into a sheath that had been wrapped around his leg. He pulled out a small dagger and placed it against a nasty cut down his forearm. The dagger's blade was covered in blood a moment later. Sky then looked up, and threw the dagger towards Lian.

It only just missed Lian's arm as it clattered against the hard wall behind him. Lian picked up the dagger, knowing what Sky meant with it. Lian looked at his brother one last time, just to be sure.

Sky nodded once. "I've got her! Go!"

Lian didn't hesitate. He dodged a Disciple trying to stab him, and ran down the corridor towards the entrance. As he ran, he dipped his finger in the blood on the dagger, and then safely put away the dagger in a sheath at his side. He brought his bloodied finger to his lips. The blood tasted metallic in his mouth.

Through his rough breathing he panted, "*Excipie magica celeritatis.*"

A black Band just like Sky's immediately appeared next to his own, and Lian didn't wait another moment. He focused on the magic quite foreign to him and thought of Matu, knowing that Sky's magic could shimmer him to any Aster. His wrist tingled as the magic started to work. Blue light appeared, and Lian vanished from the corridor.

"Keep them busy!" was all that Nathan had said before Matu dashed down the trail and found a spot so narrow not even two people could stand next to each other. It had seemed the best place to meet the upcoming Disciples, because they wouldn't be able to attack with more than one at a time.

That command from Nathan had come minutes ago, and Matu had been so occupied with killing as many Disciples as he could, that he hadn't had the time to turn around and see what his brother had come up with. He was getting tired. A Disciple had managed to cut him across his left shoulder with his sword, cutting into his skin and through the strap of the backpack. The now loose backpack bounced awkwardly with every next movement Matu made. In an attempt to unfasten the backpack completely and toss it behind him, another Disciple had the space to ram her shield against his knee, which now felt swollen and bruised. And still Matu stood firm, shifting his weight onto his stronger leg to protect the backpack behind him, which contained the blood needed for Nathan to heal him. And to buy his brother time.

To do something…

What was Nathan doing?

Matu had taken the side of a Disciple's head and smashed it against the wall to his left. His Band glowed a fierce bronze and his magic sizzled through his veins as he then picked up the Disciple to throw him as hard as he could against the others coming up behind him. The dead Disciple brought down two more; one of whom lost his balance and dropped from the trail to the depths of the Canyon below.

In the few seconds that the manoeuvre bought Matu, he turned around and even had the time to marvel at what he saw.

Nathan was making a staircase. *Making* one. His magic should've been quite drained at this point, but he was pulling out all the stops without hesitation. Great, thick, small and long vines were interlacing right at Nathan's feet, and were weaving their way upwards. They were appearing out of thin air as much as they were protruding from the rock wall. Every now and again a vine would come loose from a part of the wall that wasn't stable, but slowly and surely, the makeshift vine bridge head was getting longer, and climbing up towards the next part of the trail a hundred and fifty feet above them.

It was going slower than Matu had hoped, though. Nathan had only managed thirty feet so far. The unstable cliff wall wasn't making it easy for his brother. The seven hikers were looking nervously back and forth between Nathan and his staircase, and Matu and the Disciples.

Matu turned around and faced the next Disciple. This one was smarter. He was keeping his distance and avoiding Matu's lethal hands. With a sword in each hand, this Disciple managed to drive Matu back a foot, and then another; he buckled on his unstable knee. Matu reached for the slim sword at his side, but it wasn't enough to keep this Disciple at bay. He was driving Matu further back and towards a part of the trail that was wide enough for two Disciples to come up next to each other. There, Matu found himself only a few feet away from the backpack he'd thrown behind him.

When a second Disciple started to come up beside the first, Matu decided to go for the element of surprise, and attack. He blocked one swinging sword with his slim sword and avoided the other one by crashing against the Disciple's chest. Matu then placed both hands on the Disciple's left shoulder and arm and pulled to his own right, sending the Disciple flying off the edge of the trail. But it hadn't stopped the second Disciple from getting past him. Matu ran up behind the Disciple, swearing loudly in Swahili as pain shot from his knee through his entire leg. This Disciple might have been fast, but, luckily, he was also uncertain. He looked back over his shoulder to check where Matu was, just before he came into the humans' range. The moment he did, Matu was upon him. He grabbed the Disciple by the shoulders and threw him off the trail as well.

When Matu turned around, the other Disciples had managed to gain more than a few feet. And they were now standing on quite a wide platform. If Matu were to engage now, he would get attacked from all angles. Even worse, one of the Disciples at the front was holding the backpack. Matu knew there was no way he was getting that back now.

Matu dared a glance behind him to see how Nathan was doing. His staircase wasn't even halfway up the cliff yet.

"Nathan!" Matu yelled, jumping back further down the trail to keep the Disciples from coming too close to the humans or to Nathan. While Matu knew Nathan couldn't do anything to help him at that moment, Matu hoped his brother understood that he wouldn't be able to hold all these Disciples for much longer. Especially now that he had to face four Disciples at the same time.

"I hear ya!" Nathan called back.

Matu jumped down onto the edge of the larger platform, making sure he landed with most of his weight on his good knee. Where he was standing, they wouldn't be able to get to the humans without having to closely pass him. Matu tried to count the Disciples as they filed onto the platform, swords and daggers and other weapons out. There were too many. Too many to keep away from Nathan before he finished that damn staircase.

The Disciple at the front grinned maliciously and threw the backpack over the edge of the trail. Matu forced himself not to react, but he couldn't help dreading what it meant that Sophie's blood was now lost to him. His left shoulder was already bleeding, and he was about to face multiple Disciples at the same time, without knowing how quickly he could be healed. Instead of going all out in this fight to give Nathan all the time he needed, Matu now had to be more careful.

The Disciples broke into movement. Three of them headed for Matu at the same time, with the others close at their backs. Matu lifted his slim sword in front of him, and just then a blue light appeared in the middle of the platform.

Matu had expected to see Sky.

But it was Lian. Right in the centre, surrounded by a wall three Disciples thick, was Lian. He looked just as surprised as the Disciples did. Clearly, he hadn't expected to be landing right in the middle of a small army.

The surprise of Lian's appearance had given Matu an advantage. He himself had recovered quicker, and he managed to take out four Disciples just because they had stopped to stare at Lian and where he had appeared out of thin air.

Matu advanced onto the next group of Disciples who had now turned away from the sight of the Aster appearing right in their midst. Matu cut the throat of the first one with his knuckle knife before throwing him right off the trail, and blocked the incoming blow of the second with his slim sword, only to punch this one so hard in the face that his skull fractured underneath his knuckles.

In the brief moment of free space Matu had created for himself, he dared to look at Lian. His brother was flying through the group of Disciples faster than humanly possible. Matu didn't understand how Lian was still harnessing Sky's magic after the initial shimmer, but he didn't question it. Matu also didn't, however, miss the blood dripping onto the ground wherever Lian went. And it was getting worse.

Lian managed to use Sky's magic again and sped his way across the platform towards Matu. Once his brother came alongside him, Matu was able to see what was causing Lian to bleed the way he was. There was a deep gash from his breastbone, diagonally down to his hip. And there was a cut down his face that was gushing blood, too. Lian's skin had gone grey and his lips were turning blue. His Band was glowing bright silver as his magic of Analgesia was active, masking the pain from his wounds.

"You're dying," Matu said starkly. He pushed the panic he felt as far down as possible, knowing that he no longer had access to Sophie's blood. Only Lian could still fight with wounds like that. But without Sophie's magic, not for much longer.

Lian didn't answer him. The two of them fought shoulder to shoulder, driving back any Disciple coming their way. They were standing on a higher part of the trail, and they could see more Disciples coming onto the platform and yet more coming up from the trail below.

"Matu!" Nathan called from behind them. Matu dared to look over his shoulder. The staircase was past halfway done now, but nowhere near the top. But Nathan had got all the hikers onto it. Nathan himself was standing on the second step of his vine staircase.

"Where's the backpack?" Lian panted.

"I lost it." Matu caught a flash of alarm cross Lian's face.

"Matu!" Nathan called from behind them again.

"Go," Lian panted.

Matu cast a glance at his brother. "You need to come, too."

Lian had to come with them. He couldn't shimmer up to the top to get Sophie's blood himself. Sophie's magic could only heal others. Lian needed another Aster there to heal him, and neither Nathan nor Matu could leave right now.

"I won't make it that far. I need to find Sophie," Lian rasped through struggling breaths. And still he fought. Matu marvelled at his brother. Lian knew he was dying, and yet he would hold these Disciples back for Matu to get out.

"Go," Lian pushed again.

Matu didn't defy him a second time. He shuffled back slowly with Lian at his side, until they reached a part of the trail that was only the width of a single person. At that point Matu turned around and ran up the last part of the trail. He didn't look back. Matu scrambled up higher and higher until he reached the bottom of Nathan's staircase. All the hikers were now at the very top of the staircase, and Nathan was in the middle. Without hesitating, Matu jumped up the first few steps.

"Higher!" Nathan commanded.

Matu climbed up further until he was standing right below Nathan. His brother's Band was still glowing, and the vines at the bottom of the staircase were starting to unfurl.

"Lian!" Matu shouted.

It was all the signal Lian needed. Even from this distance, Matu could see Lian push back one Disciple to give himself enough time to reach for a dagger at his side. Lian brought the bloodied dagger to his lips, and a second later a blue flash appeared, and Lian had vanished.

Chapter 18

Matu turned his attention back to the bottom of the staircase. With agonising slowness, the vines at the bottom of the stairway were disappearing. They were hanging above the Canyon with nothing securing them to the cliff face other than the vines that Nathan had created. And yet the stairs felt steady and secure beneath their feet.

With Lian gone, the Disciples were now running unhindered up the trail and towards where the path had crumbled away. When they saw the bottom of the staircase disappearing before their eyes, they slowed to a chaotic stop, and glared angrily up at the escapees in frustration. When Nathan was sure that none of the Disciples dared to bridge the growing gap, he turned around and focused his magic on the top of the staircase. The vines there started growing again; not just from the staircase and the cliff walls but at the same time also reaching down from the platform above them.

The sight was absolutely surreal. These kinds of vines didn't exist anywhere near here, and Nathan was just summoning them out of thin air.

"Why didn't he come?" Nathan asked as the staircase grew longer and closer to the platform above them.

"He needed Sophie."

Nathan's eyes went over Matu's shoulders and chest, registering the deep cut in his shoulder and that the backpack containing Sophie's blood was missing. "We have more of Sophie's blood back in the cabin," he said. He was holding his hands out in front of him; Nathan was like a conductor, arranging his magic to respond in just the way he needed it to, to have the vines curl and tighten in just the right places to hold all of their weight.

Matu stared over the edge at the Canyon floor. "There wasn't time. I needed his help to hold back the Disciples. Shimmering to Sophie was his best option."

Nathan didn't respond.

One of the humans screamed. Matu immediately looked up to where Nathan's staircase was getting so close to the platform now that the vines had started to touch and knot together. A figure had just turned the corner and was standing at the edge of the platform. Matu immediately registered the mountain boots, the khaki shorts and the simple t-shirt.

It was David Hughes. Two more people stood behind him: Wesley and Jason.

"Don't worry!" Matu called to the humans up at the top of the staircase. "They're friends."

Finally, the top of the staircase met securely with the platform above. Nathan dropped his hands, but his Band kept glowing. Matu assumed it was so that Nathan could make sure that the staircase would hold until they were all off.

David moved aside so that the hikers could step off the green staircase and onto the solid platform of the trail. Nathan stepped off next, and Matu followed him. Only then did the Band on Nathan's wrist stop glowing.

Matu looked back, expecting the staircase to vanish or fall down to the Canyon floor, but it held steady.

Jason and Wesley weren't the only ones with David. Behind them, there were at least another five Affinites. Matu turned to David with a question in his eyes. They weren't anywhere near the top of the Canyon yet; nowhere near where Matu had told David to meet them.

David only shrugged. "Thought you might need some back-up further down."

"You didn't exactly choose the easiest trail," Matu said.

"It was the fastest," David pointed out. "We've got the humans from here, boys. I assume you need to get back down there."

Matu turned around and looked down. Where the path had ended below them, at least another twenty Disciples stood staring at them. However they were going to get back down there again, this trail was no longer an option.

"We need to find another way down," Matu muttered.

"We'll find one. Oh, and we thought you might need this, too." David motioned to his eldest son, Jason, who brought forward one of Jackson's two weapons bags. The Asters had left both of them in the truck on their way to the trail. Behind Jason, the extra Affinites David had assembled were helping the humans further up the trail.

Jason dropped the weapons bag at their feet. Nathan knelt and started working through the bag.

Then Nathan swore under his breath. Matu was so surprised that he turned to see what had caused emotion to break through Nathan's previously clinical demeanour. "What is it?" he asked.

Nathan pulled out his hand, revealing a small vile of blood. On the sticker on the side was the image of an angel's wing. Sky's blood. Which meant they could use Sky's magic. The veil was gone now; they could shimmer back down without a problem.

"How is that a bad thing? We can shimmer down now."

Nathan looked at Matu, something unreadable on his face. "Sophie's blood is in here, too."

Matu closed his eyes and tipped his head to the sky. They could've saved Lian. If they had known David had been so close with a bag that contained Sophie's blood, Lian could've stayed with them and been healed instantly.

"Are we assuming he found Sophie?" Nathan asked.

Matu opened his eyes again and looked at the two vials of blood; their access to Sophie and Sky's magic. "No. Never. Give me Sky's blood."

Nathan handed him the vial with the angel's wing on the side. Matu opened it and took a small sip. "*Excipie magica celeritatis*," he said.

A band just like Sky's appeared next to his own. Matu held out his hand to Nathan, who took it. In his other hand, Nathan held the vial with Sophie's blood. Matu closed his eyes and focused on Sky's magic. He forced it to search for its original owner; to shimmer him and Nathan to Sky. Matu felt the blue magic of Sky's shimmer soar through his body, ready to envelop them both. But then it starting ebbing away again, until nothing remained except for a slight pull on Matu's legs; just a small tug, wanting to guide him.

"What's going on?" Nathan asked.

"Something's not letting me shimmer to Sky," Matu muttered.

"But the veil is down," Nathan said.

"It must be something else," Matu replied, staring down into the Canyon. With the veil gone he could see the Disciple camp below. He couldn't see the entrance to the Underworld, but he could see a huge number of Disciples running backwards and forwards at the bottom of the *Angel Trail*.

Nathan swore under his breath.

Whatever was stopping Matu from shimmering to Sky would be blocking Lian, too. He was down there somewhere, running while he was dying. And Matu and Nathan had no way of contacting him to tell him they were safe and free from Disciples. Otherwise Lian could use Sky's blood to shimmer back to them...

Lian was in the Underworld, all alone... trying to find his sister who could be anywhere by now.

While holding Sophie under his arm and half-carrying her, Sky used his speed or his shimmer to move faster through the corridors. Only a few Disciples were on their tail; many others had gone off to warn the guards outside of the possible break-out of the humans. Sky just hoped that Nathan and Matu had made it far enough along that they'd managed to get the humans through the veil and to the other side.

But he couldn't worry about that now. Sky was too busy outrunning the Disciples behind him long enough so that he had the time to use Sophie's blood to heal her leg. For now he could only shimmer to further along in the corridor. He had never been in the North American Underworld before, and if he shimmered into the unknown, who knows where he might end up.

Despite the arrow deep in her leg, Sophie moved faster than Sky had expected. She grunted each time she had to put weight on her right leg, but she wasn't moaning or complaining. Sky had tried to keep her from having to put any weight on that leg at all, but Sophie had scolded him for trying to spare her pain instead of getting them somewhere safer as fast as possible.

She had refused to take the arrow out. It was better to keep it in and keep the blood loss to a minimum. Sky wondered if all this movement was any better, but he knew better than to question her. He just kept his eyes on the corridors ahead. He shimmered them as far as he could see in the space lit by lanterns. Sky saw a corner coming up, and shimmered them right to the end, before stumbling round to the right. He shimmered forward again, and found himself at a T-junction. There was no way of knowing which direction to take. Sky chose left without stopping to weigh his options.

He didn't have time to think.

This was what he was good at: instinct and reaction. He would get Sophie some place safe where he could heal her with her blood, and then they would find their way back out again to help Matu and Nathan. Sky assumed Lian had reached them by now, and was helping to get the humans up the trail. Sky hoped they didn't have too many Disciples to worry about outside, but he wasn't so sure they'd be that lucky.

Sophie groaned and her grip on Sky tightened, disrupting his thoughts.

The corridor Sky and Sophie were running down, started to widen. The lanterns had been replaced by chandeliers on the ceiling, and the walls were smoother and had been painted a lighter colour.

To Sky's surprise, the footsteps that had seemed to be getting closer, now seemed to be farther away again. The Disciples were still coming after them, but for some reason they were keeping their distance.

The corridor they were in was long and seemed to go on forever. Sky dared to look over his shoulder. The Disciples had now entered the same corridor, but they had slowed down to a jog. Another glance back, and they had stopped altogether.

"They're not following us," Sophie hissed through rasping breaths. Apparently, she had also managed to steal a glance. "We can stop."

"A little further," Sky panted. He could see the end of the corridor coming closer, and a great white door stood at the end of it. It was open. If Sky could only get Sophie in there, he could lock them in and he'd have the time to heal her without the fear of Disciples being able to surprise them.

The rocky floor had turned to white marble, and the light walls were now covered in elaborate paintings. They reminded Sky of the gallery back in Saluverus' castle. The island's gallery was filled with paintings that told the story of past wars and battles. These were similar. And at the heart of every army of Disciples, stood a man with hair whiter than freshly fallen snow and eyes of liquid silver.

Mitrik wasn't the Original King of the North American Underworld. If Sky remembered his history correctly, there had been at least four Kings before him, the original one dying in the Original War against Queen Aiyana. But every North American King since had the same bright silver hair and eyes; it was what distinguished them from the other six. It was how they had all recognised Mitrik the second he'd walked out of the circus tent at the bottom of the Canyon.

Only one man in the world had hair like that. It shone unnaturally brightly.

Sky burst past the white door and heaved Sophie inside. He carefully dropped her to the floor and closed the great door behind them. When he turned around, Sophie had taken up the same position as when Lian was about to heal her. She was lying on her left hip, angling herself so she could have a better look at the arrow in her leg.

Sky neared Sophie and dropped to his knees beside her. This was the first time he'd had the chance to get a better look at her. Her skin had gone slightly grey. Even though Sophie had kept the arrow in her leg, she had still lost a lot of blood. Her hands were shaking slightly as she tore away the fabric around the entry point of the arrow.

She then wrapped her hand around the arrow and looked up at Sky. While her skin had paled, her thunderstorm grey eyes were as fierce as ever. Sky reached down and held his fingers against the wound. Once her blood was on his fingers, he brought them to his lips and said, "*Excipie magica sanitatis.*"

A Band so similar to his own appeared on his wrist. The only difference was that the symbol on the inside of his wrist was the staff of Caduceus, and not the wing of an angel.

Sky looked at Sophie. "Ready to save your life," he told her with a twinkle in his eyes.

Sophie rolled her eyes. In one quick motion she ripped the arrow out of her leg. She hissed through her teeth and Sky leaned over her immediately. He placed his right hand over the wound and closed his eyes.

Sophie's magic flowed through his fingers.

It always took longer than when Sophie did it; this magic wasn't second nature to him – it wasn't a part of him like it was a part of her. But sure enough, he could feel the Band prickle on his skin and he knew it had started to glow. Sky could feel a certain warmth travel through his body and towards his right hand.

When the warmth vanished, Sky opened his eyes and pulled back his right hand. There was nothing left of the wound in Sophie's leg. Brand new skin had replaced the torn skin, and the muscles underneath had knitted together again as well.

Sky looked up at his sister, but then caught sight of the view behind her.

"Thanks," Sophie was saying. "Now let me do you."

Sky barely heard her. He could feel her hand against his skin, but he batted it away. He couldn't tear his eyes away from what was behind Sophie.

"We need to leave, right now," he said with low urgency.

"What?" Sophie turned around herself, and Sky could hear her suck in her breath. For before them was a greater space than Sky had ever seen in any Underworld before. It was large enough to fit a small village, and tall enough to fit the skyscrapers Sky had once seen in New York City. It was greater even than the cavern that held the entrance to the Sera in South America.

And they were sitting on a narrow path; the width of which would fit no more than three people, and which seemed to be suspended in the air. There was nothing either side of the path but what looked like a bottomless drop down into the darkness. In front of them, the path went on straight for about sixty feet, before vanishing downwards and appearing again a little further on. And they saw where the path led to. The sight would've been awe-inspiring if it didn't strike them with great fear.

The path led to a stunning castle. Only Saluverus' castle could compare. It was completed with high walls, with battlements at three levels, and thick towers, watchtowers and finally turrets at the top, and a drawbridge at the bottom.

But the most chilling part of it all, was the colour. The entire castle – except for the bars in the open windows, the chains of the drawbridge and the tops of the battlements and watchtowers which were a slick, glossy black – was white. Brighter than white even. It was like the entire castle shone with a light of its own.

"We need to go," Sky repeated. He tried to get to his feet, but found that he couldn't move. He looked to Sophie in alarm, and found that she was staring back at him, fear in her eyes. She couldn't move either. Sky struggled and fought against the invisible bonds that were keeping his legs firmly on the ground, but he couldn't move them an inch.

"We need to find a way out of here," Sky snapped.

"Oh, don't do that. You've only just got here," said an icy voice from down the path.

Sky's gaze snapped away from Sophie towards the voice. There was no one there, but Sky could hear faint footsteps on the white, marble path.

He saw the silver hair first. Then followed the sharp, bony face, the thin neck and then the narrow shoulders.

Mitrik walked up the staircase, his eyes locked on Sky. Sky's heart slowed as he took in the King of the North American Underworld. The colour of his eyes, just like his hair, was unnatural in every way imaginable. They were a sharp and shining silver.

The King's body was quite thin. Sky's history teacher hadn't been lying when she said Mitrik had never been a fighter. With a mere skin-and-bones body like that he wouldn't last thirty seconds in combat. There didn't seem to be any muscle on him at all. He was still wearing armour, though; black with streaks of white.

A single white dagger hung at his hip, but his hands were nowhere near it. To Sky's horror, Mitrik's hands were by his side. They seemed relaxed, but Sky quickly noticed the white glow about them. Sky then looked back at his legs and found that there was a similar glow in the shape of multiple ropes keeping him tied to the floor.

Sky! I need Sophie!

A chill went through Sky's body as he recognised Lian's voice in his head. The panic in his brother's voice was undeniable. Sky tried to fight against his bonds once more, but he couldn't move an inch. He prayed that Lian could get to Matu and Nathan; to the blood they had that could help him.

"What?" Sophie whispered as softly as she could, seeing Sky's distress.

Sky stopped his struggles, which were obviously futile, and looked at his sister. "Lian needs you."

The weight of what those words meant sank in. Sky could see the difference in Sophie's eyes. She closed them for a moment, then turned to look back at the King of the North American Underworld. Sky did the same. There was nothing they could do for Lian until they found a way to get out of this first.

Behind Mitrik, two Disciples, wearing the same black armour, stepped from the top of the staircase onto the marble path towards Sky and Sophie. One was male, and had a bone white bow and quiver slung around his shoulder, and a similar white dagger to Mitrik's at his belt, while the other was female, with a white sword strapped to her back and two whips curled around her shoulders.

"I've been told you came here by accident," Mitrik said, stopping a few feet away from where Sophie and Sky were trapped on the floor. Mitrik smiled at them. "And here I thought you came especially to see me."

Sky glared at the King but said nothing. Sophie did the same beside him.

Mitrik looked from Sky to Sophie, and then back to Sky again. He smirked and said, "Oh, we're going to have so much fun together."

With his hand clutched to his abdomen, Lian rushed through the corridors of the Underworld. Blood was running through his fingers like water and Lian could feel himself grow weaker with every step that he took.

In his free hand he clutched Sky's dagger. He'd used the blood on it time and time again to speed through the Underworld in search of Sophie and Sky. Lian had shimmered back to the place where he'd left them, but they were long gone. Only the bodies of the dead Disciples told Lian that he at least had shimmered to the right place.

Lian called Sky's name and told him he needed Sophie; his brother should hear him and be able to shimmer right to him. But no blue light appeared. Sky didn't come.

Lian brought the dagger to his lips and whispered the spell once again. Sky's Band appeared on his wrist for what seemed like the hundredth time that afternoon. Lian reached into the magic and forced it to recognise its true owner. The magic tugged at his legs as the Band glowed blue on his wrist. He had tried to shimmer to Sky specifically, like Nathan had done when escaping the explosion in the

Perth townhouse. Lian even tried to shimmer to Sophie, just like he'd managed to shimmer to Matu out on the trail. But something wasn't letting him. Something was blocking him. The only thing he felt was that little tug on his legs, guiding him.

Lian didn't waste any time. He staggered on in whatever direction the magic pulled him. He even shimmered to the ends of corridors just to save time; he imagined Sky had done something similar to get Sophie some place safe for long enough so that he could heal her. Lian wondered how deep into the Underworld Sky had gone to do that. Every time he spoke the words and the magic tugged at Lian's legs, the connection he felt towards Sky's magic didn't feel closer or farther away. The connection was just there, and it was guiding him, but nothing more.

Lian had no idea how long he still had, but he knew that this had been his best option. Lian didn't dare shimmer back to Matu and Nathan. There was no guarantee that they were safe and had the time to heal him. Not to mention Lian would first have to shimmer to the cabin to get Sophie's blood before he could go to his brothers. Even if he didn't know how close he was to Sophie and Sky right now, this still had to be his best shot.

Though now he was starting to wonder if he had a shot at all. His entire arm was soaked in blood, and his legs were starting to falter. His Band was glowing a fierce silver; his magic being the only thing keeping him on his feet right now. He didn't feel the pain; he would run until his legs would physically give out.

And his legs were starting to fail him now. With all the blood gushing out of his abdomen, not enough oxygenated blood was reaching the muscles in his legs. The energy was leaving them, and Lian could feel it. His legs were slowing down even though he willed them forward.

He called his brother's name again.

The blood was leaving his head as well. He shimmered to the end of another corridor again, reaching a T-junction. His brother's magic pulled him to the left, so that was where he turned to go. But he was starting to stumble. Dizziness had taken over and his vision was starting to get blurry.

He wondered why he wasn't meeting any Disciples. Not that he was complaining. But there had been quite a few still left when he had shimmered off to help Nathan and Matu. The fact that the magic was still pulling him somewhere and that the connection between him and Sky was strong, told him that Sky was alive and well. For now, at least.

Lian held on to that thought as he stumbled once more.

He paused for a moment and leaned against the corridor wall. His breath was coming out in short rasps. He coughed once, and found that blood was coming out of his mouth, too.

Lian forced himself to take another step forward. He needed to keep following the connection to Sky. He needed to get to Sophie. They didn't know he was dying. Only Nathan and Matu knew, but they were somewhere else entirely. The only thing to do was to keep going... to keep swallowing Sky's blood to keep the connection alive. To keep...

Lian's knees buckled.

No... not yet.

He'd been close to death before. He knew what it felt like to feel his life slipping away.

Lian tried to take another step forward. All the strength had left his right leg, and it gave way underneath him.

He crashed to the floor. With his left arm he managed to break his fall slightly, but he landed awkwardly on his elbow.

"Sky..." he rasped. His brother should be able to hear him. He should be able to come. The veil was gone. Sky should be able to shimmer wherever he needed to go.

Lian whispered his brother's name again, but no one came. No blue light appeared, bringing his salvation.

Lian felt his blood flowing from the wound, and had just enough sense left to turn onto his back to slow the bleeding.

His blurry vision was getting darker as he stared at the ceiling. He tried to press both hands against his abdomen now, but even that wasn't possible anymore. There was no energy left in his limbs.

There was no energy left at all.

His Band glowed silver as his magic made sure he couldn't feel the pain. But he could feel the end coming.

Lian whispered his brother's name one more time before everything went dark.

To be continued

What's next for the Asters?

Split up freeing abducted humans in the Underworld, the five Asters will have to use their magic in ways they didn't even know was possible, to have any chance of successfully completing their mission and quelling the rebellion of Mitrik, the Dark King of North America.

Matu has to trust Nathan that his magical abilities can find their brothers and sister in the Underworld and keep Lian alive until he can be rescued. Sky has to rely on Sophie's creative thinking to get them out of Mitrik's magical dungeon. And even if they succeed, there are still Mitrik's Disciples to face down, led by the fearsome Kali.

Join Nathan, Sophie, Lian, Matu, and Sky in the deadliest adventure of their lives as they fight to stay alive and take down the North American King, in the last in the Asters Prequel Trilogy...

A Threat To Remain

Available at https://www.amazon.com/gp/product/B0993ZWBKR

From the author

Thank you for reading *A World To Lose*, I do so hope you enjoyed it. I would greatly appreciate it if you would take a moment to rate and even write a short review, as it will really help new readers find my books.

If you'd like to be the first to hear about the progress of other books in the Asters series, free bonus content, updates to my writing and everyday life, offers from other fantasy authors, and more, sign up to my newsletter on my web site at https://francesellenbooks.com/newsletters/. As well as links to past newsletters my website also hosts my latest news, bonus content, background on the Asters, how to purchase signed copies of my books and bookmarks, and more. You can also follow me on instagram (#francesellen__), and find me on tiktok (@francesellen__), and The Asters Facebook page. Come and join me on my writing journey, I'd love to have you on board!

All the books in The Asters Series

The Asters Prequel Trilogy

A Queen To Come

A World To Lose

A Threat To Remain

The Asters Original Series

From Fury Reborn

Bonus Asters Content

Bonus content is always first announced in my newsletter and can only be found on my website:
  https://www.francesellenbooks.com/all-content/bonus-content/

Acknowledgements

Firstly, I want to thank my incredibly dream team:

Tina, for standing by me every step of the way from day one.

Carlota, for always being there to be my sounding board.

Timothy, for your everlasting energy and insights.

Peggy, for your brilliant eye for detail.

And a brilliant thank you to the newest member of this dream team: Aster! What a hilarious coincidence that your name is the same as my series. Your unique perspective and – let's face it, sometimes – just common sense, have improved my writing beyond what I thought possible.

Secondly, a thank you to my awe-inspiring parents. You are my heroes and I would have never made it this far without either of you.

Thirdly, let me thank my unbelievably talented designer, Arjuna Jay, who makes bringing my vision to life seem like the easiest thing in the world.

Finally, I am so grateful to a few more people who knew I would make it to this day:

Nick, any time I veered off course, I remembered you telling me how at heart I was an author. Those words never failed to help me find my way back.

Rob, every time you saw me you told me again of that empty space on your bookshelf where you would put my first novel. Now you can finally fill it.

Marissa, you were there at the beginning. I don't think either of us thought that those original, silly ideas would ever turn into anything. But, oh my, look at what they have become.